HOLLYWOOD BEGINNINGS

HOLLYWOOD ROMANCE BOOK 2

LIZA MALLOY

To Samantha... From your crush on Shawn Mendes to your obsession with One Direction and the Jonas Brothers, you remind me so much of myself as a tween. I'm so glad you inherited my love of music and my fascination with celebrities. For some reason, this book makes me think of you...even though you're not allowed to read it for another decade. In the meantime, keep on dancing and making me smile.

1

Sweat glistened on his palms as he cleared his scratchy throat for the hundredth time. Justin had to act now or risk losing the element of surprise. He patted his pocket again, confirming his treasure was secure, then reached his hand across the table to squeeze Courtney's long, slender fingers.

"Let's go for a walk on the beach," he said.

Courtney's sapphire eyes narrowed as she considered his proposition before quickly shaking her head. "I'm tired. Let's go back to the room. I'm sure the beach will still be there in the morning."

Justin's lips tugged upwards. He deduced from the sparkle in her eyes that Courtney was not actually tired and had no intention of sleeping when they returned to the room. The problem was, her saying that only made him more confident in his decision, more certain that he was doing the right thing. No way was he waiting any longer.

He stood, dropping the cloth napkin onto the table. "And I'm sure you'll still be 'tired' in fifteen minutes," he said with a wink, offering his hand to help her up.

Now she smiled, flashing those perfect white teeth of hers. Whatever fortune her parents had spent on braces was worth it for that gorgeous smile. "You seem pretty confident about that, Mr. Danes," she teased, calling him by the pseudonym he'd used checking into the resort. "You better not waste too much time or I might actually be sleepy."

"I don't plan on wasting a single second," he replied. They left the restaurant, hand in hand, walking immediately onto the boardwalk facing the darkened Atlantic. The air was still warm, but not muggy, and a refreshing breeze rippled across his shirt. Justin loosened his tie, feeling his throat tighten. He motioned towards the water. "Come on."

She followed him to the edge of the boardwalk before pausing to sit on a bench at the end. Justin crouched in front of her and helped her slip her foot out of the silver strappy sandals. He nearly laughed out loud at the irony of his frustration that she was delaying his plans by fiddling with her shoes, only to find himself thrust into the precise position a more traditional man might seek out for the situation.

"What's so funny?" she asked, leaning towards him.

Justin shook his head, pushing her soft, long hair behind her shoulders until it no longer obstructed the view offered by her low-cut strapless dress.

She sat abruptly, covering the tops of her breasts with her hand. "Hey, now. You're the one that wanted this walk. No previews of the goods till we're in the room."

He stood, stepping out of his shoes and rolling his gray socks into his shoes, leaving them on the edge of the wooden steps by Courtney's. They walked down towards the water and paused right where the fluffy sand began to turn damp. The tide was receding and the black water was quiet and eerily still. Courtney turned to him, placed her hands on his cheeks, and pulled his face to hers.

"This is beautiful," she whispered. "Thank you for taking me here." She kissed him before he could answer, her warm lips sending a tingling sensation down his torso. She pulled back, then began to walk parallel to the water, her fingers absentmindedly reaching for his. "So beautiful, in fact, that I might spend this whole trip right here in this exact spot instead of in the room with you. Unless of course you have more tricks up your sleeve," she added.

"Not up my sleeve," Justin said, nervously patting his pocket again.

She turned and laughed, misinterpreting his response. "I think I've seen all those tricks, buddy."

Justin wrapped his arm around her, slowing their pace considerably, and wondered how long they could walk like this before running out of beach. They were on an island, so presumably they could just go forever, circling the whole place until he got his shit together and asked her.

The night before, when his buddy, Keith, had questioned what he was going to say, Justin had been indignant. As an actor, he always had lines to memorize, but this time, it was real life. He wasn't acting, and he wanted to just improvise. He'd felt certain that when the time was right, the perfect words would just come to him then flow out like an artfully scripted scene.

But now, watching Courtney's hair dance in the breeze as she gazed at the lights of boats in the distance, Justin would've killed for a script and an underpaid assistant to subtly whisper his next lines to him. Justin was rarely nervous—not when he was acting, not when he was modeling, and certainly not when he was hanging with fans—so he hadn't expected to feel it with Courtney.

It didn't help that he had asked her before and she had technically turned him down. Then, the timing had been all wrong, and she'd correctly guessed that he was flippant. Surely she'd see that he was serious now, but if not, well, that could make for a really shitty week in paradise.

Courtney crouched down, scooping a tiny object out of the sand and inspecting it curiously before tossing it out to sea and continuing along her way. Justin debated waiting, returning to the room now for predictably good sex, enjoying a relaxing vacation with his girl, and then popping the question on their last night. It might work, except he'd already hinted at his plans on social media right before the flight. Even if Courtney didn't catch wind of that, she might find out his intentions from someone else. Besides, he didn't want to spend the whole week stressed out about losing the damn ring or keeping it hidden from her.

It was now or never.

Courtney stopped walking about ten feet ahead of him, wiggling her toes into the squishy sand. Justin took a few steps closer, thrust his hand into his pocket and shimmied the box out, confirming it was tightly closed.

"Hey Courtney," he called. "Catch!" And then he tossed it, refusing to consider what would happen if it popped open mid-flight, catapulting the precious cargo in the dark sand.

Thankfully, she caught it, effortlessly, despite being about ten years past her softball-playing days. He froze, holding his breath for a full minute before inching closer as she inspected the box. The moon cast a shadow over her face and he couldn't read her expression from beneath the hair that had fallen over her eyes.

"What's this?" she asked, her voice both casual and curious, confirming that she really didn't know.

He laughed. "Open it."

She pried the box open and gasped so softly that the sound of the waves nearly hid it.

"It's your ring," he explained, although he was confident she'd figured it out by this point. She didn't speak or move, so he tentatively stepped towards her. "You didn't think I was sincere before, but I am now. I know what I want and there's not a doubt in my mind."

He paused again, wishing she'd say something, but still she just stood there, silently, her eyes focused intently on the small ivory box clutched in both hands. He wrapped his arms around her waist, turning his gaze down to the ring.

"Courtney, I love you. I want to spend my life with you."

She glanced up, her eyes meeting his, and she smiled. "Are you sure about this?"

"I have never been so certain of anything in my entire life."

She blinked, and he realized there were tears in her eyes. "You better be, Justin, because once this baby is on my finger, I'm not taking it off, and I'm not letting you go."

He laughed, relieved, and felt himself drop to his knee for the second time that evening, despite his lifelong certainty that when he did eventually propose to a woman, he'd never resort to such a corny, cliché pose. "Courtney Lynn Robbins, will you marry me?"

She smiled wider and nodded. "I do."

He chuckled again. "I think you're supposed to save that line for the actual wedding."

Now Courtney laughed too. "I'm practicing."

Justin tugged at the ring, surprised at how tightly it had been wedged into the box, then slipped it onto her finger. Once he got past her knuckle, it fit perfectly. He kissed her hand, ready to stand, but instead she knelt across from him.

"I'm supposed to be the only one down here," he said.

"Stop being so critical," she whispered, her lips curving upward. "This is romantic."

Justin wrapped his arms around her waist, pulling her in for a kiss, and then lifted her to her feet as he stood up. They kissed for what felt like an eternity, but for once, Justin was content to simply keep on kissing her forever. Courtney was the one to finally end the kiss, immediately turning back to the ring, as though confirming its existence.

He followed her gaze to the ring, now glistening to the moonlight, then glanced around them. The beach was quiet and deserted. Aside from a few boats in the distance, the ocean was equally vacant. They were truly alone in public. For once, Justin didn't have an audience. He smiled, then picked her up and carried her back to their room, stopping only for their shoes.

2

Courtney awoke the next day with a jittery sensation. She turned slowly to find Justin sprawled out beside her. He was on his stomach, his muscled arm in front of his face, just like the first time she'd awoken next to him, nearly two years before. She smiled, then patted her stomach, uncertain of the source of the butterflies until she glanced down and saw her hand, adorned with the gigantic, gorgeous diamond. It was a clear, round cut stone—huge, but not obscenely so, with several smaller diamonds surrounding it on the thin, platinum band. The stones cast twinkly patterns on the ceilings and walls of the room as she twirled her hand about.

Courtney squealed, then bit her lip, not wanting to wake Justin. *Better let my fiancé sleep,* she thought with a grin. She closed her eyes and replayed the previous night in her head. Looking back, she was surprised she hadn't seen it coming.

Justin had clearly been off his game since he'd picked her up the day before. He was flaky and awkward on the drive to the airport. Then, he'd shared an alarmingly long, whisper-filled hug with his best friend Keith. He'd practically banished her in the terminal, insisting she go through security ahead of him, and then he'd tapped his foot and clutched her hand nervously the whole flight. In retrospect, Courtney should have figured out that something was up.

When they'd arrived at the resort, Justin's squirrelly behavior had continued. Although he was normally attentive and romantic, he'd really gone overboard at dinner. Even when he'd turned down sex and insisted they walk on the beach after dinner, Courtney hadn't suspected anything. At the moment she caught the ring box, though, it hit her that Justin was acting strangely for a reason. Her boyfriend who could casually chat with a famous talk show host in front of a live audience and however many thousands of viewers watched from home was actually nervous about something. And that told her how important it was to him.

Courtney tiptoed out of bed and snuck into the bathroom, slowly inching back under the sheets a few minutes later. She proudly glanced around the room, knowing the mess surrounding them now was simply a byproduct of the perfect night. When they'd first returned to the room the previous night, Courtney had been surprised to see the rose petals and dozens of lit candles, none of which had been there before dinner.

Now, the candles were all burnt out, and an empty bottle of champagne lay on its side next to the dress she'd worn. Matted, wilting rose petals littered the bed and surrounding floor. Justin's gray suit pants were draped over the back of a chair, but his belt, Courtney realized, was on top of the comforter at the foot of the bed. Her breath quickened as she replayed each delicious moment of the night. Then, she decided Justin had slept enough.

She tentatively kissed the back of his shoulder blade, sliding her hand down his back and resting it on his perky bare butt.

She turned her hand slightly and stroked back up his side, causing Justin to stir slightly.

"Ow," he mumbled, his eyelids fluttering open.

Courtney frowned, uncertain of the cause of his pain.

He turned to his side and reached for her hand, tapping the gem with his finger. "Watch it there, you've got a weapon now," he whispered.

Courtney traced her fingers across the ring, surprised at how sharp the edges of the diamond were, especially since it stuck out so far. "Sorry!"

He smiled, still sleepily, so that only one of his adorable dimples made an appearance. "It's alright. I just don't want a repeat of last night."

She pulled back, now thoroughly confused.

Justin laughed and sat up. "No, no. I demand a repeat of last night," he corrected, "But, uh, you sorta did a number on my arm and back with that baby." He turned, revealing a series of red scratches. He looked like he'd been attacked by a cat.

"I've got a photo shoot when we get back and I don't want the makeup artist to hate me. Otherwise I wouldn't object."

Courtney gently ran her finger across his wounds, surprised that a piece of jewelry could even do that and ashamed that she hadn't noticed in the heat of the moment.

He combed his fingers through her hair and then stood up, heading for the bathroom. He emerged a minute later, still naked, and she couldn't help but smile. There were no words to describe Justin. Well, hot, sexy, and chiseled were a good start, but really, they all fell short.

Justin was six-foot-one and roughly 190 pounds of solid muscle, although he'd put on as much as twenty more pounds of muscle when a job demanded it. He had smooth, subtly tanned California skin, the brightest blue eyes imaginable, and crazy cute dimples he used like a weapon, flashing them whenever he wanted something, confident no one could resist their power. His dark blonde eyebrows were slightly uneven, the right one raised almost imperceptibly in the middle.

His hair was currently blond—its natural hue— and short, growing back slowly from a recent buzz cut. Courtney thought Justin was equally cute when his hair was slightly longer, and nearly as attractive when it was dyed brown, but his hair style was generally dictated by his work and not her preferences anyway. Justin was rarely clean-shaven, but any facial hair he had was always impeccably manicured. His torso and upper groin were smooth, maintained by regular waxing sessions that Justin dreaded but Courtney, along with everyone else lucky enough to enjoy his shirtless appearances in magazines and movies, appreciated. He had no tattoos or noticeable birthmarks, but his body, particularly his arms, bore a plethora of pale scars reminiscent of various action stunts in movies he'd insisted on performing himself.

Having spent a fair amount of his career modeling, Justin had an inordinate interest in fashion for a guy, and the fact that he was constantly hounded by fans and the paparazzi led him to select each day's outfit and accessories with a diligence that Courtney had exercised only for job interviews, first dates, and prom.

An actor by trade, Justin had an alarming talent at reading people. He was charming but cocky, and everyone who knew Justin liked him. On the surface, he was nothing like the man Courtney had envisioned herself spending her life with, but at the core, he was every bit the man she needed and wanted.

"What's on the agenda for today?" she asked.

Justin smiled, his dimples drawing her eyes away from the rest of his naked body. "I don't know. Any requests?" He climbed over her, propping himself on his forearms in plank pose then slowly lowering until his smooth warm chest pressed into her body.

Courtney felt herself reacting to his touch instantly, her pulse racing and her mouth watering. "I have a few ideas," she replied, lifting her head off the pillow until she reached his soft, warm mouth. He took the hint, as always, and kissed her back, his tongue melting into her own until they both grew dizzy from the panting and pulled apart. He kissed her neck, his teeth raking across the skin as he worked his way lower, tracing her collar bone with his tongue, before finally reaching her breasts.

Courtney groaned the moment his lips brushed across her nipple, and she dug her fingers into his hips, pausing only to ensure she didn't snag him with the ring again. His lips found hers again and Courtney found herself beaming so widely that he pulled back, abruptly.

"What is it?" he asked, breathlessly.

She paused, waiting to catch her own breath. "I just realized I get to spend the rest of my life kissing you."

Justin smiled. "Just kissing?" He rolled her onto her side and slid his hand down to her groin, his fingers rubbing against her, softly at first, then with more and more pressure until she felt her breath pick up again.

Courtney writhed against him before reasoning that they had the rest of their lives to enjoy foreplay. She nudged Justin onto his back and straddled him, his hands groping her breasts as they made love.

A short while later, she stretched out on top of him, dizzy and content. He kissed the top of her head and she smiled, painfully aware that life shouldn't be this good.

"What's next?"

Courtney considered this, then answered honestly. "Shower then back to bed."

He laughed. "Normally I wouldn't protest, but I'm starving,

and we need to get out of here so they can clean up this room. And besides, it seems like we maybe have some calls to make."

She lifted her head, propping her chin on his chest so she could see him. "What do you mean?"

"Don't you want to tell your parents the news? And Erica?"

Of course she was dying to tell everyone she knew, but it seemed like they should figure out the logistics first. For Justin to get engaged was one thing, but for people to *know* he was engaged, well, that seemed like something his publicist Jamie should handle.

He apparently could read her thoughts. "Courtney, I don't want to keep it secret."

"Me neither, but..." Not that she didn't trust his judgment, but Jamie could be really scary. Suddenly, Courtney remembered the weird exchange between Justin and Keith at the airport the day before. She sat abruptly. "Keith already knew, didn't he?"

Justin laughed. "He helped me pick the ring. And then tried to talk me out of it."

"What? I thought he liked me?"

He sat up and shook his head. "Courtney, Keith loves you. He was only concerned about my poor ego and how I'd react if you rejected me again. For some reason, he thought you were too smart to fall for me."

She shrugged, smiling. "Sorry to have let him down. Anyone else know?"

He hesitated. "Technically, everyone might."

"Who is everyone?"

Justin reached for his phone, tapped the Twitter icon, and handed it to her. She scrolled through a medley of messages, wondering, as she did every time she glanced at his account, why he even bothered to tweet when he consistently got hundreds of responses from people he'd never met. Of course, good-hearted Justin actually replied to some of the strangers, which probably only encouraged more stalking. She finally saw his post from the day before, the one he must have sent right before their flight.

It read: "Wish me luck everybody. Here's hoping I've got some good news to share tomorrow."

"That doesn't necessarily tell it all," Courtney reasoned, despite the awareness that at least some of his 1.2 million followers clearly could figure it out. "Aww, give my fans some credit. They're not as dumb as you might think," he insisted, but he added a new tweet anyway, reading "She said yes!"

Courtney laughed, then came to a startling realization. "My mother follows you on Twitter!" Her mom wasn't exactly a techie, but ever since meeting Justin, she did everything she could to keep tabs on him.

"Then call her soon. I talked with Keith, and we decided the only way to be sure Jamie couldn't pressure us to keep it a secret was for me to publicize it in advance." Justin never crossed his publicist without running it by Keith first. It was sort of cute, the strange symbiotic relationship he had with his best friend-turned-manager.

Justin stood, headed for the bathroom. "I just didn't want something that's supposed to be exciting and fun to turn stressful. I've had friends who get engaged and then wear the ring on the wrong hand so the paparazzi can't be certain, and then they rush into a wedding just because they're sick of hiding it."

Courtney heard the shower start. She stood, but lacking the confidence of her underwear model fiancé to walk around stark naked, she wrapped a sheet around herself. "So you don't want to rush into anything," she surmised.

He popped his head around the corner, then came to her

and kissed her forehead. "Not what I said, Courtney. We can get married tonight if you want. I only thought if we took the public out of the equation, just telling them about the engagement from the start, we could make all the decisions from this point on based on what we want."

She realized again how sweet he could be. "Fine, you shower and I'll call my parents."

He started back to the shower. "Good. I'm probably already on your dad's shitlist for not asking his permission first. I'd hate for your mom to find out from someone other than you."

Courtney giggled and grabbed her phone to dial her parents. Then she hesitated, having no idea if she could even make international calls from her phone. "Hey Justin," she called, peeking around the corner to see if he was already in the shower. He wasn't. "Isn't it like long distance or something? Do I have to use a country code?"

"Bring me my phone," he instructed. She handed it to him and he typed for a moment, then handed it back once it began ringing. Justin traveled often, filming all throughout the U.S. and overseas when he could, so he had mastered all the intricacies of technology that stumped Courtney.

Courtney quickly closed the bathroom door and plopped onto a chaise on the far side of the room. She pulled the curtains back just enough so she could see the ocean. It was so beautiful that she was tempted to take the phone onto the balcony, but she figured as private as the room was, she still probably needed clothes on the balcony. Her parent's answering machine picked up before she had a chance to move anyway.

Courtney grimaced, disappointed not to reach them. She was about to hang up, but then realized Justin had switched numbers again a while back and that her parents could just be screening the unfamiliar call. She crossed her fingers. "Hey guys, it's me, Courtney. If you're there, pick up. I wanted to tell you something." She paused, and was about to click End when she heard a click.

"Hello? What's wrong?" It was her father.

"Hey, Dad. Nothing is wrong. Is Mom there too?"

"Why didn't your number show up?"

"I'm using Justin's phone. Can you tell Mom to pick up the phone too if she's home? I want to talk to you both."

There was static, and then she heard her parents squabbling about something. Finally, her mom answered.

"Hi dear, how's the trip?"

"Really good so far," she replied, smiling.

"Is Justin with you?"

Courtney had no idea how to interpret this. Her parents knew she was traveling with him. She had told them, and even if they'd forgotten, they couldn't possibly think she could afford a trip to the Caribbean on her salary. "Yeah, but he's showering right now."

Her father sighed. She figured that probably meant he realized her response meant Justin was naked in the room next to his innocent daughter. Her parents weren't exactly old fashioned about that sort of thing, but Courtney would never openly mention it to them. Justin had been to her parents' house with her the previous summer, and they'd shared a room, but it had separate beds. And it couldn't help that Justin had done some fairly provocative underwear ads which left very little to the imagination.

"We didn't expect to hear from you this week," her mother said.

"Well, yeah. I figured I would wait until I was back in Cali to call, but I had some news to share and I don't want you to hear it somewhere else first. You know how news tends to spread fast around Justin."

"You're not pregnant," her mother gushed, as though she

were both certain it was true and commanding Courtney that it not be true.

Courtney hadn't expected that response. "No, Mom." She paused, determined to ignore the distinct "Thank God" uttered by both of her parents in the background. "What I was going to say was that Justin proposed last night. We're engaged."

And then there was silence. Not just a pause, but absolute silence. Courtney tapped the phone, certain the call had disconnected, but the little ticker at the top of the screen indicated they were still on the line. "Hello?"

"I'm sorry, sweetheart. Can you say that again?"

"Justin asked me to marry him, and I said yes," she repeated, loudly. The shower turned off as she spoke, making her voice seem even more amplified.

"But you're not pregnant," her father repeated.

"No, Dad. I am not pregnant."

Justin poked his head around the corner, a crisp white towel around his waist and another smaller one in his hand. He laughed as he dried his hair and shoulders with the smaller towel.

"That's wonderful news, dear. Congratulations!" Her mother sounded genuinely happy. Her father remained silent.

Courtney cleared her throat, deciding it would be best to give them some time to absorb this new development and then talk with them next week. "Well, I better get back to Justin now."

"Oh is he there now dear? Put him on the phone so we can congratulate him too," her mother insisted.

Courtney covered the phone with her hand and turned to Justin. "They want to talk to you."

He nodded, so she switched over to speaker phone and handed it to him. He laughed, turned speaker phone off, and raised the phone to his ears. "Hi Shannon, Matt. How are you doing?"

She sighed, relieved that he at least could charm them into complacency. Still, she was dying to know what they were saying.

"Thank you, ma'am," Justin said. "Oh, well, I imagine. Yes, I, uh..."

Courtney laughed as he began to stutter. He grimaced and motioned for her to shower. She complied.

When she emerged from the bathroom, having shaved and showered, dried off, and applied lotion and makeup, Courtney found Justin on the balcony. He wore khakis but no shirt. He was still on the phone, but she could tell from his mannerisms that it wasn't with her parents. He turned, blew her a kiss, then gazed back at the water. Courtney slipped into a skinny-strapped sundress and joined him on the balcony. Justin spanked her playfully as she walked past to join him on the bench.

"Here, you can tell her yourself," he said to the caller. "Keith," he mouthed to Courtney.

She took the phone, let Keith congratulate her, and then hung up. "Should we go eat now?" she asked, knowing full well that Justin had to be starving. He ate more than anyone she'd ever known and was always hungry. He nodded eagerly, and they went inside.

"How'd it go with my parents?" she asked as he buttoned a white shirt and rolled up the sleeves.

He laughed. "I'm not sure they like me. Especially your dad."

"Everyone likes you," she replied, which was true. Justin was an exceedingly likable guy. She never knew if it was the dimples, his uncanny ability to always say the right thing, or something more complicated, but everyone liked him.

He shrugged. "Well, for people who like me, they sure seem to think I'm going to eat you or something."

Courtney smiled, rising to her toes to kiss him.

THE NEXT THREE days of vacation flew by. They had settled into a decent routine—sleep in late, sex, breakfast, lounge by the beach, lunch, sex, lounge in the pool, hit the gym, dinner, sex, sleep. It was exactly what Justin pictured in a honeymoon, except they still had that to look forward to sometime. Justin had taken beach vacations with his ex-girlfriend, Kinzie, but it hadn't been the same. He wasn't sure if the difference was the engagement, or if every vacation with Courtney would really be this good. He hadn't harbored any doubts about whether Courtney was the woman for him, but if he had, this would've reinforced his decision.

He realized it was unfair to assume every day with Courtney would be as idyllic as vacation, but he figured it wouldn't be too different. Courtney was the easiest person to love Justin had ever met. She was hardworking and smart, but modest. She was beautiful, but not self-obsessed, and she spent far less time and money on her appearance than Justin did his own. She was fun without being irresponsible or reckless.

Best of all, she was his. Justin had always assumed he'd never be able to pursue a relationship with someone who wasn't also a celebrity without questioning whether she was dating him for love, or following some other agenda. But with Courtney, there wasn't a doubt in his mind that she loved him because of the man he was, and that she would stand by his side whether or not he was popular or famous. Courtney hadn't abandoned him when a bitter Kinzie started a nasty rumor that he was abusive, even though the lies had cost Courtney her job.

Courtney lifted her head from the recliner where she was sprawled on her stomach and turned to face him before plopping back against her towel. Thanks to her thick purple sunglasses, Justin wasn't sure if she was awake or not. They hadn't been getting too much sleep overnight lately, so napping was completely understandable. When they returned to reality the next day, Justin would miss the frequent catnaps.

He wrinkled his nose, now focused on all the other things he'd miss once they were back into the grind. Namely, the free time, and the privacy. Well, the resort wasn't private per se, but as a couples' resort, everyone else there was primarily focused on their own traveling companion and, for the most part, left him alone. Justin had a grueling work schedule awaiting him at home, too. He had a modeling shoot right off the bat, and then was set to film one project after another, just like the previous year.

He didn't mind the work. He loved it, really. Learning new lines, starting to transform himself into a completely new character, it was exhilarating. And now that he had more movies under his belt, more opportunities came to him, which meant Justin could be choosier about what projects he accepted.

Still, there wouldn't be a lot of downtime. If he wasn't actively filming, he'd be working out, rehearsing for his next role, or promoting his current project.

He groaned, then realized Courtney had propped herself onto her elbows. She lowered her shades, letting her cerulean eyes pierce his thoughts.

"Are you thinking about Jamie?" she asked.

Justin laughed. "Why would you assume that?"

"Your dimples disappeared, so you must be stressed about something."

Now that she mentioned it, Justin probably should be worried about Jamie. The woman was a phenomenal publicist, but she was scary, and by proposing to Courtney and telling other people about it rather than letting her handle the news, he'd clearly crossed her.

"I can handle Jamie," he said. "But I think we need to cool

off." He leapt to his feet, lifted his fiancée, and carried her over his shoulder towards the water. Her shrieks of protest peaked as he tossed her into the water, but the moment he joined her and pressed his lips against hers, she was silent.

3

When they returned from the trip, Courtney was anxious to get back to work. After beginning her career as an attorney for a large shelter housing domestic violence victims, Courtney had abruptly lost her job following a nasty fabricated scandal about Justin. Fortunately, unbeknownst to Courtney, Justin had been offering financial support to another smaller shelter for women and children not too far from his house, and that shelter offered her a job.

Courtney was the only attorney at the new shelter, which meant she was responsible for a wide range of legal issues. The shelter was a non-profit, so in addition to the family law and criminal issues she advised clients on, Courtney also had a fair amount of business law inching its way into her daily work life. She embraced the challenge, legitimately enjoying the opportunity to broaden her horizons and learn new things. Plus, her boss, April, was a wonderful woman who really liked Courtney and was extremely flexible with Courtney taking time off.

Even though her job title, Chief Counsel, sounded fancy, Courtney was only a managerial level employee of the shelter. Someday, she wanted to be an executive, or at least hold a seat on a board of directors, but for now, she was content with how her hard work had paid off.

After missing a week of work, Courtney was overwhelmed with a slew of voice mails, emails and letters. She'd been at her desk for less than an hour when April popped her head in to update Courtney on everything she'd missed over the past week.

"How was your trip?" April asked politely, and then her jaw literally dropped. She stared at the ring, and then looked up at Courtney, beaming. "Is that what I think it is?"

Courtney nodded. "He asked me the first night of the trip. It was so romantic."

"It's beautiful. Congratulations."

Courtney waited for April to return to a work-related subject, but she just kept grinning instead. "What?"

April's shoulders jostled as she let out a short laugh. "Nothing. I just think your engagement is really good news for the shelter."

"How so?"

April sighed. "Oh Courtney, we both know you could find a much better paying job elsewhere. But if you don't need money, you're more likely to stay here long term." She paused. "And I'm banking on your husband-to-be making another donation or two in the future."

Courtney smiled and nodded. April was probably right. Without financial concerns, Courtney had no reason to leave a job she liked. Of course, she'd planned to practice this type of law long before she met Justin.

In college, she'd debated becoming a social worker or a lawyer, and, mostly since both of her brothers had gone on to graduate school, she'd decided to try law school. From the start, Courtney had wanted to find a way to use her law degree to help people, ideally domestic violence victims. But the realities of law school loan repayment and L.A. living expenses, especially when her family was across the country, might have pressured Courtney to give up.

She'd actually been so dedicated to her studies when she met Justin that she nearly missed out on a real relationship with him.

April's expression changed rapidly, dragging Courtney back to the present.

"You're not going to get pregnant and quit right away are you?"

Courtney laughed. "That's a ridiculous notion. We are like a decade away from any babies. Besides, I hear that nowadays women can be moms and still have a career."

April smirked at the comment. Courtney had met April's son multiple times, so April was a great example of being able to work and raise a family too.

Courtney's first day back flew by, with little opportunity for her to accomplish anything she'd planned on doing. At six o'clock, Justin called.

"Hey babe, where are you?" he asked. She could hear him chewing something and figured he had just finished up at the gym.

"Work," she replied.

"Are you coming over tonight?"

She considered that. Before their vacation, Courtney and Justin had never been one of those couples to spend all their time together. She worked most days, more or less on an 8-6 schedule, and Justin traveled frequently for his work, meaning they'd occasionally go weeks without seeing each other. But now, Courtney missed him a little already, not having been apart from him for more than ten minutes over the past week.

"Court?"

"Sorry. Um, no, I'm going to stay late and get back to work early tomorrow."

Justin sighed nervously. "Will you have any free time tomorrow?"

"Why?"

"I have a meeting with Jamie and Marty. They want you to come."

Courtney felt her face wrinkle into a wince. Justin's agent Marty was a nice, but pushy, guy, although he typically did a great job for Justin as far as she could tell. And Jamie, well, she was equally effective as a publicist, but she was terrifying. "Can't they just lecture you for both of us?"

He chuckled. "Please? I told them we'd be in around 11:30. I'll buy you lunch after."

"Fine." Courtney never could say no to him.

The next morning, he picked her up at work in his shiny silver Audi. It was clear Justin had already been to the gym that morning, although he was showered and dressed nicely. Justin spent hours each day exercising. He enjoyed being outdoors, and doing any type of physical activity he could, but in order to maintain his physique, he also had to lift weights, an activity generally confined to the gym.

They were mostly quiet on the short drive, and they parked next to Keith's car. Courtney was relieved that Keith was joining them also. Justin climbed out of the car, walked around to Courtney's side and wrapped his arm around her as they walked in together, instantly comforting her.

"Courtney," Marty said with a professional smile, reaching forward and shaking her hand. He paused and turned his gaze to her other hand. "May I?"

She nodded.

He held her left hand, inspecting the ring. "Nice," he said to Justin, releasing Courtney's hand.

Justin grinned. "Keith helped pick it out."

"Of course he did," Marty replied dryly. He motioned for

them all to sit while his assistant got drinks for everyone. Keith plopped into a chair, and Justin and Courtney sat on the couch. Justin placed his hand across Courtney's thigh, as though he was holding her in place.

Jamie burst into the office then, a stack of papers poking out from a manila folder. "Sorry I'm late. Busy morning," she mumbled, taking a seat by Marty. Her eyes immediately turned to Courtney's hand as well, focusing on the ring for an inordinate amount of time. Her face showed no expression.

Marty nodded. "Right. Well, good news first. I got the renewal offer you've been waiting for. I'm going to counter and see if they'll up the ante, but I think you'll be content with what they're offering now. Details are in the contract I'll leave with Keith, but don't sign it yet and don't discuss it with them at your shoot tomorrow. Assuming they like what they see tomorrow, we'll be good to go on that, and they want to start the first segment in a few weeks."

"What do you mean, if they like what they see?" Justin asked, his forehead wrinkling.

Marty licked his lips. "They've got some language about weight in the contract. They might want you to drop a little."

Keith laughed out loud. Justin grimaced, his fingers squeezing into Courtney's thigh.

"How much and how soon?"

Marty raised his hands defensively. "I won't know the details until after they see you tomorrow. Just wanted to give you a heads up. You've got a trainer and nutritionist on set with the Marks film, right?"

Justin nodded.

Courtney recalled that he was shooting something called *Hit the Marks* starting the next week, but she didn't remember any of the other details.

"I have a few more scripts for you, but that's about it. Did you go over the publicity schedule for *Days End*?"

"It's all fine," Keith chimed in. *Days End* was a series of four movies Justin had filmed, and the final installment was due out in theaters in the coming year, so he'd be doing a lot of publicity for that.

"Aren't I in New York sometime?" Justin asked. Everyone smiled. Justin was a smart guy, and obviously a talented actor and model, but he had no concept of his schedule. That was why it was so convenient that Keith had become his manager.

"Yeah," Keith said. He pulled out some notes and a calendar.

Courtney tuned out while they discussed where Justin would be over the next few months. It was mind-boggling, trying to keep track of it all. She perked up when Jamie mentioned something about a talk show in Chicago.

"My brother lives in Chicago," Courtney said. "We could visit him."

Justin nodded. "Am I free then?"

Keith glanced at a few papers. "Yeah. If you did the show on Friday, you could stay through the weekend. You're free Thursday too."

"So you want to do the talk show?" Jamie was skeptical.

"Yep. Sounds good."

Keith turned to Courtney. "I'll make the travel arrangements."

"Okay. Give me a week or so to check with my brother first and make sure I can get off work."

Jamie sighed. "Keith, I'll hold off on confirming the show until you get back with me."

Courtney exhaled and exchanged a weary glance with Justin. His life was stressful.

"My turn?" Jamie asked with a smile.

Marty and Keith both nodded.

Jamie turned to Courtney and Justin. "First off, let me congratulate you both," she began without pause. "Obviously, a little advance notice would have been nice. I always hate hearing the good news from a reporter who follows you on Twitter," she said, glaring at Justin.

"Just keeping you on your toes," he said with a distinct smirk.

"Right, well, in that vein, let me ask this. Have you picked a date, made any other major decisions?"

Justin eyed Courtney. She shook her head nervously.

"Ballpark, how long of an engagement are we looking at? Are you going to do a private or family-only wedding, some big blow out, or something overseas?"

Courtney's breath caught in her throat.

"We haven't decided anything yet," Justin said, squeezing Courtney's thigh again.

"Is there anything else you haven't told us? Any explanation for the timing of this delightful engagement?" Jamie asked, her gaze dropping to Courtney's belly.

Courtney drew her hands over her stomach. "I'm not pregnant! Why does everyone think that?"

Justin and Keith both laughed. Jamie's glare didn't falter, though, so Courtney turned to Justin for support.

"Seriously, I proposed because I like her and I actually want to be with her. She's really not pregnant," Justin said, adding, "As far as I know, anyway."

Courtney rolled her eyes at the last part, but it seemed to convince Jamie.

"Okay, so I'm fine to confirm the engagement, proposal location and date, and no plans made for the wedding yet, right?"

Justin hesitated, then nodded.

"Justin, I know you think I'm out to get you, but we're on the same team here. I can help you manage the press, keep the chaos to a minimum, and have whatever wedding experience you want if you keep me in the loop. Do you understand?"

He grinned. "No more tweets. I get it."

"Well, if you could at least run them by me first," Jamie said. "Now, I think we should get official engagement photos to the press ASAP. How's tomorrow?"

Courtney and Justin both shook their heads.

"He already has a shoot tomorrow," Keith said.

"Yeah, so unless you want me in my underwear for the engagement photos..."

"Is an engagement photo really necessary?" Courtney asked. Keith and Justin both shot her panicked looks that suggested she'd be better off not questioning Jamie.

Jamie nodded and jotted something on a notepad. "Great. Then Thursday. If we say around lunchtime, will that give you time for the gym in the morning?"

Justin nodded.

"Wait a minute. I can't miss more work. And what am I supposed to wear for these photos?"

Jamie sighed so hard that Courtney felt the ice from her breath on her arms. "It'll take an hour. Make it work. If we don't get this to the press soon, we might as well not bother because it'll be old news." She shook her head again, but not a single hair strayed from her tightly wound bun. "Had I known your plans in advance, Justin, I could have been more accommodating with the scheduling."

Justin rubbed Courtney's thigh and then squeezed her hand. "It's fine. We'll make it work. Right?"

Courtney shrugged. "I still don't know what to wear."

Jamie rolled her eyes and turned to Marty. "Send in an intern who can get her measurements." She turned back to Courtney. "I'll have a few outfits in your size sent over to Justin's tomorrow. Pick your favorite and have Justin dress to match. I assume you can handle your own wardrobe?" she said to Justin.

He nodded and snorted, as though it were a ridiculous notion for someone not to know what to wear to a photoshoot.

A frazzled looking man in a suit scurried into the office. Jamie eyed him and pointed at Courtney. "Get all of her measurements," Jamie instructed, "And text the final numbers to me so I have them on file and we don't have to mess with this again."

The man nodded and then hustled Courtney out of her chair. He led her to the other side of the office where he began stretching a cloth measuring tape around her, poking and prodding her in uncomfortably private places. She knew she was blushing, and she caught Justin watching, barely able to contain his laughter.

By the time they were out of the office, Courtney was exhausted.

"I have no idea how you do that all the time," she admitted.

Justin laughed. "Seriously? You deal with taxes and custody fights and criminal issues, but my agent and publicist are what stress you out?"

"Jamie made a strange man measure my boobs," Courtney reminded him.

"Yeah, but now you'll get cool clothes without the stress of shopping," he said. "Besides, I don't pay Marty and Jamie to be easygoing."

Justin stopped and spoke to Keith for a moment, so Courtney climbed into the car and checked her email while she waited. Finally, Justin angled himself behind the wheel.

"Did I mention my baby brother is coming to visit on Friday?"

"Luke?" Courtney had met him the previous summer, when she went to Justin's house with him. Unfortunately, she was topless at the time Luke first saw her, making for a memorable and humiliating first encounter.

Justin chuckled and nodded, probably remembering the same incident. "It's his twenty-first birthday, and he said he wanted to party in L.A."

"Ah, well how convenient then that he has a brother in the area with some decent party connections."

"He's staying through Wednesday." Justin paused. "I have no idea what to do with him that whole time."

"You probably don't have to babysit him. He could do some sightseeing during the days and go out with you and Keith at night."

Justin sighed. "I start filming Monday. I was hoping to spend the weekend with you. You'll come out with us this weekend?"

Courtney pictured Justin with his brother. Justin had two personas—the romantic or the guys' guy. When he was with her, he was the most attentive, loving guy around. He was constantly touching her, kissing her, and smiling at her. But when Justin was with the guys, he drank too much, cursed too freely, and occasionally slipped out inappropriate comments about other women. Courtney considered Justin to be a reformed partier, although he still liked to have fun. And she was fine with that, as long as she didn't have to witness it firsthand.

"Nope. I'll come over tonight and I'll drop by tomorrow to see the outfits. But I have a work dinner Saturday."

Justin parked in front of the Thai restaurant. "Wait, are you saying you won't even sleep over while he's in town?" He climbed out of the car and walked around to open her door.

"I don't want to corrupt your little brother."

"He already saw your boobs."

"Don't remind me."

"Well, seriously then, what's the issue? He already knows

we're sleeping together. Everyone does." He nonchalantly held up two fingers to the restaurant's hostess.

"How can you even say that?"

"It's true. You've been photographed leaving my place early in the morning on multiple occasions. It's all over the internet."

Courtney grimaced, but followed him to the table. "And also, why does everyone keep assuming I'm pregnant? Is it that ridiculous of a notion that you would marry me without feeling like you had to marry me?"

Courtney spotted the mischievous gleam in Justin's eyes the moment he turned to her, grinning.

"No, but is it that ridiculous for someone to think you'd have my baby?" He tilted forward across the table conspiratorially, waiting until the hostess left them alone to continue. "If you're game, we could sneak into the restroom and make a baby right now."

Between the dimples and those dangerous baby blues, Courtney could actually see him tricking her into some dubious behavior. But not that. "First of all, a public bathroom? Gross. Second, I'm on birth control. And third, are you crazy? We are both just starting out on our careers and neither of us has time for a baby!"

Justin rested back, folding his arms against his chest. Courtney knew without looking that he'd also stretched out his legs and crossed them at the ankles. He didn't say anything right away, so she waited.

After a moment, he cracked a smile. "Well, first of all, I have it on good authority that this bathroom is the cleanest in all of Venice. Second, it just so happens that I'm not really ready to share you with a baby yet anyway."

Courtney started to relax just as the waitress approached, but then Justin leaned forward again.

"We'd make ridiculously cute babies, though. You can't argue with that," he said.

He wasn't wrong, but Courtney felt the blood rushing to her cheeks regardless.

The waitress greeted them nervously, clearly recognizing Justin. When she asked for their drink orders, Courtney was about to speak, since Justin always let her order first, but then he spoke.

"Could you tell me anything about the restrooms here? I mean, are they relatively clean?" He furrowed his brows together as though posing a serious inquiry.

Courtney figured her cheeks were probably beet red by now. "He's kidding, don't answer that. And I'm fine with water. Thanks."

"No mojito?" Justin asked. "You're not pregnant, are you?"

Courtney threw her napkin at him and turned back to the waitress after shooting him her best scolding look. "Actually, a mojito sounds great."

Justin beamed, clearly proud. He wouldn't think it was so funny if he started some nasty pregnancy rumor.

4

Later that afternoon, Justin hit the gym. Nothing made him feel as well-entrenched in his usual routine as his workouts with Ryan. He'd met Ryan years ago, when they'd begun the initial cast readings for the first *Days End* movie. Ryan played Justin's dad on the movie, but in reality, less than a decade separated their ages.

"Well, you've been busy lately," Ryan said with a smirk, wiping his forehead on a towel before reaching for his water bottle.

"Not as busy as you," Justin replied. The pilot for a new forensics drama starring Ryan had just aired. By all accounts, it had been a tremendous success, so the show was guaranteed at least one sixteen-episode season, likely more. "That's great about your new gig."

"Thank you, but I was talking about your personal life. Your engagement? Congratulations."

"Oh!" Justin laughed at his own confusion. "Thanks, man."

"Have you guys picked a date?"

Justin shifted into place on the weight bench before answering. "No. We haven't planned a thing. I think Courtney is envisioning a longer engagement." He paused, exhaling hard as he pressed the weight up away from his face. "Personally, I'd rather get it over with sooner."

He finished out the set before slowly sitting upright and gazing at Ryan.

"Get it over with? Well, that's romantic."

Justin chuckled. "I didn't mean it like that, just that it seems like it might be a bit of a publicity nightmare."

"A bit," Ryan repeated, biting back a smile.

Justin sipped his water and got ready to spot Ryan. "But I am really ready to have it all official. You know, just to be done. Dating is exhausting." He paused, worried it sounded like he was still dating multiple women. "Relationships are just so much work, you know?"

A peculiar look crossed Ryan's face. "And you think marriage is easy?"

"Maybe not easy, but..." Justin shrugged. "You've got security in a marriage, at least. Whatever happens, there's still this other person by your side, cheering you on and sticking with you no matter what. And you can finally stop questioning everything. Like you don't have to wonder anymore whether you've found the right person or what the rest of your life will look like. You've decided. It's done."

Ryan snorted and ducked out from under the weights after securing the bar in its holder. "Clearly you've never been married. If you think dating is work, just watch out." He shook his head.

"Oh, stop, I've seen you and Audrey. You can't even pretend you're not happy."

Ryan's grin widened, but he kept quiet as they switched spots for the second set.

"Courtney isn't high maintenance by any means, but I've spent a lot of time over the last year feeling like I've got to convince her I'm worth it. My filming schedule, meeting the parents, her job...everything is a possible deal-breaker when you're only dating. And now that we're engaged, at least she believes I'm serious, that we are both on the same page. But there's still stuff that could happen. I just want to wake up every morning and know she's got my back, that she's mine and no one else's."

Justin tightened his abs as he pushed through the last few reps. "And I want the world to know she's off the market, I'm off the market. No more questions about whether I'm secretly dating a coworker or that crap. And no more worrying about whether she'll put up with me traveling too far or filming too much. I'm ready to know we are in it together till the end no matter what."

Ryan slowly shook his head from side to side. "Sometimes I forget you're not from around here, and then you say things like that and..." he laughed.

Justin wiped his face on his towel, certain he was blushing. "Are you implying I'm a romantic?"

His buddy laughed out loud. "I'm implying you're naïve. Just because you get married doesn't mean anything changes. Dating is the fun part. Marriage is work. If you're expecting easy, you're setting yourself up for a big disappointment."

"Easy probably isn't the right word. Security is more what I'm looking for," Justin clarified, rolling his shoulders.

"So back in the Midwest, you all don't have that thing called divorce?" Ryan taunted.

"It's easier to dump someone than divorce them."

"True, but even if you're too lazy for a divorce, that doesn't mean you're being faithful."

Justin made a face. "Seriously? Are you trying to stress me out?"

"I'm trying to paint a realistic picture for you here. Chances are, you'll live happily ever after. But getting married doesn't make any of your problems go away. If she doesn't like you shooting out of town half the year now, she's not going to like it any more after the wedding. And if she doesn't trust you to keep it in your pants now..."

"She trusts me," Justin interrupted, shaking his head. "I would never cheat on my wife."

Ryan looked skeptical. "You say that now, but after two years of fighting over conflicting schedules and child care and never sleeping ever, and only hearing about all the things you do wrong... you might run into some woman who actually makes you feel good about yourself again. And when you do, it can be really hard to remember why you were so sure you'd say no."

Justin licked his lips, trying to piece together what Ryan meant. "Wait, you're not saying you cheated on Audrey..." he said, his voice hushed.

Ryan's jaw hardened into a straight line, but he didn't confirm or deny the allegations. "I'm just saying it's hard. Especially in our line of work. You both gotta wake up every day and decide to make it work. It doesn't just happen without any effort."

He patted Justin on the back and nodded his head towards the next weight machine. "I've got a great couple's counselor when you're ready, though."

Justin cocked his head to the side. None of that sounded like the reassurance he wanted. "Gee, thanks."

He was quiet as they started on the next set, wanting to change the subject but not able to pull his mind off of the conversation just yet. He'd always idealized Ryan and Audrey's relationship, but he knew it wasn't all butterflies and rainbows. For Justin though, they'd always been the shining example of a Hollywood couple who made it work. Ryan and Audrey had both grown up in Los Angeles, both started acting as children, and both had successful careers in Hollywood. Lately, Audrey hadn't filmed much, now that they had three adorable children and Ryan's schedule was so busy, but Justin never got the impression she resented Ryan for any of that. They both just seemed so happy. Surely it couldn't all be an illusion.

Justin released the weight and rolled his shoulders forward a few times. He recalled what Ryan had told him before, about how Audrey actually got pregnant before they were even engaged. Before, Justin had assumed they'd eloped for the same reason many Hollywood couples did—privacy. But now, he wasn't so sure.

"A couple people assumed Courtney was pregnant when we told them about the engagement," Justin said, quickly adding, "She's not."

Ryan chuckled. "I could see that."

"What do you mean?"

He shrugged. "You've got a reputation as a player. True or not, many people assume you're not the type to settle down unless you feel forced. Knowing you and hearing all the sappy shit you say about this girl, I know differently."

Justin felt himself bobbing his head in agreement. That actually made sense. Maybe the assumptions bothered Courtney so much because she didn't like anyone questioning his dedication to her, not because the thought of having his baby repulsed her. "She does seem totally freaked out by the prospect of kids, though."

"Tell me you've discussed all of that, man. Look, I'm not one to give advice on what you've got to do before marriage, but agreeing on the basics like whether you want kids seems pretty obvious."

"Of course we have. We do agree."

Ryan eyed him warily, trying unsuccessfully to hold in his laughter.

"What?"

"Don't you have like eight brothers? Poor Courtney must be terrified thinking you want to recreate that shit."

"There's only six of us in my family, and I'd be fine with less than that. Three seems like a good number."

Ryan clicked his tongue. "Three is twice the work of two. And you gotta go from man-to-man to zone defense when you have the third."

Justin chuckled at the analogy. "You seem to like your third kid."

"Of course I like Stella. I'm sure I'd love kids four through six, too. That doesn't mean I have any business having that many."

"Yeah, I don't know how my parents did it. My brothers and I were not low maintenance kids." Justin tried to picture him and Courtney with a large brood and couldn't. He did like the thought of her at home with his babies, though. That whole barefoot, pregnant, and in the kitchen waiting for his return concept had a certain appeal, even though he knew it was completely sexist and backwards. He didn't actually want that, but it would be nice to know that he was her whole world.

Ryan furrowed his brows. "I don't even want to know what you're thinking."

"And you never will. I can't even say out loud the caveman-type shit going through my mind now," Justin replied with a laugh.

His friend sunk onto the weight bench and lifted his water bottle. "Well now you've piqued my interest. You have to tell me."

Justin shook his head. "No, I was just thinking about how now, Courtney has so much going on, like this whole life separate from me. Even when we get married, she's still going to be obsessed with her work. And that's cool, I mean, she should do what she loves. I'm not backwards enough to think I should get to have a career and interests apart from her while she's sitting at home raising my kids, but man, it would be nice to be her entire world for once. She's already mine."

Ryan's expression looked pained. "Dude, you sound like a serial killer, but somehow I sorta get what you mean. It doesn't work like that, though. If she's at home with fussy babies and sneaky toddlers and you're out traveling and fulfilling all your wildest career fantasies, you will not be her whole world. She will hate you." He shook his head. "Look, the girl was crazy enough to agree to marry you, so maybe you should just trust her and stop being so damn insecure."

Justin blew out a sigh and then laughed. That was what he loved about Ryan- the guy was for sure a straight shooter. And his advice was always spot on.

He nodded to Ryan. "Yeah. Alright, less chitchat and more lifting."

COURTNEY STEPPED BACK into her office and shut the door behind her. Walking to the window, she gazed out for a few moments, letting her mind wander. She always needed time to decompress after meeting with clients. Their stories were never the same, but the themes never differed. They were all women who had worked hard and loved fiercely and were completely betrayed by someone they loved. Often, it wasn't intentional. Lots of women she worked with were abused by someone struggling with a substance abuse problem or mental health issues. It wasn't always just a total jerk hurting them.

And her clients weren't always angels. Some of them dealt with their own substance abuse problems. Some of them had unrealistic expectations of the world. Many weren't big fans of adulting in general. But none of them deserved to be hurt. And the ones that had children stuck in the middle...gah. It was heartbreaking.

Courtney's phone dinged loudly, bringing a smile to her face. It was the chime she'd assigned to Justin. She swallowed one more deep, cleansing breath then turned to her phone.

"Ryan says I'm an insecure caveman. Pretty sure he thinks you could do better," his text read.

Courtney chewed her lip, welcoming the image of Justin working out that had now replaced the grittier thoughts in her mind. "He's right, but you're stuck with me. Hope you had a good workout. Send pics."

His response wasn't immediate, but when it did come through, Courtney couldn't help but smile at the image. Justin had lifted his shirt, flexed his abs, and taken a picture in the mirror.

Courtney blew out a sigh and fanned herself with an AA pamphlet on her desk. She seriously had the hottest fiancé ever. And he wasn't just a pretty face and perfectly sculpted body. Justin treated her like royalty. When it came to Courtney, Justin was totally insecure, and she found that adorable. He was universally loved—by those who knew him and strangers too—and he was funny, smart, successful, hard-working, and oh so sweet. She wasn't sure she actually deserved a man like Justin, but she wasn't going to complain either.

Especially not while staring at statistics about the recent uptick in police calls for domestic disturbances.

Courtney cleared off a space on her desk and pulled out a notepad. She could type faster than she could write by hand, but something about a physical pen and paper helped her brainstorm better. She wanted to write an article highlighting the shortcomings in current laws and how they minimized the effectiveness of the protections offered to victims of domestic violence. It wasn't an official part of her job description, but publishing in a legal journal, especially a prestigious one, could bring a lot of positive attention to the shelter. Besides, she was uniquely positioned to educate the public on some of these topics, and she didn't want to waste her talent.

Throughout law school, Courtney observed that everyone assumed the only students with lofty ambitions were those seeking competitive positions in big law firms or those hoping to someday land a political post. Courtney had never been attracted to the typical law firm schedule and had zero interest to ever be a partner. Honestly, it sounded awful.

One of her law school friends, Ashley, was an associate at a larger firm in Los Angeles, but they never even saw her because she worked all the time. She didn't do any interesting work—just grunt stuff. But every single task that a senior associate tossed her way, she'd snatch up in hopes of making partner.

Courtney could definitely understand wanting to go far with her career. Money wasn't ever the goal for her with the law, and thanks to Justin, that likely wouldn't ever be an obstacle either. But she definitely had ambitions. Someday, she wanted to head up her own shelter. She'd love to be involved on the boards of multiple nonprofits. Maybe she'd even venture into lobbying and help strengthen some of the laws she currently had to work with. Teaching also appealed to her.

So, while Courtney could sit back and do the bare minimum, she wasn't about to take that route. She was determined to get her article published somewhere, then start a new one and move up from there.

But first she had to focus enough to write the darn thing.

5

———

The next morning, Justin was struggling at his photo shoot.

"Take five," the director called, and Justin exhaled hard. He did a few shoulder and neck rolls, amazed at how stiff he felt after just a half hour of posing. Justin made his way to the long table decked out with food and grabbed a bottle of water, chugging thirstily before heading to the chair where he'd left his jeans. He glanced up as he heard a familiar voice.

"Wow, looking good," she said.

Justin smiled. "Hey, Courtney." He was careful not to rub up against her as he kissed her on the cheek. She didn't tend to be too picky about her clothes, but the Vaseline coating his upper body probably wouldn't wash out of her blouse.

He watched as her eyes scanned up and down his body, and then he reached for his jeans. They'd given him a robe to wear on breaks, but it felt strange to parade around a room of fully clothed people in a bathrobe. He zipped the jeans and stared back at Courtney.

"You're not saying anything," he noticed.

She smiled, her eyes wide. "I have no words for this."

He plopped down in a director's chair off to the side and drank more of his water. "What did you expect?"

"I'm not sure." She eyed the room warily.

Justin tried to see it from her perspective. The large, mostly empty studio resembled an abandoned warehouse. The white stage, with a white backdrop, was surrounded by half a dozen chairs and several tall lights, not to mention an abundance of camera equipment. The rest of the room, including the part where they were, near the snack table, was darker. The room was cool, but Justin was comfortable in just his jeans, probably since he'd been flexing his abs, punching the air, and prancing around as directed by the photographers for the past half hour.

"We've still got two more styles to go," he told her. "It'll probably be a couple more hours at least. Are you going to stick around for a while?"

"Do you want me to? I'd hate to distract you." Courtney traced her finger along his chest muscles, drawing down towards his bare stomach as she spoke, probably just curious about the shimmery goo on his skin.

Justin grabbed her hand and squeezed it. "Well, I was going to say I didn't think you'd distract me, but if you're going to keep that up..." he sighed, desperate to keep his mind on G-rated topics.

"Oh, sorry," she said with a laugh.

He smiled, trying to guess what they'd even do if he returned to the stage visibly aroused. Probably they'd douse him with water. Justin was also fairly certain it would end up on the internet, though, and he wasn't sure if that was a good or bad thing. It was standard practice for this type of modeling shoot to maintain a flag-half-mast, so to speak, and there were a few key tricks to achieving that, but Justin suspected nothing good could come from the effect Courtney would have on his flag.

"How long of a break do you have?"

Justin shrugged. "Dunno. They'll let me know when they need me."

"Won't you need to change?"

He nodded.

Courtney looked concerned. "Will you do that out here?"

Justin laughed. "No, I have a dressing room."

"Oh. Do you want to go there now?"

"I'm pretty sure I don't have a long enough break now to be alone with you in my dressing room."

She swatted him playfully. "I didn't mean that. I just wanted to talk."

His eyes were drawn to her chest, the casual way the thin silk of her blouse clung to her breasts, revealing a hint of her lacy white bra. "I'm not good at talking," he finally said.

"You're terrible," she said, rolling her eyes.

"I can't help it. Look at yourself!"

She obeyed, then looked back up at him, her face emotionless. "I'm wearing black suit pants and a blouse. No part of this is sexy."

Justin grinned. One of the things that had originally drawn him to Courtney was how oblivious she was to her own good looks. She could wear sweat pants and an old tee shirt and men would still ogle her, all without her noticing. He wasn't sure if it was the fiercely blue eyes, her smooth olive skin, or her long, shiny brown hair, but something about Courtney just drew the eye in.

Jana, one of the assistants, approached Justin. A pair of black boxer briefs with a red waistband was in her hands. "You ready?" she asked.

Justin nodded, finishing his water before standing. "Jana, this is my fiancée, Courtney."

Jana smiled to Courtney. "Lucky woman," she said.

Justin laughed. "Jury's still out on that one," he said, catching Courtney's eye.

"I'll meet you in your room," Jana said, walking away before mumbling something else into the headset she wore.

Justin turned back to Courtney, who looked indignant. "Wait, so she gets to go to your dressing room with you and I don't?"

"She's not going to taunt me until the briefs don't fit right," Justin said. "And besides, I need someone to get me all lubed up before I go back out there." He saw a look of panic wash across Courtney's face. "Don't worry, she's not going to help me get dressed or anything. I still have some dignity," he said.

Courtney's nose wrinkled in an adorable way, distracting Justin yet again, until he realized he didn't even know why she was there. "I thought you were swamped today. Is everything okay?"

She smiled. "Everything is fine. I had a meeting a few blocks from here and Keith texted me the address, so I figured I'd drop by." Courtney paused, again gazing around the room. "I just felt bad about ditching you again last night, well, and telling you I wouldn't sleep over when your brother came to visit. I don't want you to think I'm avoiding you."

"It is a little overwhelming, coming back to reality and having the engagement news out there," he said, certain that was what she actually stressing about.

"Yeah, it just feels so fast," she said.

Justin's stomach dropped. "You think we're rushing things?"

Courtney's eyes caught his and her expression quickly changed. "No, that's not what I meant." She reached for his hand and squeezed it. "I am thrilled and beyond happy to be your fiancée. I just wasn't prepared for questions about the wedding yet."

Her eyes were filled with so much love that Justin didn't

doubt for a moment that she still wanted to be with him. He just needed to work harder to shelter her from the chaos that went hand in hand with his career. "There's no rush on the plans, Courtney. I could marry you tomorrow or I could wait years. As long as you're mine, I don't care about the timing or the details."

She rolled her eyes but couldn't stifle the grin. "You and your lines. If this were a movie, you would totally get lucky in the next scene."

Justin laughed. "I'm okay with waiting till tonight. You'll come over after work tonight, right?"

"Yes, but we both need our beauty sleep or Jamie will kill us."

That was true. "Thank you for dropping by."

Courtney nodded and blew a kiss. Justin leaned in, pressing his lips against her forehead before unbuttoning his jeans as he trotted off after Jana.

THE NEXT DAY found Justin at a very different type of photo shoot—his engagement pictures with Courtney. She loved one of the outfits Jamie's crew sent over, so thankfully everything went smoothly. Jamie promised they could review the proofs over the weekend before she distributed them Monday.

Although Courtney sailed through the photo shoot, Justin knew she was uncomfortable with all the attention. For some unknown reason, she hated finding pictures of herself in the media, even though she always looked adorable. She insisted on returning to work Thursday and working late, but she did show up for a sleepover at Justin's Friday night.

They'd gone out for dinner, then lounged around the house, Courtney caught Justin up to speed on everything she'd been up to at work, minus all the confidential details, and then she'd helped him run lines for the Marks film he was about to start shooting. At some point, they both fell asleep.

Justin awoke suddenly, and before his eyes had adjusted to the dark, he realized that he was shaking. He turned, expecting to see Courtney bouncing around, but she was completely still. Her eyes popped open suddenly, and with her face mere inches from his, Justin could tell she was terrified.

"Earthquake!" he said the moment he figured it out. But then, the shaking stopped.

They both sat up in bed and Justin flicked on the light.

Courtney peered from side to side, her arms wrapped tightly around her knees.

"It's over," he said. "Just a mild one."

The bed began to shake again, and this time, Justin realized the movement was from Courtney trembling.

"Oh babe," he said, reaching for her. He pulled her onto his lap and roped his arms around her. He could hear the faint sound of car alarms outside, but the inside of the house was quiet. Keith was at Tara's for the night, so the silence made sense. Justin held Courtney tightly for a few minutes, until she stopped trembling.

"That was your first earthquake, wasn't it?"

She nodded.

He figured the quake had to have been relatively low on the scale. After an earthquake with a larger magnitude, there could've been aftershocks, but Justin suspected the rest of the night would be still. But he didn't want to guarantee it.

"It's done for now, and I'm sure nothing was damaged. We could go back to sleep."

Courtney tilted her head back and peered at the ceiling, as though expecting the fan to fall down on them. Justin knew she was wondering what would happen if another one hit.

"I really don't think there will be more," he continued. "And if there is, I promise to shelter you with my body."

She cracked a smile at that, but still looked uneasy.

"It's a nice night. Let's go outside by the pool," he said.

Courtney hesitated for a minute, then nodded. Justin grabbed a blanket then led her by the hand towards the patio. He didn't notice any damage, but a few smaller objects had fallen over and the pictures on the wall were crooked.

Courtney padded slowly to a pool chair. She stretched out on her back, still wearing what she'd been sleeping in—black bikini cut panties and a ribbed white tank top she'd borrowed from him. He was mostly undressed too. Seemed like a wasted opportunity, both of them being up in the night without their clothes.

Justin climbed onto the chair facing her and slowly traced his thumb down her torso. "This chair brings back some good memories," he said.

She turned to him. "How do you remember that?"

"How could I forget?" Justin was insulted that she'd think he could forget the amazing sex they'd had on that very chair early in their relationship.

She snorted. "I figured it wasn't the first time you'd had sex by the pool."

She was technically right, but it was the only time that had mattered. He remembered every key moment of that encounter. "You were so worried Keith would walk out on us that you wouldn't let me take off your bikini top," he said, smiling.

Courtney smiled back. Justin pressed his hand flat against her bare stomach and then slid it up her shirt, firmly grasping one breast, then the other. He leaned in and kissed the tender spot behind her ear.

"Keith isn't here now," Courtney said, turning in to Justin and pressing her warm mouth into his. Despite the fact that it was the middle of the night, closer to morning than not, her breath was still minty and fresh. He wondered how she always managed to be so perfect. Her fingers slipped beneath the fabric of his boxers and he immediately lost focus on whatever he'd been thinking.

He let her fingers work their magic for a minute, and then began to undress them both. Justin rolled on top of Courtney and pulled the blanket over them. She giggled, then kissed him back.

"Are you sure this chair will hold us?" she asked, breaking from the kiss just long enough for him to slide her shirt over her head.

"It did before," he reminded her.

"Good point." She lifted her hips to allow him to shimmy her panties down her legs and then wrapped her smooth thighs around his back, holding him close.

Justin peered into her bright blue eyes. He'd never understand what he did to deserve a woman this beautiful, inside and out, but he wasn't about to waste a moment pondering it. He ducked his head down, kissing and sucking his way along her neck then breasts. Courtney arched her back, narrowing the gap between them. His name escaped her lips in a half pant, half moan.

He could've continued for hours, loving the way she writhed against him as his tongue circled the firm peaks of her breasts. But after a minute, Courtney slipped a hand between them, guiding him to her entrance.

As they made love, Justin found himself wondering how he hadn't known sooner that she was the one for him. How hadn't he seen it that day, when they'd first tested the sturdiness of this chair? That kind of chemistry shouldn't be ignored.

When their bodies stilled and their breathing quieted,

Courtney kissed Justin's nose. "Did we miss the aftershocks?" she asked.

He laughed. "Hard to say. I felt something, for sure."

She laughed back and then shifted beneath him. He scooted over and pulled her on top of him, readjusting the blanket across her back.

"Can I ask you a question?" she asked.

"Yep."

"People keep asking me about the wedding, what we've planned."

"Me too."

"Well, you're a guy. You can probably get away with saying you don't know. When I say we haven't discussed it, people assume I'm either lying or that something's wrong."

"So what's your question?"

"When are we going to talk about it?"

"How about now?" he said. "What do you want to do?"

"For the wedding? I don't know."

He rolled his eyes, not that she could see it. "You're a girl. You must have thought about it."

She thwacked his head with her finger and then resumed stroking her hand through his hair. "I want the white dress. But I don't know about location."

"Are you thinking big? Small?"

"I don't know. We'd want both of our families there, right?"

He considered this. "Yeah, and that might be a lot of people to get to some island destination."

"So either here or Indiana?"

Justin laughed. "You really haven't thought about this much, have you?"

Courtney sighed. "I've thought about dancing with you and kissing you, and cake. We definitely need cake. But all the rest seems a little fuzzy. What about the timeline?"

"I think that depends on the size. The more people we involve, the longer it'll take to plan."

"And your work schedule is pretty booked the next year."

"I have openings. Pick a season and I'll make it happen," he promised.

"I'll have to think about it. You really don't have a preference?"

"If it were up to me, we'd elope tomorrow."

"Hmm...I think I have meetings then," she replied. She nuzzled her face against his neck, before settling atop his chest.

He clasped his hands together around her back and closed his eyes, just intending to rest them for a minute. But the next thing he knew, someone was poking his arm. He opened his eyes and saw Keith.

"Earthquake's over. It's probably safe to go back inside," Keith said.

Justin rubbed his eyes and tilted his head to confirm that Courtney was still asleep on his chest.

Keith started to laugh. Justin followed his gaze to the small pile of clothes beside the chair.

"Dude," Keith said.

Justin grinned. "It was her first earthquake. I had to distract her."

Keith rolled his eyes and went into the house. Justin slowly jostled Courtney awake. She'd probably want to sneak back inside before the pool cleaners arrived.

THAT EVENING, Courtney sat in the kitchen with her roommate Erica, analyzing the proofs from the engagement photo shoot Jamie sent over. Courtney wished Jamie and Justin would just choose their favorites, since they were both infinitely more experienced at this sort of task, but they both punted it back to her, insisting the bride should have the final say.

"I have to admit I did not see this coming," Erica murmured, tapping Courtney's ring as she reached for her wine.

"You didn't think he'd propose? Or just not now?"

Erica shrugged. "I'm surprised he asked and surprised you said yes. I'll be even more surprised if you actually go through with the wedding."

Courtney bit her lip, not wanting to react instinctively. Erica had always been brutally honest, but Courtney knew that while she meant what she said, she didn't always mean it to sound quite so harsh. "Explain," Courtney finally said.

"Justin is a great guy. I like him, really. And there's no denying you guys have great chemistry. He just doesn't strike me as the type to settle down, especially so young. His reputation as a player is pretty well entrenched."

Courtney opened her mouth to defend her fiancé, but Erica continued.

"I know you love him, too, but I just never pictured you with him long term."

Courtney sighed. "My mom said the same thing. She basically told me she thought I was just having fun with him and that once I got it out of my system I'd move on to a more serious relationship. She clearly doesn't think marrying him is a good idea."

"And you do?"

"Of course I do. Why else would I be doing it?"

Erica sipped her drink. "Maybe because you don't want to lose him. You love him and you want to be with him longer, but not necessarily forever."

"You're wrong."

"I hope so." She paused. "But, Courtney, you have to admit, he's a hard guy to turn down. Honestly if he flashed me that puppy dog look of his and asked me to marry him, I'd probably agree in the heat of the moment."

Courtney smiled, relieved that Erica had tried to lighten the mood. And her point was well taken since Justin, as a male, was as far from Erica's type as possible. "I never saw myself married to him either," she finally admitted.

Erica wisely kept quiet.

"I figured he'd go away for filming or something and we'd drift apart. Or his publicist would force him to date someone famous. Or he'd just get bored with me."

Erica laughed.

"I know it's hard for people to take him seriously, but I do. I truly believe he's ready to settle down. He'll be a really good husband and father someday. His family is so important to him now. People just don't see that side of him. We might not have the exact same personalities or interests, but he and I really do have the same values and we want the same things in life."

"I can see that," Erica agreed. "And if Justin were the exact same person he is now, but not such a public figure, I wouldn't hesitate to shove you down the aisle with him. But he isn't some nobody and you can't deny that his status is going to have a huge effect on your future."

"His status?"

"Oh, you know. If you marry him, nothing will be private. If you have kids, people will see everything, from your pregnancy to the baby photos to every little mistake your kids make as teens. Unless he suddenly changes careers, the paparazzi is going to be a part of your daily life."

Courtney nodded and took a larger swig of her drink, the vodka stinging as it hit the back of her throat. "Yeah."

"And you're okay with that?"

"Not really, but it is what it is. It's not like I can force him to give up his dream."

"Why not? What do you think he'd say if you asked him to pick, you or the job?"

Courtney rolled her eyes. "He'd be heartbroken and confused. One of the things he loves about me is that I'd never try to change him, never give him an ultimatum."

"Have you talked to him about it, just so he knows how you feel about the publicity?"

"He knows. And he's done his best to shelter me from it all. But I'd never ask him to give it all up. He loves what he does, and he loves the attention."

"But you don't."

"It doesn't matter. I want to be with him, and I want him to be happy. So few people ever get to live their dream, and Justin does. I don't want him to feel bad about that." Courtney polished off her drink and scooted the glass away. "Besides, it isn't all bad."

Erica raised an eyebrow.

"I always wanted to do public interest law. But I can't do that on my own unless I want to be homeless and starving. If I'm married to Justin, I can do what I love regardless of the pay. And I won't have to worry about affording childcare or a flexible job when we have kids. We will be able to afford the best schools and nannies or whatever."

"What about the travel? You'll be alone a lot, won't you?"

"So I can travel with him or stay home and miss him. That way we'll never get sick of each other."

Erica smiled. "I'm glad you're happy."

Courtney nodded. She was, too. She just hoped it was enough.

6

Justin sent a car to collect his brother from the airport, but he managed to get back to the house right as Luke arrived. They filled a few minutes with small talk before Justin showed Luke to the guest room where he could unpack.

"Mom really decorated the place?" Luke asked as soon as he emerged from the guest room.

Justin nodded. It wasn't like he could hide it. The curtains, furniture, even the lamps, were all clearly their mom's doing. Not that he was complaining. She'd done an awesome job on the place. It looked classy, but not feminine. And she'd been free.

Luke plopped on the couch. "So you guys just hang out here all day, drinking and playing video games?"

Justin heard Keith laughing from the kitchen.

"Sounds accurate to me," Cathy said as she swooped through the room with a laundry basket. Cathy had been hired as their housekeeper, but now she was more like the house mom, handling the cooking, cleaning, laundry, and grocery shopping.

"When I'm filming, I sometimes have to be on set by five a.m.

55

That means I have to be in the makeup chair by four. And I still have to hit the gym in the evening," Justin finally explained to his brother.

"But the rest of the time you just party," Luke concluded.

Justin handed him a beer and switched on the Wii. "I thought we could go out to dinner tonight and just hang out here. Courtney's coming with us another night, if that's okay. You remember her, right?"

Luke smirked. "I remember parts of her very well."

Justin punched his arm.

"You're really going to marry her?"

"Yeah. That's kind of the point of an engagement."

"Haven't you heard that expression, about not buying the cow if you can get the milk for free?"

Another punch.

"Ow. Okay, okay."

"And no calling my girlfriend a cow."

"Don't you mean your fiancée?"

"Yes, I do," Justin said with a smile. No matter how annoyed he was, Justin always perked up when reminded that Courtney had actually promised to be his forever. Although, thinking about her made him wish she would go out with them tonight.

He left Luke alone with Keith for a bit and called Courtney. She insisted she had just emailed her thoughts on the photos to him and Jamie and that she wanted him to have the night to focus on his brother without her distracting him.

Frankly, Justin would've preferred the distraction.

"What time is this work dinner tomorrow night?"

"Six o'clock," Courtney replied.

"That's early enough," Justin said, relieved it wasn't like an eight p.m. thing. "Eat fast and come meet us after."

"We're meeting with a potential donor, so I can't exactly eat fast."

"Please, Court. I'm going through withdrawal not seeing you."

She laughed softly, and he knew he'd convinced her.

"I miss you too," she said finally. They firmed up the plans to meet the following night then hung up, leaving Justin alone to entertain his brother for the next twenty-four hours.

Courtney's boss, April, pulled in front of her apartment at a quarter till six the next night. They made small talk on the way to the dinner, and Courtney was relieved to hear that April's sitter could only stay until nine-thirty. Not that she enjoyed seeing her boss stress over childcare, but if April planned to leave at nine, Courtney's plans with Justin were safe.

Courtney still didn't fully understand why they were both meeting with this guy. April usually handled all the networking, but this guy had specifically asked to meet with them both. Even more annoying was his insistence on a pre-dinner drink, then appetizers. It was nearly eight o'clock before they even received their entrees.

April was visibly panicked about needing to leave, and as much as Courtney didn't want to be stuck alone with Marshall Donovan, April's excuse for bailing early trumped. Courtney assured April it wasn't a problem and said she'd take a cab home after the meeting. Thankfully, as soon as April got ready to leave, Mr. Donovan finally began to focus on the portfolio they'd prepared about the shelter's mission.

After a lengthy silence, Mr. Donovan placed the stack of papers back into the manila folder. "I've looked into a lot of similar businesses, and yours seems to be one of the more efficient ones. You've done some great work here with the organization."

Courtney smiled. "Well, thank you, Mr. Donovan, but..."

"Please, call me Marshall," he said, lightly placing his hand over hers.

Courtney slipped her hand back and wrapped it around her wine glass, taking a slow sip. "Sure, Marshall. It's really April that has done all the work, though."

"Now tell me a little more about your role in the organization?"

Courtney began talking, growing flustered that he was dragging it out so long. He was supposed to be a numbers guy, and she'd given him all the info he needed in the folder. He should've made a decision, but instead he'd ordered a second bottle of wine.

The waiter stopped by the table. "Could I bring you some coffee?"

Marshall nodded, but Courtney silently groaned.

They sat at the table for close to another hour, Marshall asking questions more aimed at Courtney than the organization. Courtney checked her phone and saw multiple missed calls and texts from Justin. She then turned to Marshall, praying he'd take the hint. "Oh gosh, it's getting late. I'm so sorry. We didn't intend to monopolize your entire evening. I'm sure you need to be getting home."

He smiled. "It's fine, actually. I just went through a divorce, so my house is feeling very empty lately. Are you a dessert girl? I hear they have wonderful crème brûlée here."

She dug her nails into her palm under the table but smiled pleasantly. "Sure, that sounds wonderful."

They ordered the dessert and their coffee was refilled.

"Have you ever been married?" Marshall asked suddenly.

Courtney shook her head.

He sipped his coffee. "They say it's a wonderful institution, but I tell you, once you try it once, you wonder what you were ever thinking, and then a few weeks later, you just want to jump back in."

The dessert arrived, along with two spoons. Marshall nudged it towards Courtney first. She took a small bite, trying to hide her discomfort with sharing a dessert. "That is good," she said, politely.

Marshall stared back at her, his eyes glossy from the alcohol. "You don't look like you eat dessert very often. You agreed to this out of pity, didn't you?"

Courtney blushed. "No, I have a sweet tooth."

He smiled and nudged the plate back to her.

She took another nibble and tried to think of an innocent topic. They'd already discussed the business side of the organization to death, and if she didn't steer him in a different direction, the dinner was going to start to feel like a date. "I run a lot, so I can get away with having dessert every once in a while. You know, there's so many beautiful places to run here in L.A. Have you lived here your whole life?"

He ate another bite of the dessert, then pushed the plate into the center of the table. The waiter appeared with the bill, and Courtney reached for it. Marshall shook his head and handed the waiter a credit card.

"Mr. Donovan, we invited you out, and we'd love to treat you. Even if you decide not to offer your support to the shelter, we still appreciate you taking the time to listen to what we have to say."

"It's Marshall. And listen, whoever pays, it'll just be deducted as a business expense, and if I'm going to give your business money anyway, it doesn't make sense for me to make you buy me dinner."

Courtney didn't want to argue with him. "Well, thank you," she said.

The waiter returned, and Marshall signed the receipt, pocketed his credit card, and then jotted something on the back of his copy of the receipt. He slid it across the table to Courtney. "This is the amount I'm prepared to donate. I'll be honest, when I came here tonight, that was my cap. But, you were so persuasive that I anticipate a future donation."

Courtney's eyes widened at the number. It was close to twice what they'd hoped he'd offer.

"That's extremely generous of you, Mr. Donovan. I mean Marshall. We'll be sure to keep you updated about everything going on at the shelter."

He nodded, and stuck the paper in his pocket. "I should have guessed you were a runner. I noticed on the way in that you have the legs for it."

Courtney swallowed in lieu of thanking him for the compliment. Why wouldn't he just leave already? "If you'll excuse me, I should call a cab for myself so you can get home. I can't believe I've kept you so late."

"Nonsense," he said. "I'll drive you home."

She nodded hesitantly. "I'd hate to trouble you."

"It's no trouble. I'd like the company, actually."

"Um, okay. I'll be right back." She scurried to the restroom, certain Marshall was staring at her as she walked away. She shuddered once she was safely out of sight, feeling dirty and used. She tapped out a quick text to Justin, telling him that she was getting a ride home now, and then returned to the table.

Marshall had stood and was pulling his suit jacket on. For a man in his forties, he didn't look too bad. Courtney figured he wouldn't be single for long, especially with his income.

"Shall we?" he asked. She nodded and he placed his hand on the small of her back, guiding her out the door.

They waited at the valet quietly until his car appeared. It was a tiny, fire red, Porsche convertible. The valet opened the passenger door for Courtney, and she climbed in. The car was so low to the ground that there was no graceful or ladylike way to attempt the maneuver in a fitted pencil skirt, so she knew Marshall was ogling her again. He tipped the valet and then positioned himself behind the wheel. With the size of the car, they were seated ridiculously close to one another.

Courtney nervously tugged her skirt closer to her knees. When she stood, the skirt was a perfectly professional length. But somehow, whenever she sat, it shrunk up and revealed more of her thigh than she was comfortable showing to the moderately creepy, admittedly lonely guy six inches to her left. Marshall patted her thigh and Courtney startled.

"Sorry, didn't mean to scare you," he said, grinning, but thankfully moving his hand back to the gear shift.

At the next traffic light, she felt him staring at her thigh again. She turned to him, and he spoke.

"You're engaged."

She followed his gaze and realized he'd been eying her ring, not her leg. That was a relief. She nodded.

"I didn't notice your ring in the restaurant," he said.

Courtney nodded again. She had made a conscious effort to keep the ring inconspicuous. She hadn't planned on getting him to flirt with her, but she just didn't want him to see the massive ring and think she was wealthy or that the shelter didn't need donations as badly as it did.

"When's the big date?"

"We haven't decided yet."

"Some people say it isn't an official engagement until you pick the date." He snorted. "Is he a lawyer too?"

"No."

"But he's rich," Marshall deduced.

She didn't answer. Marshall patted her thigh again. "I'm sorry, now I'm making you uncomfortable again. Don't mind me. I'm just trying to think through this whole divorce thing, trying to figure out my next move." He paused. "Do you like older men?"

"Excuse me?"

"Your fiancé. The rich guy, is he older than you?"

"Two years."

Marshall glanced at her. "I bet he keeps a pretty close watch out, a pretty thing like you he probably doesn't let far out of his sight."

"Justin's a really trusting guy. He travels a lot, so he has to be." Courtney wanted to slap herself as soon as she spoke. Why would she say that? She'd only meant to defend Justin against the implication that he was overly jealous and possessive, but it came out a little more like flirting. Thankfully, they were pulling into her apartment complex.

Marshall laughed. "Well, that's good to know. If you're ever lonely when he's out of town, give me a call."

Courtney's eyes must have widened, because then he added, "We'll meet to discuss business again, of course."

She nodded and started to climb out of the car.

He reached for her hand. "Hold on there, not so fast."

Courtney grimaced, praying he wasn't about to kiss her or something. If she pissed him off now, the whole night would've been a waste, but she couldn't stomach the thought of another minute with him.

He reached into his pocket. "Let me get you the check."

She exhaled with relief.

He climbed out of the car, wrote the check on the hood, and then walked around to hand it to her. "My cell phone number is on the Memo line, if you ever need to reach me, to discuss the shelter, or for any other reason."

She took the check and thanked him. She offered her hand, which he shook, and then he kissed her on the cheek. She waved as he drove off, then raced inside her apartment.

Courtney sounded breathless when she answered her cell phone.

"Babe, it's eleven o'clock. Where are you?" Justin said. He was tired of being alone with his brother, Keith and Tara. Whenever they left him to go dance, random girls would move in on Justin.

"I'm here, but the bouncer won't let me in."

Justin shook his head, puzzled, and made his way to the door. At the entrance, he saw Courtney arguing with Brandon.

"I don't care if you got a big ring. I can't let you in looking like this," Brandon was saying. Brandon stepped to the side and Justin caught a glimpse of Courtney and immediately started laughing.

"Babe," he said, approaching her, ignoring the excited squeals from some of the women in line.

She shot an irritated glare at Brandon. "See? I told you."

Justin bit his lip to keep from laughing harder. He had told Brandon that his fiancée Courtney was arriving, and he'd described her as a sexy brunette. And here Courtney was, surrounded by girls in hot pants and tube tops, wearing a fitted suit skirt and purple blouse.

"This is really your girl?" Brandon seemed dubious.

"You look like you're going to audit the place," Justin said.

"That's what I told her," Brandon said.

Courtney rolled her eyes. "I look professional. I told you I had a work dinner."

"No offense, but you'd have better luck seducing the guy into giving you money if you at least unbuttoned the top a little," Justin said, demonstrating it for her, causing her face to turn bright red.

"He gave us a huge donation, thank you. And the car you

called was already at the apartment when I got there, so I figured I'd just change here."

Justin laughed again. He turned to Brandon. "I swear I'll have her looking sexy in no time. Until then, just pretend she's a publicist or something."

Brandon rolled his eyes as they walked past. Thankfully, when Courtney made her way back from the restroom five minutes later, she was wearing turquoise leggings, super high heels, and a low cut fitted black tank top with a long, beaded necklace that drew his eyes immediately to her cleavage.

"Much more appropriate," Justin said with a grin, placing his hand on the small of her back and leaning in to kiss her. "I'll stick the bag back in the car," he offered.

"No, I'll do it. That bouncer pissed me off," she said, clearly on a mission.

Justin watched as Courtney sauntered past Brandon and tossed the bag into the car. "Better?" she snapped as she sauntered past.

Brandon whistled and smiled. "You know it, girl," he said.

Justin smiled and led Courtney to the dance floor. "You need a drink first?"

She shook her head. "I drank way too much at dinner. Where's Luke?"

Justin pointed across the room, where his brother was hitting on a woman at least ten years his senior. He pulled Courtney closer, wrapping his hands around her lower back. "I don't like you out drinking on a Saturday night with strange rich men."

She smiled and kissed his neck, her lips lingering beside his skin. "There's some parts of your job I'm not too keen on either," she replied.

They danced for the next three songs, until Keith

approached. "Your brother's going to get himself kicked out," he warned.

Justin glanced in Luke's direction, then nodded.

Keith turned to Courtney. "Drink?"

"Club soda," she replied.

Justin watched them approach the bar before turning back to his brother.

"Sorry to interrupt here, ladies," Justin said, making his way to the table of women Luke was currently harassing. "Can I borrow my baby brother for a minute?"

He knew they recognized him, as the conversation immediately stopped and they all nodded, staring blankly. Justin flashed another smile, then guided his brother away.

"Don't tell me we're leaving already," Luke whined.

"Not if you cool it," Justin said. "You're not at a frat party. Back off a little. Either sit down and let the ladies come to you, or pick one and offer to buy her a drink."

"I can't afford a fifteen dollar drink for every chick I want to hook up with."

Justin grimaced. "Just leave a credit card at the bar and start a tab. I'll pay it before we go. And stop telling everyone it's your birthday."

"But it is!"

"Not for another hour. You're not even supposed to be in here." Justin reminded him. Luke should be grateful that Justin's presence allowed them to bypass the line—and the ID requirement, but instead he was acting like a whiny ten-year-old.

"Happy birthday, Luke," Courtney said, coming up behind them with Keith. She leaned in and kissed Luke on the cheek. Luke blushed and glanced down to her boobs.

"Jesus," Justin mumbled.

"Hey, Luke, I bet if you go dance with Courtney, you'll get a few more girls' attention," Keith suggested.

Luke turned to Courtney excitedly. She shot Keith a clear glance of disapproval, then handed her drink to Justin and returned to the dance floor with Luke.

Justin turned to Keith, who was laughing. "You should've seen your face when he checked out her tits," Keith said.

Justin sniffed Courtney's drink and took a quick sip before turning to watch in horror as his brother molested Courtney.

Courtney managed to slip away after the next song, rejoining Justin at the table. Another girl quickly snapped up Luke, and then Keith wandered out with Tara. Justin dragged Courtney's chair closer to his.

"How's my brother's dancing?"

"Honestly, he reminds me a lot of you."

"Ouch."

"Okay, you're a little more slick," she admitted.

"He didn't try anything, did he? Because I'm not above beating up family members."

She laughed. "No, and compared to the guy I was with earlier tonight, he was quite the gentleman."

"What do you mean?"

"You know how April and I met with that donor. Well, she had to leave early, and I think he was flirting with me."

"What did he say?" Justin had no trouble imagining someone flirting with Courtney. She was, after all, a very attractive woman with an overly welcoming smile. But it had been his experience that Courtney was usually oblivious to it all. Men flirted with her and she thought they were just being friendly. If she noticed the flirting it must have been really obvious.

She shrugged. "He complimented my blouse, and he said my legs were toned. And he kept touching my thigh on the drive home."

Justins' muscles tensed. "He drove you home? And he touched you?"

"He gave us a really big donation," she said.

"In exchange for what, Courtney? Did he try anything else?"

She shook her head. "He kissed me on the cheek and he said I should call him if I was ever lonely when you were out of town."

Courtney must have been able to tell how angry this was making Justin, because she quickly added, "I don't think he meant anything by it. He just went through a divorce."

"Why would April leave you alone with this pervert? You know, you don't have to let some jerk grope you just because he's giving you money. I could give the shelter money."

She placed her hand on his cheek and gently stroked it with her fingertips. "You do give the shelter money, Justin." She kissed him, her lips barely touching his and then lingering. "And I'll probably never be alone with this guy again, so you don't need to worry about it."

He finished off his drink. "Yeah, until I leave town in a week. What's his name?"

Courtney smiled and shook her head. "I'm not telling you that. And if you keep acting crazy, we're going to have to leave so I can take your mind off all this."

Justin relaxed a little. "Oh yeah? How would you do that exactly?"

She leaned forward and whispered a very tempting and surely effective way to distract him. He exhaled hard and chewed a piece of ice from his drink. If he stood up, the whole club could've guessed what she'd just offered.

"You know my brother's going to be at my house."

"Hmm," she said, twirling a lock of her dark brown hair around her finger just above her right breast. "I bet we could be alone in the car."

Justin liked this idea, but hoped she meant the Audi. His Escalade obviously had more room, but he'd had it for years, and he vaguely recalled fooling around with another girl in the Escalade, pre-Courtney. No sex, but he still wasn't comfortable getting her naked in the same vehicle.

"You know, if you're into cars, I'm sure we could go outside now and get the driver to take a walk around the block while we had some alone time in the Denali."

She smiled. "I think you'd have to tip him really well for that."

He turned to the dance floor again, where his brother was now making out with a girl in a short, fur-lined skirt. He sighed. "Fuck. He's probably going to try to bring her back to my house." He caught the waitress' attention and ordered more drinks, then followed Courtney back onto the dance floor.

Sure enough, an hour later, Luke sauntered over to him, eager to leave. Justin gazed past him, at the drunken brunette he'd been dancing with. "Yeah. We can go," he said. "Let me find Keith. Is anyone else coming with us?"

His baby brother grinned proudly and nodded at the brunette. "Carrie is."

"Jesus," Justin mumbled under his breath. "Okay, meet us out at the car in five minutes." He glanced around for Keith.

"Can I borrow you for a minute?" he asked.

Keith nodded and stood.

"Luke's ready to go and he's bringing a girl back to the house. I told him Courtney and I would meet him at the car. Do you want to stick around or are you done here?"

"We'll head back with you," Keith said.

The car was crowded, so Justin rode in the front. He felt bad sticking Courtney in the back with a couple on the verge of a hook up, but he couldn't stomach watching his brother flirt any longer.

When they got home, Keith and Luke led their women inside, but Justin motioned for Courtney to wait with him.

"I'm sure he'll take her straight to the guest room and you won't have to see them anymore," Courtney said.

"Yeah," Justin agreed. He figured he should be proud that his brother was having some luck with the ladies, but it was just weird. He was used to being wingman for Josh, Rob, or Chris, but Luke had always been the baby and they'd never really prowled for girls or hit the town together before. "But you promised me a ride in the Audi," he said, a sly grin on his face.

Courtney's lips parted into a subtle smile. "A ride, huh?"

He nodded, and she led him to the car. They both stared at the car dubiously for a moment before climbing in.

"You know, there's more room in the Escalade," Courtney said.

"But this one's my favorite," Justin replied.

Courtney pushed him into the passenger's seat and he reached down to scoot the seat as far back as possible before she straddled him. He started to kiss her, but she pulled back.

"Maybe I should still be mad that you made fun of my outfit earlier tonight," she said.

Justin made a pouty face. "You looked hot. Just not dance-club hot." He slipped his hand under her shirt and stroked his thumb across her nipple. "I think I can make you forgive me," he said, gradually increasing the speed and pressure of his thumb.

Courtney's breath quickened, so he didn't wait for further instruction. He pulled off her shirt, revealing her perky, cream-colored breasts peeking over the top of a lacy black and white bra. Courtney followed suit by tugging his shirt off over his head, both of them giggling at the cramped quarters inside the car.

"Hang on," Justin said, shifting Courtney so her legs were both on the same side of him, allowing him to awkwardly shimmy her pants and thong down to the floor. She smiled and swung her leg back over him.

"This would've been easier if I were still in the business skirt," she teased, unzipping his fly.

He pulled her bra down and craned his neck until his mouth could reach the peak of her soft breasts. She groaned softly as he ran his tongue across them, sucking at her firm skin before tracing his tongue back and forth across her nipple.

She wriggled her hands down, rubbing him through his boxers. He lost focus for a moment, digging his teeth into the soft flesh at the side of her breast, and she raised up on her knees.

"This won't work," she said. "These need to come off."

Justin lifted his hips and managed to maneuver his remaining clothes down. Courtney grinned, her blue eyes sparkling in the darkened car. She licked her fingers and then reached them around him again. Justin contentedly watched her breasts sway slightly side to side, inches from his face, as her hand moved.

He was growing impatient, so he moved his mouth to hers, thrusting his tongue into her open mouth. He moved his hands across her perfect body, his fingers lingering again on her breasts before pushing around to her back and then roaming up towards her head, tousling her soft brown hair. She shifted her hips and lowered herself over him, a soft groan escaping her lips as soon as he was inside her.

Justin grinned, kissing her harder, shifting his hips to meet hers as their rhythm increased and their breath came faster and faster. They came together, Courtney's nails digging into Justin's skin at the precise moment that his teeth scraped along her shoulder. He moaned, kissed her again, then let his head fall back against the headrest. Courtney collapsed against his chest, leaving her hips in place.

"I have a new favorite experience in my favorite car," he whispered.

They waited a few more minutes before climbing out of the car, pulling their pants up, and sneaking back into the house. The house was dark as they tiptoed up the stairs to Justin's room.

Courtney stepped into the room first and gasped.

Justin flew in front of her, half expecting an intruder. But instead, it was Luke staring up like a deer in headlights.

"What are you doing in here?"

Luke blushed. "Sorry, I uh, needed to borrow some, well, I didn't have any..."

"Spit it out."

"I don't have any condoms," Luke finally said, staring at the floor.

Justin sighed, grabbed several from his nightstand, dropped them in Luke's hand, and nudged him out the door, locking it behind him. He plopped onto the bed, sighed, and rubbed his forehead. Why had he agreed to this visit?

Courtney sat behind him, pressing her breasts into his back as she rubbed his shoulders. "Hey, you better not be getting stressed out. I just finished relaxing you and we can't keep this up all night. You're running out of cars."

"I still have one more," Justin said, grinning.

7

____

Justin was due to start filming again the day before his brother left. They were shooting locally, but thanks to some union rule, filming began earlier and earlier each day of the week. Since Justin was also attempting to drop weight for his next gig, he had to eat less than normal and increase his cardio. His trainer ordered him to jog a full hour five days a week instead of his normal weight lifting routine.

In short, Justin was busy, tired, stressed out and hungry. Courtney kept her distance, dropping by a few nights only long enough for sex and sleep, the two things that seemed to relax Justin.

It was a strange dynamic, since Courtney was accustomed to being the stressed, overly tired one of the pair. Justin was normally so laid back about everything that Courtney was tempted to blame his tension on the diet and not the work. But then again, she'd never really spent much time with him while he was filming a movie because he'd done most of his filming out of town since they'd become involved.

By the following Friday night, Justin was so exhausted that he fell asleep by nine o'clock, a record for him. Courtney had only arrived at eight, so they'd barely had time to catch up and make love before he'd conked out. She initially tried to sleep too, figuring she could always use the extra rest, but she was fidgety and worried she'd only wake him up if she stayed in bed any longer.

Courtney slowly inched off of Justin. Without turning on a light, she was able to locate her panties, but then decided to just put on Justin's long-sleeved shirt instead of risking waking him by rummaging around for her own clothes. She stepped into the hall as she finished buttoning the buttons, then rolled the sleeves up, smiling as she noticed his familiar scent on the shirt.

She flipped on the small light above the sink once she reached the kitchen and filled the kettle with water for tea. Then she plopped down at the table to browse through the latest stack of screenplays Justin had received from his agent. When the kettle began to screech, Courtney quickly hopped up and poured the steaming water into a mug. Just as she raised to her tip toes to reach the tea in the cabinet, she heard a loud thump. She turned abruptly, and there was Keith.

He whistled. "Nice ass," he added, dropping his keys on the table and heading straight to the fridge for a beer.

Courtney chalked the out-of-character comment up to drunkenness, since Keith was rarely so crass. She grabbed the tea while his back was turned, plopped the bag into her mug, and then tugged the shirt back down so it covered to her mid-thigh. "I didn't hear you come in. I thought you were staying at Tara's."

"Nope. Won't be staying there anymore." Keith started into the living room and then paused, returned to the fridge for two more beers, and then stretched out on the couch, placing all three bottles on the coffee table beside him.

Courtney switched off the light and followed him, wrapping both hands around the oversized mug for warmth. Keith moved his feet as she approached, so she sat on the opposite end of the couch.

"Is Justin asleep?"

She nodded.

"That's ironic."

Courtney laughed. "Yeah, I felt bad that I was always tired when he wanted to go out, but he's been getting up so early this week that he was out before we even turned the light off." She paused. "So did something happen with Tara?"

"You could say that," he replied, swigging freely from the first beer.

She suspected he did want to talk about it, but she didn't want to pry. Whatever was bothering Keith, Courtney knew Justin could cheer him up.

"We broke up," Keith finally explained.

"Oh." Now she really didn't know what to say. If he were a girl, she'd offer a hug and then chat about it until they'd overanalyzed every mundane detail of the relationship, but something told her that wasn't exactly how guys dealt with this situation. "Like for good, or just a break?"

"Permanent." He opened the second beer. "It's sort of your fault, really."

"What?" Courtney was grateful the room was mostly dark. She knew she was blushing now.

"Well, indirectly. Tara and I had already been dating for over a year when you met Justin. Did you know that?"

"I guess so."

"When Justin told me he was proposing, I knew that would piss off Tara. She wanted to be engaged first since we started dating first. Sure enough, she started dropping hints shortly after."

"So why didn't you propose?"

He laughed. "I don't want to. I thought for a while maybe I

just didn't want to get married at all, but the more I tried to picture marrying Tara, I realized I just didn't want to marry her."

"Oh." Again, Courtney was speechless. She'd never particularly loved Tara, but she didn't hate her either. To her, Keith and Tara seemed to make sense together. "I'm sorry. Did you tell Tara that?"

"Geez. Do I look like I have a death wish?" He shook his head. "I just told her I didn't think I was the marrying type and that if she wanted that, she should probably look for someone else."

"That seems reasonable."

Keith chuckled. "Tara didn't think so. She threw a plastic bottle at my head and told me to go fuck myself."

"Oh."

"I feel like a jerk. I could tell she was hurt, but what else was there to say? I should've told her sooner, before she wasted over two years with me."

"Then why didn't you?"

He shrugged. "I didn't know. I liked her, and up to a point, it didn't seem weird that I didn't want to get married to her. I figured I'd wake up someday and that would change." Keith went into the kitchen and fixed himself another drink, although he hadn't yet finished all his beers. "You want anything?"

"No, I'm good with tea," she answered.

He returned to the couch. "I probably never would've figured it out if it weren't for you and Justin."

"What do you mean?"

"Oh, you know," he said.

"No I don't."

He rolled his eyes and slurped his drink. "Justin knew he wanted to marry you. It wasn't like he just figured it was time to settle down or that he had to propose to keep you around. He wanted you and even when I tried to convince him to hold off, he wouldn't."

"I can't believe you tried to talk him out of it." And she couldn't believe she hadn't already been pissed off over that.

He flung his hands up defensively, spilling his drink. Courtney hopped up to grab a cloth. She crouched on the floor and tried to sop up the whiskey before it soaked through the rug.

"Seriously," he mumbled.

"What?"

"If I'd seen your ass before, I would've been much more understanding of Justin's need to get you locked for the long haul."

Courtney sat back on the couch and shot him a look. "First off, don't think for a second that just because you're drunk and depressed, you can get away with being a creepy jerk. Second, you've seen my ass plenty of times. This is much more covering than my bikini."

"I meant it as a compliment. I wasn't trying to hit on you."

They both sipped their drinks quietly for a minute.

"I wasn't sure you'd say yes," Keith finally said. "When Justin popped the question. I couldn't tell if you were that serious about him yet."

Courtney laughed. "He could've asked me the first night we met and I would've said yes. You know how he is."

Keith shook his head. "Nope, I have no personal experience of the intimate sort with Justin."

"Keith, I don't mean how he is in bed." Although, he was very persuasive in that department too. "I was talking about his charisma. No one could ever say no to Justin. From the moment I met him, I couldn't stop thinking about him."

He groaned. "You're making me nauseous."

"That could be the alcohol."

He eyed his growing collection of glasses and bottles skeptically.

"So, how do you deal with breakups, aside from drinking to excess?"

"What do you mean?" he asked.

She quickly raised then dropped her shoulders. "I don't know. Do you just wallow in your misery for a while, or do you get right back out there? Do you look for a rebound girl?"

He cocked his finger at her. "That sounds like a fantastic idea. Although, usually I'm more the wallowing type."

Just as Courtney remembered she was never again going to have to deal with a breakup, Keith continued.

"I haven't been single for so long, I don't even remember what type I am. Or maybe it's changed. Maybe now I'm into screwing a different chick each night." He snorted, then laughed so hard he nearly spilled his drink again.

"I really can't picture you being that type."

They kept talking for a while, and at some point, Courtney fell asleep.

JUSTIN AWOKE EARLY, refreshed. He wasn't about to start going to bed early every night, but it did feel good to catch up on sleep. He rolled over quietly so as not to wake Courtney, but she was already gone. When he finally made his way downstairs, Justin expected to find Courtney in the kitchen, or maybe on the back patio. So he was more than a little surprised to find her sprawled out on the couch next to Keith.

They were definitely in a compromising position. Keith was fully clothed, but Courtney appeared to be wearing nothing but Justin's shirt and her skimpy panties. A blanket was draped over her legs, which were partially covering Keith's lap, but her head was at the opposite end of the couch from Keith's. Justin leaned down and kissed her on the forehead, eager to hear her explanation.

Courtney's eyes opened slowly, and she greeted him with a groggy smile. Justin glanced at the row of beer bottles lining the coffee table before turning back to her. She raised her head quickly, apparently aware of the perturbed expression on his face.

She turned to Keith, who was still asleep, then stood slowly. "Sorry, I came down here for some tea and then I guess I fell asleep."

Justin turned and headed to the kitchen. While he was confident nothing shady had gone on between his fiancée and roommate, there had to have been more to the story than that. He started to make coffee, aware that Courtney had followed him into the kitchen.

"Looks like you two had quite the party last night," he said.

Courtney frowned and perched onto the table beside him. She looked so hot in his shirt that it almost irritated him. He had at least wanted to give her a hard time about ditching him for Keith in the night, but now all he could think about was ravishing her on the kitchen table before breakfast.

"That was all Keith," Courtney said. "He was a mess."

Justin didn't believe that for a second. He'd known Keith since middle school, and the guy had never been a mess. He was always the rational, level-headed, in control guy that everyone else went to when their own lives were falling apart.

"He and Tara broke up," Courtney explained, raising her arms to twist her hair into a loose knot, inadvertently inching the shirt up even further, until Justin could see the lace lining her black panties.

"Oh shit." Justin looked over at his sleeping friend, with a new pity. He'd suspected that was coming. Things hadn't been right with Keith and Tara for a while. Still, it was a shock. They'd been an item nearly since Keith moved to L.A. Their breakup was truly the end of an era.

"Yeah, so we started talking, and I guess we both fell asleep. Or at least I did. He might've just passed out." She reached for Justin's hand and pulled him closer. He cooperated, stepping in between her thighs and squeezing one in each of his hands. "I'm sorry I snuck out on you. I just couldn't sleep and I didn't want to wake you."

Justin nodded and undid the top button on her shirt. He smiled at the improved view before kissing her. She kissed him back eagerly, her warm lips pressing into his own with the same fervor as her hands squeezing into his hips. It took every ounce of restraint Justin had not to push her back onto the table, knock the papers to the floor, and make love to her there. He was immediately glad he hadn't, though, because it wasn't much longer before Keith stumbled into the kitchen.

"Dude," Keith grumbled, shielding his eyes.

Courtney pulled away quickly, rebuttoning the top of the shirt. Justin remained where he was, safely nestled in front of Courtney where his bulging hard-on couldn't further offend his hungover, newly-single roommate.

"It sounds like a trip to Vegas might be in order," Justin said, uncertain how else to broach the topic of Keith's new singleton status.

Keith poured himself some coffee and nodded. "I'm in," he mumbled, stumbling back out of the kitchen.

"See? He'll be fine," Justin assured Courtney, stepping away to get his own coffee.

～

THE NEXT EVENING, Courtney came over to help Justin practice lines. Keith joined them on the back patio and they took a short break to eat dinner. Justin wolfed it down then swore and declared he was still famished. As Keith headed back inside, Justin peered around, wild-eyed, as though looking for something else he could eat.

"Don't take this the wrong way, Justin, but you've been really cranky lately. People are starting to get scared of you."

Justin snorted. "Keith, you mean?"

Courtney shrugged.

He sighed. "I can't help it. I'm hungry and tired and really stressed out and hungry."

"You said hungry twice."

"Well I feel doubly hungry."

"Maybe you should postpone the diet and extra cardio until after you're done filming. Then you won't have all the stress and sleep deprivation."

He shook his head. "I can't lose fifteen pounds in three weeks."

"But you can in five?" She was no mathematical expert, but it seemed like a lot, especially for someone like Justin who didn't have much fat to lose. It would have to be almost entirely muscle.

"I have to." He slumped down on the couch. "They said they still want me muscular, just not as bulky. Don't worry about it, okay? I already went over this with my trainer."

Clearly, Justin didn't realize how miserable he was making everyone around him with his new diet. Courtney slid onto the couch beside him and stroked her fingers through his hair. It was longer now, and she liked that. She wondered what they'd do to it for the ad campaign.

"Justin, maybe you should just forget the whole campaign.

You said you wanted to focus more on acting, so why not just let this go?"

His eyes widened. "Are you insane? This is an incredible opportunity for my acting. The last ad series had five billboards total. This one is fifty, maybe more. This one has TV ads, print ads, everything. I'll get my image in front of more casting directors from this campaign than anything else I've done."

She frowned. "Oh. I didn't realize that. I thought it was more about the money." She took a long swig from her water bottle.

Justin laughed. "Well, I'd be lying if I said I wasn't excited about the four mill."

Courtney choked on her water. "Four mill? You mean million? Dollars?"

He grinned and squeezed her thigh. "As opposed to pesos?"

She tried to collect her thoughts calmly, but all she could see was an image of Justin swimming in a tub filled with dollar bills. "Wait, what exactly are they paying you for this?"

"One million for the initial photos, another three million minimum in royalties over the next three years."

Courtney couldn't believe it. She didn't understand anything about how royalties worked for ads, but she figured that didn't matter at the moment. She was in shock.

Justin kissed the tip of her nose. "Babe, say something."

"Like what?"

"I don't know. But you're freaking me out looking at me like that." He paused and snickered. "Oh shit, you knew I made more money than you, right?"

Courtney swatted him playfully. "I didn't realize you made that much. Is that normal?"

He shrugged. "It's more than I made for the last ad campaign I did for them. Almost four times as much. And David doesn't pay me much of anything for the stuff I do for him, but that's cool."

"What about the acting? Are you making that kind of money acting?"

Justin laughed again. At least she was cheering him up, albeit inadvertently. "Courtney, I'm pretty sure you could do a quick internet search and find out what I'm paid for most movies."

"Well, I never have. I figured it was a lot, but I never thought about how much exactly." She paused. "Never mind, it's none of my business."

Justin smirked. "When we're married, will it be your business?"

"No. We'll have a prenup."

Now he looked offended. "Okay, we can get into that discussion another time, when I'm not so hungry that your thigh is starting to resemble food."

Courtney covered her thigh and smiled. "Fine. What are you getting for this movie?"

"Just shy of two mill."

"Upfront, or total?"

"Total."

"Is that good?"

He nodded. "Marty does a good job negotiating for me."

"Is it based on how long the filming takes?"

"No, I think it just depends on the film's budget."

Courtney did some mental math. "So if this takes you sixteen weeks to film, you're still making roughly twenty thousand dollars more in a week than I earn in an entire year?"

Justin smiled. "I think this marriage is really going to fuck with your tax bracket."

Courtney smiled. And then she hesitated.

"What?"

"How did this never come up before?"

"I figured you knew. You've seen my cars, the house. That

stuff isn't free." He laughed, then paused. "And there's the apartment in New York. Even with Andi paying half, it's still insane."

Courtney winced. "I feel terrible. All I have is a crappy salary and loads of debt."

"What debt do you have? I know you're not making car payments." He tickled her side, clearly trying to transition away from the conversation.

Justin had paid for the majority of Courtney's car, a BMW sedan, when she graduated law school. Her old Camry was dying at the time, so she'd accepted what otherwise she probably would have seen as an inappropriately expensive gift. Around the same time, Justin had treated himself to a flashy new Audi, but held on to the black Escalade he drove before.

"Student loans for law school," she finally explained. "I'm making payments, but it might take a while at this rate."

Justin shook his head. "That's ridiculous. Fax the info over to my accountant in the morning and he'll pay it off. Then we can go into marriage debt-free." He leaned in to kiss her.

"I'm not comfortable mooching off you, Justin. I can handle it on my own."

"Courtney, come on. Don't make me set up an appointment with the guy so he can talk sense into you. He's a nerd and it'll be so boring. I don't know shit about finance, but I'm sure it's easier and cheaper to pay off your damn loans now than to string it along."

He paused. "I'm not going to spend the rest of my life feeling bad that you don't have money even though you work just as hard as I do. As long as you're broke, I can't enjoy my money. So really, you don't have a choice. You have to start mooching off me so we can both have fun."

It wasn't that Courtney worried he'd think she was using him for his money, so she didn't know why she was so insistent on buying things herself. She just figured that she was supposed to support herself, at least until the wedding, whenever they got around to that.

"Fine, you can pay off my law school loans, but only if you come up with something I can do for you to pay you back."

His eyes widened and a mischievous smile crossed his face. His hand shot into the waistband of her jeans.

She giggled. "Something I wouldn't do anyway."

Justin appeared to consider this for a moment. "Got it. You come visit me on the weekends when I'm out of town. I don't care how busy your week is, if I want to go out on Saturday night in New York, you're coming with me. And I want booty calls on command."

Courtney smiled. That actually was a reasonable compromise. She wasn't a fan of flying, and she knew he wanted her to visit him more when he was out of town, so it made sense. Except for one thing. "I like that plan, except there's the whole issue of financing my travels."

The pesky grin spread across his face again. "Perfect. I wanted to get you a credit card anyway. Your name goes on it, and the bills will go straight to the accountant." And before she could protest, his mouth was on hers.

8

———

Thanks to some production delays, Justin had an unexpected four-day break from shooting. He had briefly considered being responsible, spending that time at the gym or maybe trying to hash out wedding plans with his fiancée, but in the end, he chose a different route. He treated Keith to a long weekend in Vegas, hopeful it would help his friend recover from his recent breakup.

Not surprisingly, Courtney was completely supportive of his plan. Reason number 748 why she was the perfect woman. Any other girl would be hurt or jealous, but Courtney actually praised Justin for being such a thoughtful friend.

After three days in Vegas and a slight break from the grueling diet and workout regimen, Justin felt refreshed, relaxed, and ready to tackle the week. Courtney's car was in the driveway, and Justin was eager to kiss his girl.

Unfortunately, the moment he walked in the house, he was greeted by a gossip magazine on the floor by the door, complete with post-it note indicating his publicist had seen, and disapproved of, his weekend in Vegas. She wanted to know if he and Courtney had broken up, and if there was any other news he'd failed to share with her. Given the magazine's unavoidable placement, Courtney must have seen it too.

He swore under his breath. He quickly considered which woman would be easier to appease, then pulled out his phone to text Jamie.

He typed, "Vegas was fun. Took K bc he broke up with gf. Nothing happened other than what photos show. Still w C. All good."

He hit send, then glanced around for Courtney. He finally spotted her outside. She was standing in the pool, wearing a simple black string bikini and reading a book. Justin laughed. Only Courtney would read in a pool. He switched into his swim trunks then jogged outside to join her.

She gazed up and smiled when he appeared, which he took as a good sign. But he also knew that sometimes she felt angrier than she acted.

He sat on the edge of the pool. "You leave work early?"

She nodded, placing her book on the side of the pool. "I did a lot of work over the weekend while you were gone, so I left early today and had a late lunch with Erica."

It was bad if Erica saw the photos too.

"Did Erica come back here with you?"

Courtney nodded. "Is that okay? She just left."

"Of course. Your friends are always welcome here. It's your house too. Or it would be, if you'd finally move all your stuff in." He slipped into the pool beside her. The water felt cool and refreshing.

Courtney didn't step closer or make eye contact. She was definitely pissed.

"You saw the photos," he said.

"Erica saw them. The magazine was on top of a stack of stuff on your counter."

"Yeah, I think Jamie must have dropped it off. She wanted an explanation."

"Can't imagine why," she retorted.

"I'm sorry Erica saw that."

"And me?"

He shrugged. "You would've seen them anyway. I wasn't trying to hide it from you."

"Okay," she replied, in her dismissive tone that was supposed to mean they could change the subject but Justin knew meant she was still upset.

"What do you want me to say? It was a fun trip. We partied, we danced, we flirted. The pictures captured it all pretty well, I guess." He paused. "Well, actually, there was also chicken fighting. I'm surprised they didn't get a photo of that dumb blonde on my shoulders. That would've been a terrific shot."

"Not that, Justin," she interrupted. "I don't want to hear any of that."

He inched closer as she turned, wrapping his arms around her waist. "But it's the truth, Courtney, and that's all that happened."

"I know that," she said meekly.

"Do you? Because I don't think you realize how much I thought about you over the weekend. I missed you. I kept thinking how much more fun it would've been with you." He paused and pulled her closer. "I didn't touch anyone else when we were dancing. I didn't encourage anyone in any way. I talked about you nonstop. And there were no girls in our entire suite at any point."

She turned slightly. "You expect me to believe that Keith didn't bring someone back to his room?"

Justin laughed. "I'm not saying he didn't disappear to some girl's room for a few hours the second night, but I'm serious. There was never any girl in our suite."

Courtney sighed. "My parents are going to see that."

"I'm sorry. Want me to call them? Explain everything? Maybe bring your dad along on my next boys' weekend?"

Courtney's stomach tightened as she giggled.

"I love you. I want you. No one else." he whispered, smiling as Courtney finally relaxed against him.

"I wasn't expecting photos in Vegas," she said. "I thought they couldn't have cameras in the casinos."

"We didn't stay in the casinos the whole time."

"Because you ran out of money?"

Justin laughed. "We sure as shit didn't come out ahead."

"No more chicken fighting next time, okay?"

"Okay."

"You can always say no, you know? To the girls, I mean."

"Yeah. Although the chicken fighting was Keith's idea. He begged. I couldn't say no to him. You've seen that face he makes."

Courtney giggled again. Justin slowly lowered himself down and placed his mouth over the back of her bikini.

"What are you doing?"

He tried to answer, but the suit strings were in his teeth by that point, so it all came out garbled anyway. A moment later, though, he had succeeded with his task and her suit was untied, hanging loose around her neck. He immediately slid his hands up from her stomach to her breasts.

"Keith still isn't home?" she asked.

"Nope."

"I can't believe you untied that with your teeth."

"I'm a talented man when properly motivated," he replied.

"You better not have practiced that skill in Vegas."

Justin smiled, content that Courtney was so tolerant of his indiscretions. He just had to hope that her parents and brother were equally forgiving, since they'd be seeing them in Chicago in a few days.

EAGER TO GET AHEAD of the game at work before her long weekend in Chicago, Courtney rolled into the office at seven a.m. She was completely in the zone when she heard a tapping at her door.

April popped her head inside. "So now you're the early worm plus you handle those late nights."

"I haven't had a late night here since the meeting with Mr. Donovan."

April raised her eyebrows. "Funny you should mention that." She let herself into the office and tugged the door shut behind her, sitting in one of the two chairs facing Courtney's desk before continuing. "I told the Board about how helpful you've been and we thought that you might be interested in a different job title."

"Different how?" Courtney pressed her tongue against the roof of her mouth, unsure where the conversation was headed.

April handed her an envelope. "Executive Director of Legal. How does that sound?"

Courtney opened her mouth to answer but didn't know what to say.

"Read over the offer. I'll be honest, it's really not much different from your current job, but it sure sounds better, and I like to think there's some merit to being on the Board of Directors."

April smiled warmly and was gone before Courtney could answer. She opened the envelope and read the single typed page, signed by all current members of the board. April was right—it was basically her current job duties, plus a few more, and only the slightest of pay increases. But to be a director? That was an amazing opportunity.

She planned to tell Justin the moment they were alone, but Justin was so busy wrapping the film that they didn't even see each other until they met up at the airport. And then, Justin was so exhausted from filming that he slept the entire flight.

They arrived in Chicago late the night before Justin was to be interviewed by Courtney's favorite daytime TV talk show host. She was surprised that the show, which was known for the involvement of the live studio audience, filmed in the morning, even though the episodes aired late afternoon.

Courtney stayed backstage with Justin until shortly before they started shooting, and then someone from the staff showed her to a corner seat in the front row of the audience. She was beyond excited. Not only had she never seen Justin do an interview in person before, but she'd actually never even been to the filming of a talk show. She couldn't believe he'd almost turned down the interview.

The show opened with a quick, witty monologue from the host. The first guest was an actress from a TV show that Courtney hadn't seen before but apparently, based on the clapping of the audience, was pretty popular. Next, was Justin.

As soon as the host announced his name, Courtney was overwhelmed by the volume of the screaming around her. Women had popped up out of their seats and were literally jumping up and down, clapping and squealing. It was insane. She wondered how much of the excitement was a result of his willingness to wander around the audience for about a half hour earlier in the day, signing autographs and posing for photos as they all waited for the taping to begin.

Courtney loved the enthusiasm, but really just wanted to focus on Justin. As soon as he walked out, she couldn't help but smile. Justin had such a natural stage presence. He waved at the audience, flashing his widest smile—complete with both adorable dimples—and raised his eyebrows at Courtney before greeting the host with a hug and sitting in the chair across from her. Courtney was amazed at how calm he appeared, and wondered if he ever panicked, even just for a moment, about tripping and falling during his grand entrance.

The audience quieted down at the request of a series of signs held up by the staff, and the host began asking him a few generic questions, focusing on his work since he last appeared on the show.

"So it's fair to say you've been keeping pretty busy since I last saw you," the host summarized. "Anything else new with you? I think the last time you were here you mentioned a dog."

He laughed, looking even more irresistible. "Yeah, Bella's still doing well."

The host nodded. "Now I see you're wearing a shirt today," she said, the audience erupting into laughter. "What? It's a legitimate observation. You see this man in movies and plastered all over magazines and billboards, and he never has a shirt on." She lowered her voice and leaned towards the audience. "He doesn't always keep his pants on either."

Justin raised his hands jovially. "I think the costume designers are just trying to save money is all, and that's why they never give me a shirt."

She nodded. "So it isn't your call, about the clothes? You don't just say sure, I'll take this role, but only if I don't have to wear a shirt?"

Justin waited until the audience stopped laughing before he answered. "No, honestly it's really cold on some of those sets. I'm just really glad when I get to keep my clothes on, like today."

The audience booed. Courtney smiled as Justin blushed even more. He was cute when embarrassed. The host reached out and tugged on his shirt curiously.

"Oh come on now, that's more than one shirt. Just how many shirts are you wearing there? Two?"

He laughed. "Three, actually."

"Then just humor us a little, surely you don't need all of

those shirts. Could we get you to take the top two off? I'm sure someone here will keep you warm if you get too chilly."

He hesitated for a moment, then nodded. "One, I'll take off one." And the audience cheered uncontrollably as he stood up and lifted his long-sleeved shirt slowly up over his head, his two tee shirts pulling up just enough to offer the audience a flash of his bare stomach. An assistant came up and quickly reclipped his mic to his tee shirt and then Justin walked to the edge of the stage, the audience still whistling like crazy, and tossed his shirt.

Courtney was so absorbed in the show that she nearly missed it, not having realized he meant for her to catch it. He laughed and winked as the cameras flashed briefly over to Courtney. Justin returned to his seat by the host.

"Oh, wow, now that lucky fan gets an extra special souvenir. A dirty shirt. Who wouldn't want that?" the host teased, groping his biceps as the audience laughed.

Justin grinned. "Eh, I'm pretty sure she'll give it back to me."

The host shook her head. "You won't even let her keep it? What, you're giving shirts away so often now that you're running out of them? Come on, let the poor girl take it home with her."

He shook his head again, still laughing, and arched his back so he could turn to see her. "Alright, she can take it home with her," he finally began, holding up his finger so he wouldn't be interrupted. "But only if I get to come with her, too."

The host's eyes grew wide and the audience's screeching was now ear-piercingly loud. Courtney realized that the host had no idea she was his fiancée. She watched Justin lean forward and whisper something to the host. A moment later, the host quieted the audience.

"Okay, apparently he's not just picking up random women here. Tell them what you just told me, Justin."

He grinned and glanced over at Courtney again. "She's my girlfriend."

The audience all "awww'd" in unison now and the cameras flashed back over to Courtney. Acutely aware that everyone was now staring at her, Courtney waved, praying she didn't pass out from anxiety.

The host frowned and stood, leaning closer to the audience. She turned back to Justin. "Wait a minute, you said girlfriend, but unless the tabloids have lied, isn't there a giant rock on her left hand?"

Justin laughed, nodding. "Alright, my fiancée. I'm just not that used to saying it yet."

The host nodded, clearly pleased. "Now wouldn't that have been something to mention when I asked you what was new?"

He shrugged, those perfect dimples still popping.

"So how'd you pop the question?" the host asked, then she shook her head. "Nope, actually, I want to hear it from her. What's your fiancée's name?"

Courtney couldn't hear Justin answer, because all of a sudden, two of the assistants were helping her up onto the stage. It was all happening so fast that she barely had time to panic. Justin hopped up and grabbed her hand when she reached the stage, confirming her fears that she looked like she was about to pass out.

"I'm so sorry babe, I love you," he whispered, one hand over his mic. He guided Courtney to the seat he'd been in and scooted one chair down. Courtney tried to remember what Justin told her about interviews, how he stayed calm by treating it just like a conversation between two people, and she attempted to ignore the recurrent thoughts that everyone in the audience was staring at her trying to decipher what exactly a hunk like him saw in her.

The host introduced herself and Courtney shook her hand, excited to actually be able to meet her. "No one told me he was bringing you along or we could've planned this better."

Courtney smiled. "I love your show, so I made him take me."

"Thank you. So tell me about this proposal. Was he as romantic as in the movies?"

Courtney turned to Justin and they both grinned. "Yeah, he did pretty well. He was nervous, though, which is unusual for him. He actually threw the ring at me."

The audience laughed at this.

"I caught it," she quickly added. "And then he went through the whole proposal thing after that."

"Now are you from the Los Angeles area? I mean, have you had other celebrity boyfriends?"

Courtney laughed. "No, I moved to Los Angeles after law school, and he is my one and only celebrity boyfriend."

"Dating an actor, I'd imagine you must like movies. What is your favorite movie?"

She panicked, hating being put on the spot. "You mean my favorite movie overall, or my favorite one that Justin's in?"

The host grinned. "Are you saying that your fiancé is not in your favorite movie?" The audience laughed, as did Justin. Courtney blushed. "Which actor is in your favorite movie?"

Flustered, Courtney blurted out the first good movie that came to her mind, along with a slightly older well-known actor.

"Lucky for Justin I don't think he's single."

Courtney shrugged, still blushing. Justin squeezed her thigh.

"Well, we're running out of time now, but I was planning on offering you a check to donate to the charity of your choice if you'd show us a little skin today," the host told Justin, eliciting more shrieks from the audience. "I don't think this qualifies, though," she continued, squeezing his chest through his shirt. "If we can't get you to reconsider on the shirt, how about you show off those muscles instead?"

"What do you have in mind?" Justin asked, smiling.

They turned as two stage hands wheeled out a large contraption.

"Can he do ten pull-ups?" the host asked Courtney. "Can he do more?"

Courtney nodded.

"Alright, you give us fifteen pull-ups and I'll give you a check for five grand to pass on to whatever charity you want. Deal?"

Justin laughed, and Courtney now realized he was blushing. He headed over to the pull-up bar and tugged on it tentatively. "You sure this thing's sturdy?" The host nodded. He wiped his hands on his pants and rolled the short sleeves of his tee shirt onto the top of his shoulder, flashing the entire length of his toned arms to the audience, who responded with appreciative whistles.

He jumped up to grab the bar and quickly did fifteen pull-ups, paused, and then did five more. He was laughing and blushing as he dropped back to his feet and swung his arm around Courtney's waist, pulling her closer. "You could've agreed to ten," he whispered, smiling.

The host thanked him, handed him an oversized fake check, and then they went to commercial break.

"You're a good sport," she said to Courtney, who simply blushed.

Justin kissed her on the cheek and the audience screamed even louder, and then he waved again and they left the stage.

Justin and Courtney spent the day sightseeing around Chicago before meeting her family for dinner. They arrived at the restaurant first, thanks to Justin's insistence that they not be late. Especially after the pictures of his Vegas escapades landed in the tabloids, he wasn't about to give Courtney's brother or father any reason to be irritated with him.

He kept his sunglasses and winter hat on as they glanced around the lobby of the restaurant, equally unwilling to risk running into fans who might bother Courtney's family.

"I don't see them," Courtney confirmed. Then she giggled. "Babe, you look ridiculous. It's nighttime and you're indoors and you're wearing sunglasses. This isn't L.A. No one does that here."

He reluctantly slipped his sunglasses off, smiled at the hostess who was now wide-eyed and blushing. "Hi. We had a reservation for five, under Robbins."

The hostess fumbled with a notepad and her pen flipped to the floor. Justin bent to retrieve it.

"Thanks," she mumbled. "Do you want to wait at the bar for the rest of your party?"

Justin winced. The whole point of a reservation was to proceed directly to the table. Courtney was already pulling her hat and gloves off. He helped her slip out of her coat and waited for her to reply.

"I think a drink would relax you," she said.

"Yeah, but," he began.

"I think you're worried for nothing. There's no paparazzi in Chicago." Courtney turned to the hostess. "You don't know who he is, do you?"

The poor girl turned awkwardly from Justin to Courtney, clearly uncertain of how to reply. Finally, she cleared her throat and answered quietly. "He, um, looks a lot like Justin Erikson."

Justin nodded, flashed a pointed stare at Courtney, then turned back to the hostess and smiled. "Nice to meet you," he said.

"Oh, whatever," Courtney said. "I'll be at the bar."

He laughed. "I guess we're going to the bar."

"I'll let you know when the rest of your party arrives. Can I take your coats?"

Justin handed her Courtney's coat, then reluctantly slipped out of his own, wedging his hat and gloves into the pockets. "Thanks," he said, quickly bringing his hand to his head to fix any damage done to his hair by the hat, having forgotten how short his hair was now. He followed Courtney, who was already seated at the bar, two martini glasses in front of her.

"That was fast," he said, taking one of the glasses and sipping hesitantly. He knew the alcohol would relax him, but he also worried that a dirty martini before the meal might relax him a little too much.

Courtney grasped the cocktail spear in her drink and bit off one of the blue cheese-filled olives in her drink, drawing his eyes to her mouth. He sat beside her and kissed her before she finished chewing. "God you're sexy," he said.

She smiled. "So what was the deal with the hostess? You're being weird. Why do you care if anyone recognizes you?"

He shrugged and took another swig of his drink. "I don't know. I just don't want your parents to think I'm being rude if people try to get an autograph or anything. They already think you can't have a normal life with me, I just..."

Courtney laughed again. He wondered if she was already tipsy and then noticed she had nearly drained her drink. "Justin, if you stop acting crazy, then they'll see that you're normal. And they won't think you're rude if other people interrupt you. You're just nervous. It's not like they haven't met you before."

He knew she was right, but he still felt inexplicably nervous. "Christ it's cold. You really miss this weather?"

"Yup. I miss sweaters and leggings and cute hats."

"You do look cute in hats." He grinned. "The only thing I miss about this weather is hockey. And snowboarding, not that there's any hills near here."

Courtney finished her drink and took a sip of Justin's. The bartender appeared to offer her a refill, but Justin shook his head dismissively and paid for their drinks instead.

"So why are you drinking so fast if I'm the nervous one?" he asked.

"My parents like red wine."

Justin knew Courtney hated red wine, so he figured she was just planning on abstaining during the meal. "What kind of red wine?"

"Merlot, I think," she replied just before jumping out of her seat. "Eric!"

Justin turned as she ran off towards a guy that had just walked in. He stole one last quick drink and then followed her. Courtney was still squealing and hugging her brother as Justin approached. Eric was tall and thin, with short brown hair. As soon as Courtney released her brother from the hug, Justin could tell he shared the same facial features as Courtney, minus the blue eyes.

Eric faced Justin and held out his hand. "So you're Justin. I'm Eric," he said.

They shook hands. "Nice to finally meet you."

"Where are Mom and Dad?" Courtney asked. "I thought they were staying with you."

"They're parking the car. Dad thought the valet looked like that guy in Grand Theft Auto, so he took off looking for street parking." Eric turned back to Justin and gave him an obvious once over. Then he leaned in to Courtney. "Geez, when Mom said you were dating a hunk, she wasn't kidding, huh."

Courtney and her brother both laughed, leaving Justin feeling even more nervous than before.

Eric seemed to pick up on his discomfort before Courtney did. "Nah, I'm joking, man. I mean, Mom did say that, but I won't hold it against you. So what do you guys have planned when you're in town?"

Courtney thankfully reappeared by Justin's side and he wrapped his arm around her, feeling himself relax as his body touched hers. "Just hanging out, really. I haven't spent much time in Chicago since I was younger."

"He was on a talk show this morning," Courtney added, making Justin blush more.

Eric clearly didn't know how to respond to this, so he changed the subject. "Court says you grew up around here?"

"The South Bend area," Justin replied, then paused, as he saw Courtney's parents walk in the door.

After another round of awkward greetings, the hostess took everyone's coats and showed them to a table in the corner. Justin, thankfully, was able to sit with his back to the main part of the restaurant.

They ordered drinks, Justin winning points with his future in-laws by suggesting a bottle of merlot for the table.

"Holy shit, is that thing real?" Eric suddenly asked, reaching over Justin and grabbing Courtney's hand. He turned to Justin. "Nice. What are your intentions with my sister?"

"Oh stop it," Courtney said. "You promised you'd be nice."

Eric grinned mischievously. "I was being nice, but now that you mention it, I have a question for you. How far along are you, anyway?"

Now Justin knew he was blushing, but Courtney clearly didn't comprehend what her brother was insinuating yet.

"I see you're not drinking and you clearly couldn't land a guy like that unless..."

Courtney leaned across Justin to swat her brother with a napkin, but thankfully, then, the waitress returned with a martini for her. "Jerk," Courtney mumbled to Eric.

"Courtney says you just finished med school," Justin said,

desperate to change the subject. One of my older brothers is doing his residency in Indianapolis."

Eric smiled, and they talked about med school until the waitress brought the appetizer and took their orders.

"I just watched all four of the *Days End* movies last week with a friend," Eric said.

"Girlfriend," Courtney corrected, eliciting a glare from her brother.

Justin laughed. Although the subject matter of those films, zombie werewolves, sounded like a guy's movie, the focus was actually a romantic love triangle. So when a guy watched the whole saga back to back, it was generally because of a girl. "Oh yeah? What did you think?"

"Honestly it wasn't as bad as I was expecting."

Courtney's mom, Shannon, shushed her son at this, but Justin merely smiled. It was a truthful response, and he appreciated Eric's candor. "I know what you mean. It was a lot of fun to shoot those, but I generally prefer more action. They were definitely a big hit with the fans, though."

"Yeah, so what are you working on now?" Eric asked.

Justin opened his mouth to answer, but then noticed a shadow hovering over him. He turned to see a woman, probably in her late twenties, standing there.

"So sorry to interrupt, but I just had to tell you I just love your work," she said nervously.

Justin smiled politely. "Thanks. What's your name?"

"Marcie."

He reached out, shook her hand, and smiled again. "Nice to meet you Marcie. Thanks for saying hello. You have a good night."

The woman beamed and scurried off after the guy she'd been dining with.

Justin turned back to Eric. "Sorry, what were you asking?"

Eric laughed in response, and Courtney's parents quickly followed suit. Courtney squeezed Justin's hand.

"Are you that nice to all the fans, or just the cute girls?" Eric asked as the waitress cleared away the appetizer plates and brought another bottle of wine.

"All of his fans are cute girls," Courtney answered for him. "And he's always that nice."

Justin shrugged. "I don't get work unless the fans buy tickets to my movies. Can't hurt for them to like me."

"Have you thought about any wedding dates yet?" Shannon asked, turning to Courtney.

"Um, no, not really," Courtney said.

"Well, have you decided if it'll be in L.A. or Indiana?"

Courtney shook her head. "We haven't really planned anything yet. It's complicated."

Justin sighed, relieved that she didn't explain why it was complicated or mention that any way they did it, it was going to be either a publicity or security nightmare.

"How well do you know Andrea Taylor?" Eric asked.

Courtney groaned, presumably knowing where he was going with the question.

"Andi's a good friend," Justin said with a smile.

"You've done a lot of movies with her, huh?"

"Yeah. She was in all the *Days End* ones with me and then we've done two others together. We might do another one next year, but we're still working out the contract issues and timing."

"I saw the photo shoot you guys did, the one with the elephant. You know the one?" Eric paused until Justin nodded. "That bathing suit of hers, was it..."

Justin laughed. Courtney groaned again and started talking with her parents. "Paint. It was just body paint."

Eric grinned. "You're telling me that the whole time you guys were doing those photos, she was basically just naked. Right beside you."

Justin lowered his voice, really not wanting to get into the details with Matt and Shannon right there. "Well, she had on a skin-toned thong under the paint, but that was about it."

"Damn. Talk about job perks." Eric gulped his wine. "She's probably a little young for me anyway, but man is that girl hot."

Justin shook his head. "Andi's a year older than Courtney. That's the same as you, right?"

Eric raised an eyebrow. "So how much fun was it filming that last one, where you got to hook up with her like, what was it, three times?"

Actually, there had been four sex scenes in that movie, but Justin wasn't about to correct him, especially with Courtney right there, even if she did appear to still be engrossed in conversation with her parents. He opted to change the subject instead. "Hey, well, as a doctor, you get to do checkups on naked women all day, right?"

Eric laughed. "Yeah, pretty much. Except they're all older, ugly, and sick."

"Well, the whole filming process for those scenes is nothing like the finished product. There's multiple guys standing right around the bed with cameras, lights and clipboards, and then the director critiques your every move. Plus Andi had a nasty cold during the last one we filmed. She could barely breathe through her mouth and she was trying not to blow her nose much because she didn't want it to get all red. It was just gross."

"I knew it!" Courtney suddenly exclaimed.

Justin winced.

"You said you had no idea where that cold came from, that it must just be some superbug."

They all laughed. Justin finally relaxed, confident that Courtney's brother and parents seemed to like him enough, and they all finished the meal without any drama.

Justin insisted on paying the bill right as Courtney turned to Eric. "We wanted to go check out some clubs after dinner. Think you and that girlfriend of yours could show us a good one?"

Eric laughed. "I'm not bringing any girl I'm interested in within two miles of him."

Courtney rolled her eyes. "Come on, it'll be fun to hang out and you guys can get to know each other better without Mom and Dad around."

"I heard that," Shannon said with a smile.

Courtney blushed, but successfully convinced Eric to join them.

They had a great time out with Eric and his girlfriend that night, and the next day he and Courtney tackled the majority of their holiday shopping followed by a little more sightseeing and a Bulls game. He had a fun time on the trip, but really didn't feel as refreshed as he would've expected. Between filming and Vegas and now this trip, the last eight weeks had been a blur.

He settled lower in his seat and rested his head on Courtney's shoulder. She patted his head much like one would pet a dog.

"How is it possible that I just spent an entire long weekend with you and feel like we haven't actually had any time together at all?" he asked.

She snickered. "Probably because you slept every minute that we were alone."

"Not every minute! I recall at least five minutes that I was very awake."

"Hmm, that was a fun five minutes," she teased.

Justin let his eyes slip shut just as Courtney jumped.

"Hey! I forgot to tell you. I have news," she said.

He lifted his head and turned to face her.

"The shelter offered me a position as a director on the board."

Justin furrowed his brow.

"Executive Director of Legal."

"And that's different from your current job?"

"Yes!" Courtney paused. "Well, I mean, the title is. And it's a much more prestigious position. My duties will stay basically the same, except now I'll also attend board meetings and do... whatever else directors do."

"That's awesome, Court. Why weren't we celebrating this weekend?"

She shrugged. "I don't know. Maybe because we were busy. And I sort of forgot. Or because it's more work and not much more money?"

"Well, if one of us doesn't start making more money soon, we might have to cut back on something. Like maybe have the lawn service come less often," he teased.

Courtney nodded, her smile widening and looking more natural now.

"When did you find out?"

She hesitated. "Well, last week. Before we left for Chicago. I was going to tell you right away but then you were working and then you were tired, and..."

"I'm never too tired or busy to hear about your day," he interrupted.

"Well, you're hearing now."

He tugged her hands onto his lap, squeezing them as he kissed the top of her head. "Congratulations. You're officially too smart for your own good."

9

———

They enjoyed a few uneventful weeks together, and just when Courtney was starting to accept that her life actually was perfect, she woke up with a terrible headache. She wasn't surprised, since a sore throat had kept her up most of the night. Still, she wasn't one to get sick. Not even with a cold. She took a couple Advil, wincing at the pain of swallowing, and left for work. By noon, she was achy all over and shivering. Worried she had the flu and would spread it to the whole office, she packed up her stuff to work from home.

The shelter wasn't too busy this time of year, at least in the legal department, so Courtney wasn't too worried. She figured she'd take a nap and work a few more hours after she woke up. But instead, when she woke up, her whole body felt like it was on fire. She called Justin to whine.

"You sound terrible," he said. "What's your temperature?"

"I don't have a thermometer," she said.

"Why don't you go to the doctor?"

"I don't have a doctor."

"What?"

"Well, I haven't been in L.A. that long. I mean, I have a gynecologist, but I hardly think a sore throat falls within her specialty."

Justin was quiet for a minute. "I'm coming over," he said.

"No. I'm probably contagious."

"I'll wear a mask," he said, and he disconnected.

Courtney sighed, but was too achy to move. Justin arrived less than an hour later. He had a bottle of juice, a box of popsicles, canned soup, and a thermometer.

"You went shopping," she observed, pleased with the gesture.

He handed her the thermometer. "Want me to make the soup?"

She shook her head. Her throat was way too sore for soup. She popped the thermometer in and Justin rubbed her back while they waited. The thermometer beeped and they both glanced at it. 103.

"Come on, I'll drive you to one of those pharmacy clinics," Justin said.

"No way. I look terrible. I'm not going with *you*." She started to stand, her body now trembling uncontrollably. "I'll drive myself." Courtney envisioned the photos that would surely appear if Justin went with her to the doctor, her puffy eyes and grotesquely shaking body.

He left the room without speaking, and returned a moment later. "I called you a car. Do you need help getting dressed?"

She shook her head.

An hour later, she climbed back into the car, a diagnosis of strep throat and a bottle of Penicillin in hand. She took one of the pills and closed her eyes until they returned to her apartment, but when she felt the car stop, she opened her eyes and saw Justin's place. "Not here," she told the driver. "Take me back to the apartment where you picked me up."

"Mr. Erikson said to bring you back here," the driver replied.

"Well I want to go home."

"I have to follow his instructions. He's paying for the service."

"It's kidnapping to take me someplace against my will. I'll pay you for the rest of the drive," she said. "Now take me home."

By that time, Justin had appeared at the side of the car. "Here, I'll help you out," he said.

Courtney shook her head. "I want to go home."

"I'll take care of you here," Justin said.

"No," Courtney replied, her voice more forceful now.

Justin walked around the car and climbed in. "Fine, then I'll come with you."

"You're not wearing shoes."

He winced. "Give me five minutes, okay?"

He returned a few minutes later and they drove to her place. Justin helped her back into bed, made her some tea, then left so she could sleep. He returned later with soup, which Courtney sipped painfully before taking her next dose of antibiotics. They watched a movie together on her tiny bedroom TV, and Justin even refrained from griping about the size or quality of the picture. And then, Courtney realized she was feeling infinitely worse.

She climbed out of bed and barely made it to the bathroom before vomiting. Justin, thankfully, waited in the bedroom until she reemerged. He eyed her pitifully.

"Okay, now you've got to go home," she grumbled, crawling back into bed. "You're making me feel self-conscious."

He patted her head like she was a dog. "I'm sure you're all better now."

She shook her head. "I feel like maybe I'm going to die in five minutes. Seriously, just go. I'm never sick, and I'm not good at it. I just need to be alone. I'll call you tomorrow morning."

He reluctantly left, but not before bringing juice and

crackers to her bedside. Courtney was sick again, and then decided a hot bath might cheer her up. She took the bath and then felt a little better by the time she crawled out. She toweled off and then turned to the mirror as she slipped back into her pajamas, and then gasped. A patchy white and red rash was spreading across her neck and chest. She turned, and the same rash was all over her back.

"You've got to be kidding me," she grumbled, right before vomiting again. She stumbled back to bed and called the number of the clinic she went to earlier. They initially wanted her to return, but when she reemphasized the frequency with which she was throwing up, they agreed to prescribe a different antibiotic instead.

Courtney knew she couldn't drive herself to pick it up, so she reluctantly dialed Justin.

"Sorry to bother you, but apparently I'm allergic to penicillin. I'm still sick and now I've got a rash. The clinic called in a new prescription for me."

"Want me to get anything else?"

"Ginger ale."

Justin arrived an hour later with the items. Courtney hid under her bedspread so he couldn't see the rash, but she could tell from the look on his face that she must look terrible. Thankfully, he left quickly.

The next two days, Courtney felt progressively better, but still pretty horrible. Her head was throbbing from lack of sleep, her stomach was still wacky from the medicine and the lack of food since it still hurt to swallow, but she no longer had a fever. Justin had dropped by each day to check on her, but now Courtney was panicked.

He was leaving for work the next day and wouldn't be back until Christmas. It was a busy trip, with international publicity touring for the last *Days End* movie.

That was a long time to go without seeing Justin. Courtney knew she wasn't contagious anymore, courtesy of the miracle of modern medicine, so she showered, styled her hair and makeup, and pulled on a fresh pair of sweatpants to head over to Justin's.

~

COURTNEY LOOKED BETTER when she arrived at his house that morning. The color had returned to her cheeks, and her stomach didn't seem quite so hollowed out.

"I figured I might as well recover here, with you," she said, adding, "I'm not contagious now."

"I wasn't worried about that," he replied, kissing her forehead and taking the bag in her arms.

They spent the day snuggled together on the couch, watching movies, and then Courtney took a long hot bath while Justin did his workout. When he returned, he showered and then found her curled up in his bed, asleep. He crept under the covers slowly, careful not to wake her, but she shifted and inched closer to him the moment he lay back.

"I hate that you're leaving tomorrow and I've hardly seen you this week," she said.

"You could visit me," he replied, knowing it wasn't a really viable option. He was going to be busy on this trip, traveling to multiple cities. Besides, she was working and she'd never agree. But then, he realized what she could do in his absence that was sure to cheer them both up.

"I figured out what I want for Christmas," he said, waiting until she gazed up to continue. "Move in with me."

"That's not a present."

"Is too. When I come home and see my bedroom and bathroom completely overtaken with all your pink girlie crap, it'll be like Christmas morning."

"First off, I don't own any pink crap and you know that. Second, you'd really want me moving all my stuff in while you're gone?"

"Absolutely. And I'd be even happier if you'd just let me pay someone to pack and move all your stuff so you don't have to mess with it."

Courtney wrinkled her nose. "I don't have that much stuff that I really want to bring. I mean, the couch in our apartment is mine, and so is the furniture in my bedroom, but I figured I'd leave it all and then Erica wouldn't have to buy new stuff and could advertise a furnished place for a roommate."

That made sense. Courtney's furniture was all cheap anyway.

"I hate leaving her before she finds a new roommate," Courtney continued.

"I'll pay her your portion of the rent until she finds someone. It's not a big deal."

"It's not about the money. I don't want her to be all alone."

"You're here most nights anyway," he reminded her. "Besides, I promise to let you have unlimited visitation with her after you move." He tickled her until she laughed at his stupid joke.

Then she sighed, nestling her head into his chest. "I'm still gross, aren't I?"

"No, you're perfect."

"Then why aren't you trying to take advantage of me?"

He debated whether it might be a trap. He was pretty sure that the gentlemanly thing to do was not to pressure a sick girl into having sex with you. "Because you're not feeling up to it."

"Well I really don't feel like waiting three more weeks either."

Justin smiled and kissed her, tentatively at first. She kissed him back, but Justin waited for a more obvious sign before proceeding further. Once her hands slid down his stomach and slid under the thin material of his boxer briefs, he knew she was serious. They made love once that night, and again in the morning, right before Justin left to catch his flight.

OVER A WEEK LATER, Courtney was just returning to her desk at work when Justin called her cell phone. They'd managed to talk at least once a day since he'd left, with random texts and emails filling in the gaps. Still, she loved hearing from him.

"Hey, how's it going?" she asked, smiling.

"Good. How are you?"

"Better now. Isn't it late there? Aren't you supposed to be on a plane?"

"I'm on the plane now, but we have a half hour layover. And yeah, it's late, but I'll sleep on the plane. I've got my neck pillow and an awesome airline blanket."

She smiled, picturing him snuggled up in his first class seat.

"I think we need to go to Europe together," he said. "I keep thinking of stuff you'd like over here."

"Like what?"

"Hiking in the Alps, exploring castles in England, gondola rides in Venice."

"Okay, I'm jealous."

"Well it's not like I'm doing any of that stuff on this trip. I'm just getting ideas."

"Sounds good."

"Seriously, we should hit up Asia too, maybe even Africa. And definitely Australia."

"Justin, you know I'm not that big of a fan of flying."

"You get used to it," he said. "Besides, I'd distract you."

She shut her office door and settled back in her chair. "Oh yeah? How?"

She could hear the smile in his voice as he spoke. "Well, you know how I mentioned that big airplane blanket I've got now? It's plenty big for two. And if you... ow!"

Courtney waited, confused, for Justin to continue.

"Ryan says hi," he finally said.

"Ryan's there?"

"Yeah, he's in the aisle seat next to me. Hang on, I'm giving him the phone."

Courtney spoke to Ryan for a minute before he returned the phone to Justin. Ryan was Justin's frequent gym buddy, as well as a costar on the *Days End* series. He had three kids with his wife Audrey, who happened to have starred on Courtney's favorite TV show growing up. It had been strange for her to meet Audrey in real life, but now they'd become friendly. They were about ten years older than Courtney and Justin, which also made them a good example for a Hollywood couple that actually was working out, so far.

"Where was I?" Justin asked.

"I think you were talking about cuddling with Ryan during the flight."

Justin laughed. "So whatcha wearing?"

Courtney glanced down. "Long sleeve shirt, floral skirt, brown boots."

"Boots?"

She smiled. Justin thought women in boots were the sexiest thing ever.

"And?"

"White bra and matching panties."

He sighed audibly. "The lacy ones with the little bow?"

"Yes." She wondered if he was questioning her faithfulness when she admitted to wearing his favorite of her underwear when he was overseas. "And you?"

"Grey sweatpants, red tee shirt, black sweatshirt. Red boxers. Ouch!"

"You okay?"

"Yeah, somebody keeps smacking my arm," he said.

Courtney smiled, easily picturing Ryan growing frustrated at the conversation.

"You're really wearing sweatpants? On an airplane?" Courtney knew Justin had an excessively high standard of fashion, even on an overnight airplane.

"Yeah, we're in Europe. No one seems to recognize us." He paused. "So tell me more about these lacy things you're wearing. Have you taken them off yet? Ow!"

She laughed. "Sorry babe. I'm with Ryan on this one. No phone sex when you're seated right next to someone we know."

He sighed audibly again, although she knew he had only been teasing. Probably.

"I miss you," she said.

"Me too."

"Get some sleep. I'll talk to you later."

"Okay. Love you." He hung up.

Courtney sighed and leaned back in her chair, closing her eyes to picture him for a moment. It had to be rough, flying around the world at all hours of the day and then needing to smile and greet fans like he'd slept all night, but Justin relished any opportunity for travel. And she loved when he came up with future travel plans for the two of them. It always made her feel like she really was part of his long term plan. Not that the engagement didn't signal that too, but in a different way.

While she was thinking of him, she reached for her purse to take her birth control pill. She used to take them in the morning, but then realized she wasn't that alert in the mornings and might as well take them in the late afternoon each day, especially since she'd been carrying them in her purse ever since she started spending nights at Justin's.

Courtney popped one of the pink pills in her mouth and scooted her purse back across her desk and then paused. Something wasn't right. She tugged her purse back and opened up the packet of pills. She glanced at the calendar. It was Friday, but the pill under the label of Friday was still in place. So was Thursday's. Courtney heard a crunch sound and realized she'd just bitten off the tip of her fingernail.

She pulled up her calendar again. She distinctly remembered taking her pill Thursday and the day before that. In fact, she was nearly positive that she'd taken it at work each day that week. What made more sense was that she'd forgotten the pill over the weekend back when she was sick. Courtney turned back to the small blue package of pills. She wasn't just one day behind, but two. And while she didn't remember missing either of those days, what she did remember was the first day she was on Penicillin, when she took her pill and then promptly threw up.

There was a knock at her door and she jumped, nearly dropping the pill container in the trash. She wedged it back into her purse, tried to calm her breathing, and called for her next appointment to come in.

JUSTIN SPENT the next four days promoting *Days End* in various cities in England. The whole cast wasn't there—just Justin, Ryan, and three of their female costars. The three big stars somehow managed to skip out of the distance publicity gigs. Justin had been to England once before, but he'd had no more opportunity to explore then than he did now. They'd check into a hotel, have at most an hour or two to get situated, and then they'd leave to go meet fans, sign autographs, do interviews, or talk at various conventions.

When they finished that, they'd move on to the next city. It was grueling, and frustrating. Justin loved exploring new towns, but he felt like the whole trip was a big tease. He could see lots of cool places to visit, but couldn't actually get out of the plane, train, or car to actually experience or touch anyplace. He'd definitely have to come back with Courtney.

He hadn't been able to hang out with this group since they'd finished filming, and it was fun to travel and eat with friends. Over the weekend, they were returning to New York to do an extra week of promotions there. His publicist Jamie would meet up with him then, so he'd have even less time for his friends. So Justin was determined to enjoy his time.

10

———————

The next weekend, Courtney stared at the plain, flat stick as it lay on the already overcrowded bathroom counter. She had read the directions enough times to memorize them since opening the package fifteen minutes earlier. Still, she felt compelled to review one last time before peeing. She couldn't possibly be pregnant, and it would be a travesty to mistakenly think she was, even for a moment, by misreading the test.

She told herself that it wasn't that big of a deal to be late. Lots of women had irregular periods. Being a couple of days late probably meant that she was stressed out. Besides, her doctor had said that, over time, she might stop getting her period altogether on the progestin-only pills. Maybe it was finally her lucky day. She really shouldn't be so negative.

She took a deep breath and ignored the voice in her head reminding her that her pill also had a reputation for being less effective when not taken at the exact same time each day. It was all just so crazy. In all the years that Courtney had been on the pill, she'd always been careful. Whenever she took antibiotics or anything else that might affect her pills' effectiveness, she remembered back-up protection. She took her pills at the same time each day, always with sufficient water. And, until recently, she'd never missed a pill.

According to the internet, estrogen-progestin combination pills were still 97% effective even if you skipped one pill. If you missed two though, the number dropped to 93%. What concerned her most was her recollection of vomiting right after taking her pill the day before she skipped the first of two pills. Well, that and the fact that every chart she found online had a handy little asterisk noting that missing progestin-only pills had a greater chance of resulting in pregnancy.

Ugh.

Really, it was Justin's fault. If he hadn't been leaving town, she wouldn't have even considered sex so soon after strep throat, but she hadn't wanted to wait another three weeks. Besides, she had felt nearly good as new once the antibiotics—the ones she wasn't allergic to—kicked in.

Courtney checked the expiration date on the package one last time. She'd had a pregnancy scare once before, in college, and the worst part had been the waiting. She'd vowed then to always keep a pregnancy test on hand, so she never again would have to worry and wonder about the unknown and could just test whenever she thought of it, no matter how ungrounded her concerns were.

She yanked down her jeans, grabbed the stick, and peed. Her hand shook so much that she ended up dousing her fingers. She placed the cap back on the stick and set it flat on a clean paper towel before scrubbing her hands and then turning her back to the counter, checking the time on her phone. As she set her phone down, it buzzed, and she jumped in the air, the phone nearly flying out of her hand.

Courtney glanced at the phone. Justin was calling. She

answered without thinking about it, hearing the uncertainty in her own voice.

"Hey babe, what's wrong?"

"Oh, nothing. I was just thinking about something with work. How's it going?"

"Good. I just got to the mall, and I guess I'm going to be signing autographs and stuff for a few hours, so I thought I'd check in first."

Courtney smiled, picturing him in his element, surrounded by fans, clowning around and flirting harmlessly. She turned slowly, almost forgetting what was behind her. But there, reflected in the window, she saw the plus sign, as clear and easy-to-read as the packaging promised.

Her breath caught in her throat. "Oh, God," she murmured.

"Court? You still there? It's loud in here, so I can't hear you well."

"I'll talk to you later," she mumbled, hanging up and sliding slowly to the floor.

When she heard Erica calling her and knocking on the door, Courtney realized nearly an hour had passed. Courtney considered ignoring her, but that technique wasn't too effective when she was holed up in the small, shared bathroom of their two-bedroom apartment. Unable to speak, she reached up and unlocked the door, nudging it a few inches open. She didn't look up, but didn't need to.

"Oh my God," Erica said, immediately joining Courtney on the floor.

Courtney couldn't look at her, didn't know how to explain or even what to say. But Erica wasn't fazed. She leaned in, wrapping Courtney in a tight hug, then released her.

"I take it this wasn't planned," she deduced.

Courtney snorted in response.

"Does Justin know?"

She shook her head.

"It is, um, his, right?"

"Erica!"

Her roommate shrugged. "Okay, I figured, but I just wanted to ask. No judgment here."

"I can't have a baby," Courtney said, so quietly that she wasn't certain if she'd thought it or actually spoken aloud until Erica answered. She thought of her recent conversation with Justin, where he was rambling about all the places he wanted to go, and she thought of his career and how it was just picking up...having a baby now would ruin him. And worst of all, she knew he'd never have the heart to admit it.

"Okay. Then don't."

Courtney turned, surprised. "What do you mean?"

Erica shrugged, then looked at her watch. "If you don't want to have the baby, you don't have to."

"You mean, like an abortion?"

"Well, yeah." Erica's tone remained nonchalant. "They even have pills you can take now if it's early enough."

"I don't know if Justin would go for that."

"It ain't up to him."

"But I'd still have to tell him," Courtney said.

"Only if you want to." Erica paused. "You don't even have to tell the doctor who the father is."

Courtney wasn't sure how to respond. "I'd have to tell him," she finally repeated.

Her phone buzzed again, this time a text message from Justin. "Just got a proposal from a teen. Too bad I'm taken," it read. A smiley emoji with its tongue sticking out punctuated his final sentence.

Erica eyed the message, then glanced back up. "You're sure he's never done anything he hasn't told you?"

Courtney didn't answer.

Erica launched into a matter-of-fact discussion of the various methods of ending a pregnancy. She spoke in the same tone Courtney would expect from someone evaluating the pros and cons of organic produce.

Courtney rubbed her eyes, wishing it were all just a nightmare. "How do you know so much about this?"

"I had an abortion in college," Erica replied casually.

That confused Courtney further.

"How do you know men aren't for you if you don't give them a try, right?" Erica joked.

"I'm sorry, I didn't realize you'd ever..." Courtney wasn't sure what she was trying to say.

Erica shrugged. "It was a long time ago. Even then, it was tough, though, and it took a while to get over." She paused. "I mean, if I could go back in time, I'd still do it, but you know, it was just a lot to process."

Courtney nodded. That she could understand.

"Why don't you sleep on it, then go to the doctor tomorrow? They could do another test, just to confirm, and talk about all your options. Then once you know more, you can decide what to do and whether to tell Justin."

Erica left then, returning a few minutes later with the numbers of a few clinics Courtney could call if she didn't feel like using her regular doctor.

At some point that night, Courtney made it to bed, eventually falling into a light, dreamless sleep. She called her doctor on the way to work, but still couldn't get an appointment until the next afternoon, even after insisting it was an emergency. Erica offered to come, but Courtney refused, feeling this was something she, as an adult, should be able to handle alone.

April, her boss, was out of the office the day of the appointment, to Courtney's relief, so she was able to avoid conversation with everyone in the morning. A half hour before her appointment, she told the receptionist she was taking a late lunch and would work from home the rest of the afternoon.

By the time she reached the medical office, Courtney was in a panic. She had assumed she'd be more comfortable talking with her regular doctor, the same one she'd gotten to know at her annual checkups over the past two years, but now, she was worried. What would her doctor think of her? Would she have to switch doctors after this? What if Justin stumbled across her medical records and found out about all this in the future?

Courtney nervously glanced around the office, feeling like a fugitive. She reminded herself that no one knew why she was there, that no one could possibly know she was pregnant. The nurse showed her back to a quiet room in the corner, stopping at a bathroom on the way to have her pee in a small plastic cup. When she reached the room, the nurse checked her blood pressure and then let her know the doctor would be in shortly.

Twenty long minutes passed before her doctor finally appeared. Dr. Patel knocked quickly, then entered without awaiting a response. Notwithstanding the name, which Courtney suspected indicated only that she'd married a man of Indian descent, Dr. Patel was a tall, middle-aged blonde woman, with a soft voice and a forgiving smile. She plopped on the rolling stool in front of Courtney and scooted closer.

"How are you doing today Courtney?"

Courtney shrugged in response. What a loaded question.

Dr. Patel sighed. "Before we get started today, I want to let you know we tested the urine sample you left, and it did confirm what you indicated on the phone."

Courtney frowned, not certain she understood. "So I am pregnant?"

The doctor nodded. "Congratulations!"

Courtney burst into tears.

Dr. Patel scooted closer, handing an entire box of cheap hospital-grade tissues to Courtney. "Do you need a moment?"

Courtney shook her head. "No, I've known for over a day now. Another moment won't help."

Dr. Patel nodded. "Unplanned pregnancies are much more common than you might think. I understand it can be an extremely stressful situation, but let's go ahead and discuss your options." She quickly flipped through Courtney's medical chart before continuing. "I don't see anything here in your medical history that would complicate a pregnancy," she began. "Are you still taking your birth control pills?"

Courtney rolled her eyes, tempted to say "not very well," but instead she answered honestly. "I missed a couple pills about two weeks ago when I was sick."

"And since then?"

"I kept taking them until yesterday."

The doctor nodded. "Well, regardless of your decision, I'd like you to stop taking the pills until further notice." She paused again to flip through the papers attached to her clipboard. "We just ran your labs and did your pap at your annual appointment two months ago, so I don't feel a full exam or more bloodwork is necessary."

"You don't need a blood test to confirm I'm p...p..."

Dr. Patel smiled. "No. Blood work can tell us the quantity of certain hormones in your system, but the range of what is normal varies so widely that unless we repeat the labs in two days, we really can't infer much from the results. If you'd feel better knowing, we can go ahead and draw a sample now but you'll need to set up another appointment for later this week."

Courtney shook her head. Missing more work certainly wasn't the answer.

She closed the folder and looked up. "I have a whole packet of information I'll give you on pregnancy and childbirth. I'd like you to read through it all and let me know if you have any questions. If you decide to continue the pregnancy, I'll want to see you again in about another month to do a quick ultrasound. We can draw blood then to confirm everything still looks good."

The doctor paused, and Courtney wondered if she was supposed to jump in yet. But she still didn't know what to say, so she just kept staring at her feet.

"Look, Courtney, the first decision you'll need to make is whether to continue the pregnancy or not. The sooner you decide, the better. If you carry the fetus and deliver, you can either keep the baby or pursue adoption. If you're interested in considering that route, I can give you contact information for different agencies that could handle that."

Courtney shook her head. She couldn't imagine spending nine months with a baby and then giving it away. Not to mention the difficulty she'd surely encounter in hiding a pregnancy from Justin for that long. "No, if I have the baby, I'll keep it. I just..." Courtney couldn't say out loud what she was thinking, that she didn't think she wanted to have the baby.

Dr. Patel nodded calmly and proceeded with her spiel. "If you decide to terminate the pregnancy, we'd need to do a quick ultrasound to confirm how far along you are. And then I can either prescribe a medication that you would take at home or we can perform a quick procedure in the office. Both methods have side effects, but neither should affect your ability to have a successful pregnancy and delivery in the future. I'll give you some information on each option that you can read over."

Courtney nodded, expecting the doctor to stand and fetch the information she kept referencing, but instead, she remained seated and patted Courtney's hand gently.

"I understand this is a tough situation, Courtney. You can do your research and think about everything tonight, and then you can come in later this week to discuss any questions you have or to set up an appointment to terminate the pregnancy if that's your choice."

"How quickly can that be done, if I decide to go that route?"

If the question caught the doctor off guard, she hid it well. "I could prescribe the medication today and it usually works within forty-eight hours, or we could schedule the procedure today."

"And do you need, um, I mean, can I decide that alone? Or do you need anyone else to consent?" Courtney couldn't even make eye contact on that question.

"No. Because you are an adult, you can make that decision on your own."

"But do you ever notify the father?" Legally speaking, Courtney was sure she knew the answer, but it just didn't seem logical to her that the mom, who couldn't have made the baby without the dad, could terminate the pregnancy without telling him.

"All of it is completely confidential. I cannot share any of the privileged information in your health file without your consent."

Courtney nodded, satisfied.

"Have you, um, discussed any of this with your fiancé?" The doctor nodded pointedly at Courtney's oversized engagement ring.

Courtney winced, regretting not having left the ring in her purse. "No. He's out of town now. He doesn't even know I'm pregnant."

The doctor inhaled audibly through her nostrils, but her expression showed no judgment. "Okay. Do you have any questions regarding the paternity?"

"No! It's definitely my fiancé's. I didn't cheat on him!" Courtney slouched down further, feeling guilty for having raised her voice. But still, was screwing up with birth control really on par with having an affair?

Dr. Patel cleared her throat. "I didn't mean to imply anything or offend you, Courtney. I'm only asking because it seems that maybe you are considering terminating the pregnancy without telling your fiancé."

"You just said I don't need his consent," Courtney reminded her.

"And you don't." She licked her lips. "I need to ask, though, has there ever been any violence in your relationship, or do you have any reason to believe your fiancé would hurt you?"

Courtney shook her head. "He's a wonderful, amazing man and I love him so much, but I can't have a baby now." She realized she was crying again. "I just need to get this done and over with so things can go back to how they were."

"I'm going to give you the contact information for a pregnancy counselor also. I really recommend you speak with one before making a final decision. You are not the first patient I've had who has considered abortion. For some people, it's the right decision."

She paused. "But you need to make sure it is the right decision for you. Once it's done, it's final. You can't change your mind or undo it, but it's also not going to take anything back. It won't be like you were never pregnant, just that you're no longer pregnant. It's a hard decision to make, and the chances of you being satisfied with your decision are highest when you have a good support system."

"So you think I should tell him?"

Dr. Patel smiled. "I think you should talk with someone."

Courtney wasn't satisfied. "Are you married?"

Dr. Patel nodded.

"Do you think I should tell him?" she repeated.

The doctor hesitated. "I would tell my husband," she finally said. "But it's your choice." She scooted back in her chair before standing. "I'll be back with all of the pamphlets we discussed."

She sent Courtney home with an oversized plastic bag filled with information. Courtney pored over it all that night, discussed it all with Erica, and then devised a plan. She'd tell Justin as soon as he returned home. They'd discuss all of the reasons why it was bad timing. She'd convince him not to feel guilty, assuring him that she, too, thought the best solution was to end the pregnancy. She'd be better about taking her pills, they'd get married, and then they'd start having all of the kids he wanted in five or so years.

Everything would work out.

11

Justin took the red eye from New York on Saturday, and Keith picked him up at the airport early Sunday morning. He'd slept a little on the flight, but definitely needed a nap before seeing Courtney that afternoon. She'd been strange on the phone the night before. No, actually the whole last week. She sounded stressed out and distant. Justin hoped that wasn't how it was going to be whenever he traveled, especially since he'd be home for less than a month before leaving for another three months.

Justin showered and changed, then lounged out by the pool in drawstring sweatpants and a tee shirt. For some reason, he took the best naps outside, and it just made him feel more at home. He popped in his headphones and immediately zonked out. When he awoke, Courtney was sitting beside him, gently rubbing his arm.

He yawned, stretched, and pulled out the headphones.

"Sorry to wake you," she began. "I can't imagine you'll be able to get to bed at a reasonable hour tonight if you sleep much later, though."

Justin couldn't imagine ever being too pissed off at her

waking him up. Sure, he could've thought of better ways for her to do it, but a gentle arm rub worked too. He sat up and kissed her, breathing in her fresh, sweet fragrance. "You smell good," he said.

"I missed you, too," she replied, her voice quiet and uncertain.

"Is something wrong?"

She hesitated. "No."

He gripped her chin, tilting her head backwards until he could see into her sapphire eyes. "What is going on in that beautiful mind?" he mused. He pressed his lips to hers again, this time lingering but still not deepening the kiss. Kissing him always relaxed Courtney, so when she still looked tense after they separated he knew something was definitely on her mind.

"I can tell you're worrying about something," he said.

She tilted her head to the side. "No, I've just been busy. And I didn't move my stuff in. I thought you might be mad."

"Disappointed, yes. Mad? Hell no. As long as you sleep in my bed tonight, I couldn't care less where your stuff is."

Justin meant what he said. He wasn't mad, but he was confused. Courtney acted strangely the entire day. He'd wanted to take her directly to the bedroom, but she'd resisted, instead insisting on making him dinner. She was quiet when they ate, and then after dinner she went back to the patio and claimed she had to read through a few legal documents before nightfall.

Every time they had a moment alone, she'd come up with some excuse to avoid any actual intimacy with him. That night, she declined his invitation to shower with him. It didn't make sense. Every other time he'd returned from a trip, Courtney was as eager as he was to reunite physically. This time, she seemed to be avoiding it.

He went into the bathroom and started the shower, then shut it off. He needed to think. She had to be mad at him. But why? Justin scrolled through his calendar, confirming he hadn't missed their anniversary or any other significant occasions. Then, unable to think of any other explanation, he texted Jamie and asked if there'd been any press about him lately that might bother Courtney.

Luckily, her response was immediate. "Not that I've heard of. Why? What did you do? I want to get ahead of it, whatever it is."

"NOTHING," he replied, a bit insulted at her assumptions. Then, he decided she deserved more of an explanation. "Courtney is mad. I don't know why."

"Sorry. Not my job," she replied. "Try jewelry."

Justin snorted. Courtney was not the type to forgive someone who bribed her. No, he needed to be direct.

"Babe, what's going on?" he asked, draping the towel around his waist and reemerging from the bathroom.

She gazed up slowly, then frowned. "Did you shower already?"

"No. I'm worried."

"About?"

"You. Why don't you want to shower with me?"

"I don't want to get my hair wet before bed," she said, avoiding eye contact.

Justin ground his teeth together. If she were any other girl, Justin could believe that excuse. But not Courtney. She wasn't obsessed with her hair and besides, when she slept with wet hair, she woke with it bent into gorgeous waves.

He crawled onto the bed, leaning over the laptop where she was working. "Court, we've been together all day and you haven't yet tried to jump my bones. Something is wrong."

She hesitated, then gazed up. "I'm sorry. We can...if you really want to."

Justin suppressed a wince. As much as he wanted to be with

Courtney, he had zero interest in doing it if she didn't actually want to do it.

"It's just...bad time of the month, and I'm all distracted by this law review article. They want me to get the final version to them by tomorrow, and I need to make sure all the cases I cited are still good law."

Justin sighed. She'd never before used her period as an excuse, so he didn't for a moment believe that was truly it. But work, that made sense. Courtney was more dedicated to her job than anyone else he knew.

"So do you think it'll be published?" he said, backing away and sitting on the edge of the bed.

"Yeah, they've already agreed to publish it. And it's my first choice law review, too."

Justin listened as she yammered on about the merits of various publications, trying not to read too much into the fact that her work relaxed her more than he did. It was nearly a half hour later when he finally got into the shower, and when he returned to the bedroom, she was sound asleep.

COURTNEY AWOKE EARLY the next morning and enjoyed a full minute of serenity before she remembered about the pregnancy. Then, suddenly, she felt nauseous and excessively warm. She wriggled out from underneath Justin's arm and grabbed the bottle of water she'd left on the nightstand. After a moment, the icky feeling passed. She gazed over at Justin, who was still snoozing calmly. Just like a baby, she thought.

Bleh. What a dumb expression. Everyone knew babies didn't sleep soundly. Babies never slept. And if she had one, she would never sleep again, either. And after too many late-night study sessions in law school, Courtney knew she liked sleep.

Without adequate sleep, she became cranky, anxious, and whiny.

She was sure that Justin would be the type of dad to split the night shift evenly with her. Actually, she suspected he'd do it all if she asked, and probably without ever complaining. Except in order to share the night shift, he'd have to actually be home at night. That would mean he'd have to rearrange his entire schedule for the next year.

Justin's career was just starting to pick up. He'd killed himself the past several years shooting as many films as he could, just to gain enough recognition so as to become popular enough to be able to turn down offers. If he slowed down now, right when he was so close to reaching the point in his career when he could be more selective about projects, he'd probably never get there.

And the worst part? Justin would absolutely turn down a movie if Courtney asked him to. He'd risk pissing off directors or producers or whoever if she wanted him at home to help out. That wasn't fair. Even if he didn't end up resenting Courtney for that, she'd resent herself.

But the only other option would be for her to back off of work. And Courtney didn't love that idea either.

She slid out of bed slowly, dressed quietly, and then snuck out of the room. Once she was safely in her car, she texted Justin that something had come up with work. She couldn't lay in bed next to him, couldn't gaze into those adorable blue eyes, all the while not knowing what she was going to do about the pregnancy. She needed to make a decision.

As soon as her doctor's office opened, she would call and make an appointment for the ultrasound. Then, she would decide whether she could actually go through with an abortion and if so, whether she could really do it without telling Justin. She cringed just thinking of that possibility, except really, it was a gift. If he knew about the pregnancy, he'd either want her to continue it and thereby ruin his life, or he'd agree they should end it, but then he'd feel guilty and sad over it too.

No, it was better for her to just bear the burden alone. She was doing him a favor by leaving him out of it.

And until she decided, Courtney wasn't going to let herself think about it, even for a moment.

12

———

Justin's schedule was jam-packed. Between two interviews and a reading for a part in a new movie that Marty had scheduled for him, Justin barely had time to breathe the first day back. The next day, he had a modeling gig and an evening meeting with Marty at his house. Courtney arrived just as the meeting was ending.

Justin, Marty, and Keith were all seated outside by the pool. It was a nice day, cool, but with clear skies and no wind. Courtney came outside and politely said hi to the group, then retreated inside.

"We done here?" Justin asked, eager to join Courtney.

Keith laughed.

"I can finish up with Keith," Marty said, excusing Justin.

Justin nodded and stepped inside. He perched on the kitchen counter next to Courtney as she rinsed off an apple.

"You want to go out for dinner?"

She shook her head. "I'm exhausted. I'd rather stay in."

"Me too. Thai food sound okay?"

Courtney hesitated, then nodded. They figured out what

they wanted, offered Keith and Marty some, then called in the order for delivery.

"It'll be an hour," Justin said. "Precisely how exhausted are you?"

She smiled. "I don't think I could make it up the stairs right now if I tried."

He frowned, then picked her up. "Guess I'll have to carry you," he said, heading up to his room. He gingerly placed her on the bed and lay beside her. "You smell good," he said.

"Wow, you really do know how to woo the ladies," she teased. But then she licked her lips, which Justin knew was his cue.

He leaned in to kiss her, and minutes later, most of their clothes were in a pile beside the bed. He was relieved, since the last time they'd been together, she hadn't seemed interested in any form of intimacy. Justin kissed her breasts then moved lower, to her smooth abdomen, before working his way even further south.

Twenty minutes later, they were both significantly more relaxed. Courtney gradually inched off of him and curled up against his chest. Justin pulled the sheet up over her, realizing it was cold in the room.

"How was your day?" he asked after a long silence.

"Better now," she replied. "I had a rough morning. Remember that woman I told you about, who was staying at the shelter and found snakes in her car?"

Justin nodded. It was pretty hard to forget stories like that, although Courtney always had some pretty depressing shit to tell about at the end of her days.

"Well, I spoke with the prosecutor this morning, and apparently the cops screwed up the chain of custody with the evidence and they don't have enough to charge the guy."

"Want me to pay someone to beat him up?"

"Yes."

Justin smiled. He knew they were both kidding, but he liked that Courtney wasn't so gung-ho about the criminal justice system that she couldn't appreciate the best ways to put a jerk in his place. "I got some good news today," he said, changing the subject.

She perked up instantly. "You got the part?"

He grinned and nodded. It had only been between him and two other guys, but they'd cast the female lead first and wanted each of the men to do a chemistry test and reading for the part.

"When do you shoot? And where?"

He kissed her forehead and nudged her over so he could start dressing. Surely it was almost time for their food to arrive. "I don't know exactly. Keith and Marty were going to get back to the studio with my availability next year. They've got all my calendar stuff, so they'll make it work."

Courtney's eyes widened. "So you're not going to be around much next year."

"Don't worry. It's all going to be local." Justin said. Keith would have an easier time working with his schedule if he knew the wedding date, but Courtney had been resistant to discussing that at all lately.

"Aren't you filming one other thing next year too?"

He nodded. Technically, he had signed contracts for three films total for the next year, but one of them was only a bit part.

"And you're still on your modeling contract, and you're probably doing stuff for David too, right?"

"I'll be done with all the *Days End* publicity stuff by then, though. And I won't be traveling much at all." He tossed Courtney her clothes. She looked like she was about to cry. Justin suddenly felt panicky. "Courtney, don't worry. It's all going to be fine."

"You don't know that," she said. "I hardly ever see you now."

"I've been traveling a ton lately, I know," he interrupted. "But come spring, I'm going to be here, in L.A., with you."

"Even when you're in L.A. we hardly see each other. Justin, I know you. If your schedule for next year really isn't that busy yet, you'll just take on more projects. You can't say no, and you shouldn't have to. You're not going to have time for me next year and you definitely aren't going to have time for anything else."

She was definitely crying, but Justin still wasn't sure why. Five minutes earlier she'd seemed excited about him getting the job.

"Is this about the wedding?"

Courtney hesitated then shook her head. "No. I don't know. I'm sorry. I'm just tired and it feels like we have so much going on. When are we even going to fit in a wedding?"

He kissed her on the forehead and wiped the tears off her cheeks. "Whenever we want. Courtney, I promise. It is going to be fine. If you need me to turn down this project to prove that to you, I will. I can tell Marty to tear up the contract right now."

"You know that's not what I want."

"Okay, then trust me. I'll be there for you when we're planning the wedding. And I'll be there after." He finished dressing. "Besides, it's probably better for both of us to indulge in our workaholic sides now. A few years down the road, we might want to start having kids, and then we will both need to back off from work and free up more time."

She shook her head, and snapped her bra.

Before he could say anything else, the doorbell rang. Saved by the dinner.

COURTNEY FELT an odd mixture of relief and dread when she awoke the morning of her ultrasound. On the one hand, she was glad the day had finally arrived. By the end of the day, she'd have a game plan. On the other hand, ignoring reality had worked better than she'd expected. Pretending she'd never gotten the positive test had enabled her to focus on all the great parts of her life. She really loved her job, and her law review article that just came out was already getting some attention. And Justin was just perfect. She had the ideal life, aside from that one tiny thing floating in her abdomen.

Courtney arrived at the doctor's twenty minutes ahead of schedule. She was about to head inside in hopes of getting in to her appointment early when her phone rang. She didn't recognize the caller, but the call was forwarded from her work phone and she had nothing better to do than answer.

"Hi. Is this Courtney Robbins?"

The male caller sounded so suave that she instantly feared it was a reporter calling for info about Justin. Usually the shelter's receptionist screened those calls, but not always.

"Yes. I'm out of the office at the moment, though, so if you hold on, I can forward you back to our receptionist," she finally replied.

"Oh no need. My name is Dale Everett. I'm on the Board of Directors with the Fifth Street Legal Aid Clinic. Are you familiar with our work?"

She hesitated. "Um, generally, yes."

"Great. Well, I just wanted to touch base. We are about to have a vacant seat on our Board and your name came up in our initial discussions of people who might be interested in filling it."

Courtney felt her eyes widen. This was exactly what she had hoped would happen after her article came out, but she'd figured it wasn't realistic. Especially not this soon.

"I, uh, I..." she stammered.

He chuckled politely. "Listen, I realize I'm catching you off guard. Is there a time we could sit down to discuss?"

"Definitely. I'm actually about to head into an appointment outside of the office, but if you could email me some times that work for you, I can get back to you and confirm this afternoon."

He politely agreed and disconnected the call. Courtney squealed loudly and dialed Justin without thinking. He answered quickly and sounded appropriately excited for her, even though she suspected he had no idea what all this position would entail.

"You sound like you're in a cave. Where are you?" he asked.

And just like that, Courtney snapped back to reality. How had she forgotten where she was? Or why she was there, for that matter?

"Shoot, I'm going to be late for an appointment babe," she said. "Call you later?"

He agreed and she disconnected without another word.

Ten minutes later, Courtney found herself inside an exam room while a nurse took her blood pressure.

"A little higher today," the nurse commented.

Courtney wasn't surprised. It hadn't exactly been a relaxing couple of weeks for her.

"Hey, uh, I didn't leave another urine sample. Don't I need to do that so they can test it?"

The nurse smiled and shook her head. "They just wanted to get a baseline for your blood sugar and proteins at the last appointment. They won't start making you leave a sample at every appointment until the second half of pregnancy."

"But don't they test it to make sure I'm pregnant?"

The nurse paused and glanced down at the file. "They did that last time, too."

Courtney felt her face heat up. "But what if that one was wrong? My period was barely late then, so isn't there a good chance it was a false positive?"

"No worries, sweetie. Sometimes we see false negatives if

someone tests too soon, but once that stick turns positive, it's positive. You'll get some reassurance at the ultrasound, though." She patted Courtney's arm and then made her way to the door. "The tech will be in with you shortly."

Courtney waited patiently for five minutes, then ten, then fifteen. Finally, she pulled out her phone and started working. As the clock ticked to 45 minutes past her appointment time, she blew out a sigh. This had to be a sign. She was not meant to get an ultrasound without Justin. What was she even thinking?

She stood up and shimmied into her clothes, wadding the paper gown on the table. She poked her head out, quickly spotting the nurse who'd led her into the room.

"Oh sweetie, I was just about to come let you know. We had two separate patients come in with some urgent concerns so we're running behind. They should be with you in a few minutes, though."

"It's fine. I am a bit swamped at work so I can't wait anymore today. Can I call and reschedule?" She left without waiting for an answer.

13

ourtney was so distracted at work the next day that she got nothing done. And then when she got to Justin's, she immediately picked a fight with him about the wedding. She was simply trying to point out that with his film schedule, they didn't have time to plan a wedding, let alone to participate in one. He had to go and throw it back in her face, promising to quit whatever he had going on that interfered with the planning or the actual event. The worst part was knowing he'd actually do it.

Courtney stood up and grabbed a bottle of water from the fridge before storming up the stairs. She needed to sleep, and she needed to get away from Justin.

She stripped and crawled under the covers of his bed, wondering if her sudden exhaustion was something she'd have to live with for the duration of the pregnancy. She literally felt like she could sleep for days at this point, and it was barely even nine o'clock. Just as she started to fall asleep, though, she felt Justin's warm body press against her back. She smiled sleepily and started to fall back asleep.

"You okay?" he asked, jolting her back awake.

"Just tired," she mumbled.

"You just finished dinner."

"But now it's bedtime anyway, right?"

"It doesn't have to be," he said, rolling her onto her back and climbing on top of her in one fell swoop.

"Justin, I'm tired."

He paused, and she noticed the look of hurt on his face. Was this really the first time she'd turned him down?

"Are you sick?"

"No, Justin. I'm..." she stopped herself and shook her head. She couldn't tell him she was pregnant. Not now, and not like this.

He rolled onto his side with a sigh and pushed a stray hair out of her eyes with his fingers, his hand lingering on her cheek. "I meant what I said. I want to help with the wedding planning. I'll do as much or as little as you want. You can handle all the fun parts like picking the cake and I'll go to all the meetings with the coordinator and DJ or caterers or whoever."

"When you're around." The bitterness in her voice startled Courtney.

"Courtney, I'm not traveling much next year. I told Marty I want local work."

"You're too new at acting to screw up your career."

"I'm not screwing up anything. Most films shoot in L.A. I can find plenty of interesting work here. The only reason I traveled so much before was because I liked seeing new places."

"And now you don't?"

He laughed. "No, now I like seeing you."

Courtney groaned. "Why? I'm a total nutcase. All the wedding talk has made me insane. I don't even like me lately. I just don't feel like myself."

He was quiet for a minute. "Roll over," he instructed. She complied, and Justin straddled her lower back and began massaging her shoulders. Courtney wondered how many more weeks she had until she could no longer lay on her stomach with a 200-pound man straddling her midsection.

"I don't think it's the wedding," Justin finally said.

Courtney lifted her head. "What? You think I'm just a bitch all the time?"

He chuckled. "No, but you always get a little nutty before I leave town for a long time. You've always been that way. You subconsciously think you'll miss me less if you spend our last few days together fighting."

Now Courtney laughed. "So now you're a shrink?"

"No, but I can read you like a book, baby. And I think it's sweet."

"You think it's sweet when your fiancée acts crazy?"

"I think it's sweet that you hate when we're apart, even though you're always acting like Little Miss Independent who doesn't need anybody."

"I do hate when you're gone for so long," she admitted.

"Why don't you come visit me more? Or let me fly back to see you some."

Courtney considered this. She'd already agreed to visit him a couple times, plus they were meeting up in Indiana for the Superbowl. With how much work she'd need to do to get on track before having a baby, she certainly didn't feel like committing to even more travel. And it would be tricky for Justin to stay on task with his filming if he were taking red-eyes back and forth to visit her.

Courtney shook her head, her face still buried in the mattress. "No, because then I'd just waste what should be a romantic overnight being stressed out about you leaving again. It wouldn't work."

He climbed off her back and stretched beside her again. She turned to face him. "You're crazy, you know that?"

She smiled. "So you tell me."

"Maybe that's why I love you."

Courtney heard him, and she would've answered, but she was already drifting to sleep.

~

JUSTIN WATCHED his fiancée sleep for a few minutes before inching away. He figured a good night's sleep wouldn't kill him, but he just wasn't tired. He was about to head downstairs to see if Keith wanted to play a round of pool when he heard a shrill ding emanate from Courtney's phone.

He lunged for it, quickly entering the passcode and switching the phone to "Do Not Disturb" mode before it woke her. He didn't mean to snoop, but the incoming text was from Courtney's roommate.

"R U coming home tonight?" it read.

Justin quickly replied, letting Erica know it was him and that Courtney was already asleep. She thanked him and he was about to set the phone on the nightstand by her side of the bed when he noticed she had other unread texts and a voicemail, both from the same number. He didn't read the message, but the sender was saved in her contacts as Dr. Patel.

He assumed this was a doctor she dealt with at work, but then again, she had been acting a bit off lately. He peered over at the message again, not willing to cross the line of actually clicking on it to read the full message. But the first line of the message asked her to call the office to reschedule her appointment.

So, not a client matter.

Justin dropped the phone, already regretting snooping. She was allowed to make her own doctor's appointments, and it was none of his business. But he was a little hurt that she didn't even mention to him that she was having some sort of health issue.

He ambled down the stairs and found Keith already playing a video game, so he joined him. A few beers later, all memory of the mystery text message was erased. When they finally agreed it was time to call it a night, Justin started up the stairs with an uncapped bottle of water in his hand.

"Hey, Courtney left her purse down here," Keith called.

Justin turned slowly. She did usually take it into the bedroom with her, but since she had her phone already, she really didn't need it. He was about to say as much when Keith chucked it to him. He lunged for the purse and caught it, but spilled water on it in the process.

"Dude!" Justin chastised.

Keith shrugged and headed off to his own room.

Justin carried the purse into the bathroom and dumped the contents onto a towel. He'd only spilled an ounce or so of water into it, but virtually every item seemed a little damp.

"Thank God she had her phone," he mumbled. He shoved each item back into the bag as soon as he dried it. The process went quickly until he reached a wad of folded up magazine pages. They'd gotten considerably wetter than everything else, so he unwrinkled them, trying to decide if it was anything worth salvaging.

When he saw what they actually were, his breath caught in his throat. It wasn't a page from a magazine. It was a pamphlet about pregnancy. Multiple pamphlets, actually.

Suddenly, it all clicked. Courtney's fatigue, her weird moods, her sudden obsession with his schedule over the next nine months...

He started rifling through the items he'd already stuck back in her purse. He didn't recall seeing her birth control pills when he was drying things, but maybe he just hadn't noticed. When

Justin confirmed they weren't in her purse, he shoved everything back in and opened the bathroom door.

Courtney was stretched out on her side, her arm curled in front of her chest and her dark eyelashes tickling the tops of her cheeks. Justin watched her chest rise and fall as she slept, and suddenly he was overwhelmed with the need to wake her. They should be talking—not sleeping. He had so many questions. When had it happened? And how?

He doubted she would've stopped taking her pills without telling him, but he also would've never thought she'd let a moment pass without telling him of her pregnancy. Yet, here they were. He'd always assumed they'd be one of those couples taking the test together, nervously clutching hands while awaiting the appearance of the magical pink plus sign.

Not that he'd spent a ton of time picturing it...

Justin stepped closer just as Courtney sighed peacefully. God he was a jerk. Here he was, about to wake his sleeping fiancée—his pregnant fiancée—and she was probably planning some cutesy way to tell him the news. Maybe she'd ordered a onesie or one of those personalized beer cozies. He didn't need to wake her. He needed to be supportive. And patient.

He grimaced. Patience had never been his strong suit.

It was harder than usual for Justin to leave Courtney the next day. He wasn't sure if it was because of how long he'd be gone, how pathetic she looked during their goodbye, or the fact that he felt guilty abandoning her when she was pregnant. Normally, he'd get psyched about his upcoming project as soon as the flight was in the air, but this time, he was still missing Courtney when he arrived at his apartment.

Luckily, his mom had flown out and met him there. She hadn't seen the apartment before and wanted to do some sight-seeing in the Big Apple. The timing was perfect.

"I really could go to the supermarket for you tonight to get you stocked up on some more things," his mom said, nervously peering into the amply filled cupboards.

"No, Mom, it's fine. I don't even think there is a supermarket around here. And we arranged for the cleaning lady to do the shopping and some cooking."

"Cleaning lady? You don't even know her name. Is this how I raised you? You can't even take care of yourself?"

"I am capable of doing it all myself, Mom. I just don't have time and I don't need to get mobbed every time I buy produce at the Piggly Wiggly."

She sighed, clearly convinced she'd failed as a parent. Justin located organic herbal tea bags near the stove and offered one to his mother. She nodded, and he filled the kettle with water. The tea was from Andi's stash, but she wouldn't care. Besides, this was an emergency.

"Does Courtney know you're this helpless?"

Justin laughed. "Yes. She and Keith tease me about it regularly." He went to the living room and plopped down on the couch, and his mom followed.

She sighed loudly as she sat, a sign that she had something to say that he wouldn't want to hear. He considered ignoring it, but that never worked for long.

"You said you share this apartment with another woman?"

"Yeah. Andrea Taylor. You've met her."

"What about once you're married? Are you still going to stay here with Andi?"

He nodded. "It's a good arrangement. And it's not often that we're both in town at the same time."

"I just wonder if your arrangement gives people the wrong idea."

"My publicist loves when people in general get the wrong idea about me and Andi," he said with a laugh. "Courtney doesn't mind me sharing the apartment with Andi. They're friends. And Andi has her own bedroom."

As he spoke, the tea kettle began whistling loudly. Justin popped up and poured his mom a cup of the tea and brought it back to the couch, resting it on top of one of the floral coasters Andi had bought.

She thanked him for the tea. "Oh, Justin. You know I just worry about you. You moved out to L.A. when you were so young, and now you're flying all around the country with people throwing money and everything else at you. You have so much opportunity to get mixed up with the wrong things."

Justin nodded. It had been hard on his mom when he'd rejected the college route and moved to Hollywood. Several of his brothers had left town already, either for school or with the military, but when he left, it was shortly after his father died. And he'd always been closer to his mom than some of his brothers anyway.

"Well, you don't have to worry about me anymore. I'm settling down and getting married."

His mom winced. "Are you sure you're ready for that?"

"I don't understand. You said you liked Courtney."

"I do like her. She's a remarkable young woman. I think she's good for you."

"So what's the problem?"

She shook her head. "I only want you to be sure that you're ready for marriage, that you're good for her too. Marriage means a lot more than just dating someone. A marriage is forever."

Justin knew now was not the time to play devil's advocate with his mom, so he refrained from mentioning the D-word that ended more marriages than not. Instead, he picked at the rest of her statement. "You don't think I'm good enough for Courtney?"

His mom smiled and sipped her tea. "You're a very good man,

Justin. You're hard working and generous and thoughtful. But sometimes, you get carried away. We all do, only you have a few more resources at your disposal. I worry about you choosing to do things because you can, and not necessarily because you should."

She paused, but not long enough for him to interrupt her lecture. "Just because you live in Los Angeles doesn't mean God expects any less of you in the morals department than if you were back on a farm in Indiana."

He had to laugh at that, but the conversation was stressing him out. "I'm not going to cheat on Courtney, Mom. We're going to get married, she's going to move in, and everything is going to work out fine."

"You missed the point of my lecture. What I was trying to tell you is that you are good enough. You have worked very hard and made good choices in your life, and I want you to remember that." She smiled and stood up to hug him. "Congratulations!"

"Thanks," Justin mumbled.

Justin's cell phone buzzed, and Courtney's name popped up. She must be getting home from work. He glanced at his mom for confirmation of whether he should answer.

She stood, kissed him on the forehead, and started out of the room. "I'm going to bed. Tell Courtney I said hello."

14

Before she knew it, Courtney was on her way to meet up with Justin for the Super Bowl. Typically, when Justin was gone, time crept slowly, but the past few days had flown by. Courtney didn't think that was a good sign. Keith occupied the seat beside her, but as much as Courtney would've preferred to talk with him to pass the time, she didn't want to say the wrong thing and alert him to her awful secret. So, she closed her eyes and, thankfully, she fell asleep.

When she awoke, Courtney briefly forgot where she was, thinking she was cuddled up next to Justin. She opened her eyes and realized she was slumped over on Keith, drooling on his shoulder.

"Sorry," she said, sitting up.

"You're just like Justin," Keith said, grinning as he leafed through a magazine.

"He drools on you, too?"

"Not lately. But he can sleep through anything." Keith set the magazine on his lap and glanced around the plane. "This has been the rowdiest flight I've ever been on. Everyone is heading to the big game, and somehow you managed to sleep through shouting, chants, and even singing. It's insane."

Courtney smiled. Now that he mentioned it, she did notice the atmosphere seemed a little more frat party than business class. "I'm not usually like that. I've always been jealous of Justin's ability to sleep on command. But I'm just so tired lately."

A woman from the row in front of them popped her head around the seat. "Sorry to interrupt, but you're Courtney Robbins, right?"

Courtney nodded cautiously, trying to place the woman's face. On a flight to her hometown, there was a chance she'd run into someone from her high school.

The woman smiled. "I thought it was you. I saw you in a magazine with Justin Erikson."

Courtney winced, as she did every time she thought of her picture appearing in a magazine. It hadn't happened often in print, generally just around the time of movie premieres, but online, photos of her and Justin all around town popped up regularly.

"You're his fiancée, right? Justin Erikson's?"

Courtney glanced at Keith, who was now pretending to read his magazine, a bemused grin plastered on his face.

She finally nodded, and then briefly panicked, wondering if this woman was going to run to the press and say she was cheating on Justin by sleeping on some guy on the plane. "This is his manager, Keith," she explained. Keith glanced up, raised his eyebrows as a greeting, then returned his gaze to the magazine.

"Oh my God, so he's going to be in Indianapolis then, right?"

Courtney hesitated. She didn't want to blow Justin's cover by giving away his location and adding one more stalker to the mix, but anyone who knew him could guess that he'd be there. He'd gone to the past three Super Bowls, and this one was in his home state. She nodded.

The woman shrieked. "Okay, so I'm sure you can't tell me where he's staying or anything, but can you give me any clue as to where he'll be? I'm such a huge fan and I'm dying to meet him."

"I'm sorry, but I don't really know what his plans are, aside from the game. He's been in New York filming, so we haven't really discussed the details." Courtney turned to Keith, desperate for help.

Keith set the magazine down. "She'll call him when we land and you could say hi," he told the woman, whose eyes instantly lit up. "But I actually need to discuss some business with Courtney here now, so..."

The woman took the hint and after thanking them again, ducked back into her seat.

"Thanks," Courtney said. "Do we really have business to discuss?"

He shrugged. "At some point before I move out, I need to go over some info with you."

"You don't have to move out," Courtney reminded him. It wasn't that she didn't want to be alone with Justin, but especially when he traveled so much, that big house would get lonely. And she hated feeling like she was kicking Keith out to the curb.

Keith just gave her a look and patted her leg.

"What kind of info?"

"Mostly just names and numbers for different people who do work for Justin. He's not involved per se in the running of the house," Keith explained.

Courtney frowned. "So you're still essentially doing the personal assistant stuff even now that you're also his manager?"

"Sort of. I mean, I don't get him coffee now."

She laughed, although she knew for a fact that he often did

get Justin coffee. Of course, Justin probably got coffee for Keith on occasion, too.

"What is your arrangement with him, exactly? If you don't mind my asking. He's never really discussed the business side of it, just that you guys are old friends and you came out here and studied business. What exactly does a manager do? And how's that going to change if you move out?"

Keith handed his empty glass to the flight attendant as she walked by. "As Justin's manager, I help him select scripts, coordinate with his agent and publicist, set up meetings with directors or producers, cover meetings for him when he can't make it, and hire interns to deal with his fan mail and that sort of thing. I also handle all his travel arrangements and oversee his schedule."

"I knew that part," Courtney said. On countless occasions, she'd asked Justin if he was free on a certain date, and he would have no idea until he either asked Keith or checked the calendar on his phone, which Keith updated regularly. "So what about Jamie and Marty? Isn't there some overlap with them?"

"Well, Jamie handles all things publicity. Obviously Marty and I have a vested interest in keeping Justin's reputation clean too, but she's in charge of filtering the information that gets out to the public and molding his image. Marty does some of the same stuff I do, but he has more contacts in the industry, so he gets most of the scripts for Justin and then when there's one Justin likes, Marty negotiates the contract."

Courtney considered this. It all made sense, really, and she was surprised she'd never given it much thought before. "How are you all paid?"

"Jamie gets a monthly fee. Marty and I both get a percentage of Justin's gross pay." Keith paused. "But then the other stuff I do for Justin that doesn't really fall under the manager hat is all a separate story."

"What kind of stuff is that?"

"Checking in with his accountant, dealing with his mail, making sure the bills get paid on time, keeping tabs on the gardener, the pool guy, the car company, and everyone else Justin pays to make sure they're doing their jobs correctly."

"And he pays you separately for that?"

Keith laughed. "He doesn't pay me at all for that. It wasn't that big of a job when I first came out here, but over the past couple of years it's gotten to be a lot to manage. But it's basically just running a house, and since I live there too, it's not a big deal." He paused. "I don't pay rent, so it evens out."

Finally it all made sense to Courtney. "So when you move out, you're not doing any of that anymore. And we both know Justin can't handle those details, so that means I'm supposed to take over?"

Keith shrugged. "There's no way you could do it if you're still working. Especially with wedding planning."

Courtney sighed and bit her lip. How had she not considered that before?

"Well who else works for Justin? You mentioned an accountant, a gardener and a pool guy. And I know he has a car company on retainer, right?"

He nodded. "You know Cathy, and she does all the cleaning, laundry, grocery shopping, and a lot of the cooking. She's on salary. And then when he uses a bodyguard, they're usually paid by the hour. Oh, and so is his trainer." Keith paused again, folding his magazine back into his messenger bag. "I told Justin he needs to hire a personal assistant and then I can get them up to speed on all this before I move out. I don't think he realizes how much it is or that you're going to get stuck with it if he doesn't hire someone."

Courtney frowned. "Can he afford to hire a personal assistant?"

Keith laughed. "Oh yeah. Justin's not really a numbers guy,

so he rarely makes the meetings with his accountant, but even he knows he's got money to spare."

She closed her eyes and took several deep breaths. A bout of nausea washed over her, but Courtney didn't think she could chalk it up to morning sickness.

Keith patted her leg again. "Hey, don't worry about it. If Justin doesn't hire an assistant, I'll set up some interviews and you and I can pick someone."

"I just feel bad. If you move out, Justin's losing someone who does all this useful stuff for him and he'll have to pay someone to replace you. I'm just going to be moving in and taking up space while contributing nothing."

He shook his head. "I don't think Justin looks at it that way. And like I said, Justin can afford to hire the extra help. Besides, once you guys are married, won't you be contributing your income to the mix?"

"I probably make less than Cathy," she said.

Keith laughed and pulled out his phone while the flight attendant spoke over the loudspeaker, asking passengers to remain seated until they reached the terminal. "Have you ever considered a new profession?"

He dialed and then spoke quickly. "Hey man, we're here. Courtney got recognized by one of your fans. She can call you in a minute, but we promised the fan you'd talk to her. You got a minute?"

Keith stood and leaned over the seat in front of them, where the woman was eying them expectantly. "Here's Justin," he said. "I need my phone back in one minute."

The woman nodded eagerly and snatched the phone. Courtney and Keith both laughed.

Justin had told Courtney to look for the guy with a sign bearing her name on arrival. She ducked into the airport bathroom to try to salvage her hair and makeup while Keith went on to the baggage claim area. Just as they were about to look for their driver, Courtney spotted Justin. He was grinning wildly, and holding a large sign reading "Courtney."

She laughed and ran to him, nearly knocking him over with the ferocity of her hug. "I missed you!" she said, relieved at how happy she was to see him.

Justin wrapped his arm around her, pressed his lips into her hair and whispered in her ear. "Come on," he said, guiding her towards the door. "You can relax in the car. Keith and I will wait for your bags."

JUSTIN COULDN'T BELIEVE the chaos when they pulled up in front of the hotel. The windows to the black Suburban were darkly tinted so no one could see in, but the mere presence of the vehicle in a highly secured area outside the best hotel in the town was enough to alert the crowds that someone had arrived. He should've listened to Keith about having a security guy ride in the car.

"Hey, can you talk to the valet guys and see if we can get checked in from here so I can go right up to the room?" He leaned over the seat of the car. Damn, it was a big fucking vehicle.

Keith nodded and snuck out of the car. He returned a moment later with a bellhop, two private security guards and a uniformed police officer. Clearly, Indianapolis wasn't used to celebrities walking around. It was insanity.

"You ready?" Keith asked.

Justin nodded, then swung the massive SUV door open and immediately heard shrieks. He turned to one of the security guards. "This is crazy!"

He let Keith shelter Courtney as they walked in, certain that would be less chaotic for her. Justin started in towards the hotel, hearing his name shouted in every direction. He got the impression the security guards were trying to rush him in, but what was the fun of that?

"Hang on a sec," he said. He waved at the crowd, grinning, and swung by to shake a few hands before the glare on the faces of the police barricading off the hotel entrance encouraged him to keep moving.

Once they were in the privacy of their own hotel room, Justin turned to Courtney to greet her for real. He kissed her on the mouth and then ran his eyes down her body, pausing on her stomach, which seemed even flatter than he remembered it.

"Are you sure you're eating enough? You look like you're losing weight."

She scowled.

"We could stay in tonight, so you could rest," he offered.

Her eyes widened. "Are you insane?"

"We've got dinner reservations at eight. It's supposed to be the best local steakhouse. Then the party starts at nine, so I figured we'd drop in around ten. Is that too late?"

She shook her head. "I'm on L.A. time, babe."

"Okay. You sure you're okay if I head to the gym now?"

"Yes. I'm going to nap."

Justin waited a minute in case she changed her mind, but she looked exhausted, so he left.

He and Keith were the only people inside the hotel's fitness center. Compared to many of the places he'd stayed over the years, the workout area was impressive. A handful of high-end cardio machines lined the windows overlooking the city below, with the strength training machines and free weights taking up the rest of the space.

"I'm surprised there aren't more people here," Justin said as he stepped onto the treadmill for a warmup jog.

"Really? You don't think most people in town are too busy partying and enjoying life to exercise?"

Justin grinned. He'd mastered the art of staying fit while still partying. He winked at Keith before switching on his music. "It's all about balance, man."

He caught Keith rolling his eyes before he turned back to the view. He was excited about the weekend, for sure. He and Keith had made it to three of the last Super Bowls, and this would be the best yet. It was in his home state, and his girl was with him.

His mind flitted to images of Courtney sleeping back in their suite. He'd googled pregnancy symptoms when he was waiting for his flight to take off, and he'd learned fatigue was pretty normal for first trimester. Although Courtney had enjoyed naps before, too, so maybe this was no different.

He hopped off the treadmill before the belt fully stopped, grabbing a folded towel from the shelf nearby to wipe his forehead. After a cursory stretch, he moved on to weights. Justin glanced over at Keith, noticing that he kept reaching for his phone every couple of minutes, grinning at whatever he was reading, then tapping out a quick reply.

"What's up?" Justin asked, curious what had brought the smile to his friend's face.

Keith shrugged and shook his head dismissively.

Justin sighed, desperate for a distraction from Courtney. Surely she'd tell him this weekend. And when she did, he'd be ready. He'd already prepared his congratulatory response. He would be the best dad ever, from the very first moment.

"What's up with you?" Keith asked.

Justin set down the weights and turned to Keith. It was probably an innocent enough question, but it was all the opening he needed. Justin had to tell someone. He glanced around to confirm they were still alone, then stepped closer, lowering himself onto the bench closest to Keith.

"Courtney's pregnant," he said, his voice quieter than he intended. Keith didn't respond immediately, but Justin knew he'd heard since his eyes widened.

"Your Courtney?" Keith finally asked.

Justin nodded.

"With a baby?"

Justin nodded again, clarifying, "My baby."

Keith's expression remained a mix of confusion, concern, and disgust. It reminded Justin of the face someone might make when first tasting some unique food combination, like cinnamon and lemon. He waited for Keith to say something, anything.

"Like on purpose?" he finally asked.

Justin blew out a sigh. "Of course not on purpose."

His friend's grimace deepened.

"You're supposed to say congratulations."

Keith's eyebrow shot up. "Really? Um, okay. Congrats. That's, uh, awesome?"

Justin tried to hold in his laughter but it shot out like a snort. He didn't blame Keith for the response, it was the same way he'd reacted initially. It was probably good he'd told him alone, as opposed to having waited until after he and Courtney actually talked about it. She might've been offended by Keith's tempered, less than enthusiastic response.

"Maybe practice the excitement before you talk with Court-ney," Justin said with a chuckle.

Keith shook his head. "I'm sorry, man. I just...that is not what I expected. I knew you were acting strange and I thought it was something totally different, and... Congratulations, really. You guys will have an insanely cute little kid." He paused. "Do you know, like boy or girl? Or is that later?"

"Later," Justin said, feeling like an expert from his cursory internet research, at least compared to Keith.

The awkward silence reminded Justin why he'd needed to tell his best friend the news. "So listen, you can't say anything to anyone. Courtney doesn't know, and..."

"Courtney doesn't know?" Keith interrupted. "How is that even..."

Justin shook his head. "No, I mean, she knows she's pregnant." Then he paused. That was true, right? She had to know. She had the pamphlets. And it was her body. If it was obvious enough for him to figure it out, surely she already knew. "She doesn't know that *I* know. She hasn't actually told me yet."

Confusion colored Keith's face. "Then how do you know?"

Justin told him about the pamphlets he'd found, and her weird behavior. Then once he'd gotten him up to speed on everything, he went in for advice. "What should I do?"

"What do you mean?"

"Like, do I tell her I know? Or wait for her to tell me and pretend to be surprised?"

Keith wrinkled his nose. "Can you even do that? Act surprised?"

Justin's head dropped to the side. "I'm literally an actor, man. Thanks for the vote of confidence."

Keith chuckled. "So you think she's planning some big surprise or something and that's why she hasn't told you yet?"

Justin nodded. "Yeah, or..." He paused, feeling like he'd jinx it or something by saying it out loud. "I guess she could be waiting, just in case something goes wrong. Like, I was reading about how miscarriage is a lot more common than people think and some people don't really tell anyone they're pregnant until after the first trimester. That's twelve weeks," he added, again priding himself on his newly gained expertise.

"Twelve weeks? How many weeks is it now?"

Justin shrugged. Since he'd been out of town, he'd assume at least three or four but he didn't fully understand how they calculated the weeks in the book anyway. It didn't seem like it actually started on the day you made the baby.

"Well, don't you think that only applies to other people? I mean, you're the father. Pretty sure you get to know before everyone else."

Justin shared that sentiment, but what other explanation could there be? "The timing isn't great," he said after another pause. "She might be waiting to tell me because she thinks I'll be mad."

"I can't imagine any scenario where you'd get mad at her."

"I wouldn't!"

"I think she knows that."

"Well, yeah. Not mad at her, but just not thrilled about it all. She's made a lot of comments lately about how busy my schedule is over the next year, so I'm wondering if she's worried a baby will mess everything up."

"And you're not worried about that?"

Justin rubbed his forehead. "Of course I am, but it's a little late for that. It happened now, so..."

Keith nodded.

"So what do I do? Do I tell her I know? Or keep waiting for her to tell me?"

Keith raised his shoulders. "I don't know man. I guess wait?"

"It's driving me insane. I can't think about anything else."

"Well, then don't wait. Maybe tell her you know."

Justin didn't love that option either.

"Okay, or don't do either. Tell her she seems distracted or something and give her a chance to tell you. Or talk about how much you like babies or some shit like that."

Justin laughed, but he did think that idea made a lot of sense. "Yeah. I could do that. Thanks." He sighed and stretched his wrists. "So what's new with you?"

"Nothing," Keith replied quickly. "Definitely nothing."

Courtney fell asleep immediately, but awoke groggy. She changed clothes and trekked down to the lobby, planning to buy some coffee then check out the gym and see if she could spy on her man working out. She was standing by the muted Monet in the lobby, trying to determine whether a hotel would really have such valuable originals, when she heard the crowd outside shriek. She was curious, but she couldn't see over the security guards blocking the door. The door swung open and two security guards were blocking a petite woman as she walked to the front desk. They backed off once she reached the desk.

The woman was thin, wearing jeans tucked into expensive fur-lined boots and a long, olive-green pea coat. She had a black knit hat with a flower stitched to the front of it, and, as she reached in her purse for something, Courtney saw that she wore black gloves with the fingertips cut out. There was something familiar about the woman, but Courtney still couldn't quite figure it out.

Then, the woman turned and lifted off her oversized rounded sunglasses. It was Andi.

"Courtney! I thought that was you!" Andi walked over and hugged her. Courtney flashed the security guard a victory smirk.

"I didn't know you were coming to town. Are you staying here?" Courtney asked, despite the obviousness.

Andi laughed a sing-songy laugh. "I thought I was staying with you guys. Justin said you guys had an extra room in the suite?"

"Oh yeah, of course!" Courtney tried to recall if Justin had actually told her that, but she couldn't have imagined forgetting.

"I was going to get an extra key, but I didn't know which room you were in or what name he used to check in."

"It's in Keith's name," Courtney answered.

They both returned to the desk. "So is this your first Super Bowl?"

Courtney nodded. "You?"

"I've been to two others. I'm not a huge football fan, though."

Courtney spotted Keith out of the corner of her eye and waved. He jogged over to them.

"Hey there, Andi, how are you?"

"No complaints," she smiled. "What about you?"

"Good."

Courtney noticed an awkward exchange between the two of them, but she didn't have time to dwell on it because Justin appeared suddenly.

After another round of greetings, they all returned to the suite upstairs. Justin showered while Andi unpacked then made drinks for everyone.

Andi carried over the drinks, handing one to Keith and Courtney, then making a second trip to the bar to retrieve one for herself and Justin.

"There you go, the best champagne cocktail you will ever taste. Drink up!" Andi said.

They clinked their glasses together. The pale purple, bubbly liquid smelled so good. Courtney raised her glass to her lips and took the slightest of a taste—really just a drop on her tongue and not enough to even swallow. She caught Justin glaring at her out of the corner of her eye and shrugged. Keith began eying Courtney warily too, glancing back and forth from her and Justin.

Courtney set her glass on the table.

Andi plopped on the couch beside Keith and flung her hands up. "Don't tell me you don't like it? No one has ever had any complaints about my Purple Fizz."

Courtney shook her head, and Andi pressed the glass back into her hand.

Andi sensed her hesitation. "This is a party weekend. You have to drink." she paused. "You're not on a diet, are you?"

Courtney's eyes widened. "Do I need to be on a diet?"

Andi stared back at her, clearly considering this.

Justin flew out of his seat. "No, you don't need to be on a diet. You look perfect."

Courtney ignored Justin. "With the wedding coming up, I don't want to gain anything," she said, deciding that could be the perfect reason for her refusal to drink.

"Yeah, good call. Well, you should try egg whites and spinach for breakfast, and maybe a grapefruit and salad for lunch," Andi began.

Justin threw a pillow at her head before she could finish. "Shut up, Andi," he said.

"We'll talk later," Courtney whispered.

"Does this mean you all picked a date?" Andi asked.

"Why don't we all watch a movie until it's time to head to dinner?" Keith cleared his throat, clearly uncomfortable, and flipped on the TV. He clicked on the first movie and then paused. Justin laughed.

Andi glanced up suddenly. "Oh, geez. Yeah, that will help clear out the awkwardness here. Let's watch me fake an orgasm with Justin while his fiancée sits beside me."

They all must have eyed Andi suspiciously then because she added, "You know, the second sex scene in this one is kinda graphic."

"There's more than one?" Courtney turned to Justin. His face was beet red.

"Hey Keith, wanna go find a Starbucks with me?" Andi asked.

He nodded and they left.

Justin moved over to the couch where Courtney sat. He gingerly leaned her back and crawled on top of her. The weight of his perfect body pressed against hers made Courtney's mind go blank. He brushed a kiss across her lips and then slid his upper body slightly to the side of her, leaving his legs draped across hers.

"You're not really worried about getting fat, are you?"

Courtney wasn't sure how to answer this. As a female, the answer was, in general, yes. Thus far, she'd never had any problems with her weight. She was blessed with a high metabolism and the compulsive drive to jog regularly. She'd never had a huge appetite, and her stomach didn't tolerate greasy or fattening foods very well, so she never went for chips, fries, or heavy desserts. She'd always assumed she'd be very skinny if she gave up alcohol, which is probably why she'd lost a couple pounds the past few weeks.

When Courtney and Justin were dating, she knew she was much heavier than his previous, waif-like girlfriend, and while she was still probably thinner than the average American woman, she looked like an elephant next to the models and actresses buzzing around Justin.

Since the engagement, Courtney realized she was photographed more with Justin, and she hated constantly stressing about sucking her stomach in whenever they were in public, just in case someone was sneaking a photo. It was easier to just drop a few pounds.

At present, Courtney had a narrow waist, flat stomach, and lean, toned legs, with all of her fat going to her butt and boobs, thankfully. But that wouldn't last during pregnancy, and she feared it would never go back to normal.

Justin kissed her again, surely as a prompt for her to answer.

"I just want to look good for our wedding."

"Okay, when is that?" he asked.

She blew out a sigh. "Justin, when we're together, people

look at us and see how perfect you are, and then they wonder what you're doing with me."

He laughed. "Courtney, you have that completely backwards. I don't even know what you're doing with me. Even my own mother says you're out of my league."

"But I'm talking about people who don't know us, who just see us and think I look like a fat cow and wonder why I can't bother to even try to look good for you."

"You can't worry about what other people think Courtney, it'll kill you. And you look perfect to me." He paused and his hand grazed the side of her breast.

"Justin, you spend all day with super skinny models and actresses fawning over you. We're almost never in the same town, and if I let myself go, what if you start thinking about them and not me?" Courtney hated how insecure she sounded, but it drove her crazy that he didn't understand.

"I love you, Courtney. I'm not going anywhere. Even if you gain a hundred pounds and never lose it."

She smiled, picturing Justin with a wife who outweighed him.

He scooted completely off her, onto his side, and grasped her hand in his. "You have my ring," he said. "You're stuck with me."

She sighed. He could be so romantic. "I know."

He kissed her again. "You're still thinking about what other people think, aren't you?"

She nodded.

Justin sighed. "You're everything to me, and I'm not there to take care of you now. I hate that, but you know I'm never too busy for you, right?"

"What do you mean?"

He shrugged. "If there's ever anything you want to talk about, I have time."

Courtney chewed her lip, determined not to read too much

into his statement. Instead, she opted to distract him. "If you have time to talk, you have time to make love to me."

Justin was up in a nanosecond, sweeping Courtney up in his arms, carrying her to their bedroom. He kicked the door shut behind them and plopped her onto the bed, covering her in kisses.

Courtney slipped Justin's shirt over his head and ran her fingers across his muscled chest. "In fact, we might have to make time for this a second time before Keith and Andi return."

Justin raised his eyebrows excitedly and began tugging her clothes off.

15

The next morning they ordered room service, then Justin played in a celebrity flag football game for charity. It had been a blast, but immediately after the game, Justin started acting strangely.

Back at the hotel, Courtney followed Justin into the bedroom and plopped behind him on the bed, massaging his shoulders while he inhaled a trail mix bar.

Justin reached up, squeezing her hands. Then he turned to face her. "There were a lot of kids at that game. Did you notice that?"

She shook her head. She'd been seeing babies everywhere the last few weeks and she truly hadn't noticed any at the stadium.

He looked disappointed. I just hadn't realized how many people like us already had little kids. Stuff like that would be a lot of fun for families."

"I had a lot of fun watching you play on my own. Honestly, you look like you'd be amazing at football, but then…"

"Hey, I was plenty good!" he interrupted.

Courtney giggled, pleased to have successfully distracted

him. He had actually been really good, but his ego sure didn't need that confirmation. "You looked sexy playing today."

He frowned. Not the reaction she'd anticipated. After a moment, his hand reached out and slid across her belly over her tee shirt. "You would look very sexy pregnant."

Courtney's heart rate skyrocketed. What the hell was he talking about? She shoved his hand away and averted her eyes. "I guess I maybe do need to consider that diet if that's what you think about when you look at me." She stood, desperate to go anywhere else, but he tugged her back to the bed.

"Court, come on. You know that's not what I meant at all. I've just been thinking about it a lot lately."

"You've been thinking about me being fat?"

His eyes narrowed. "No, I've been thinking about us having a baby. I've been thinking about how much I love you, and how attracted I am to you, but how I think I would fall even more in love if you were carrying our baby."

Courtney didn't dare make eye contact, didn't even want to risk breathing. She needed to change the subject before she burst into tears.

"I'm not trying to freak you out. I just think we'll make super cute babies. Why not get started sooner than later?"

"Justin, you're leaving in a few weeks to film for three months. Then you've got another project scheduled for the end of the year. And you'll have more next year and the year after that. Your career is picking up now. This is your time to focus on that."

"I can find plenty of work here in L.A. over the next two years. That's not an issue."

"Well, there's my career. I didn't spend three miserable years in law school so I could work two years then quit and stay home with a baby."

"We'll get a nanny. Or I'll quit work and stay home," he

teased, really concerned when she didn't even crack a smile. He didn't exactly have enough in savings to cover the mortgage on a two million dollar house and his half of the Manhattan apartment without some form of employment.

"What about your travel dreams?"

He shrugged. "We'll all go together."

"You want to tour Europe, Asia, and Africa. We can't exactly hike the Alps with a baby in tow. And I think the flight to Australia might be hard with an infant."

"Then we'll wait a few years to travel there. That's not a big deal."

"We just got engaged, Justin. We're not even thirty yet. We're supposed to have a long engagement, get married, and then have a baby after a few years of enjoying married life without kids."

"So we'll get married." he said. "I'm just saying, we'd be great parents. This is something I want. I just thought you should know."

She didn't know what to do with any of this information, so she switched tactics. Full on distraction would work better. She kissed his neck, groaning softly.

"Courtney, I just played football. I stink. Just tell me why you hate babies."

She inched her hand up his leg and began rhythmically kneading his groin. She paused just long enough to slide her shirt up over her head and then smiled mischievously. "Sorry. What were you saying?"

Justin had no clue what he'd been saying. "Your boobs are amazing," he said instead. And it was true. She'd always had nice breasts—rounded, perky, and firm. He reached out and touched the right one.

Courtney finally began to relax a bit.

He pressed his lips gently into the pale skin on the top of her breast while unfastening her bra. She slipped her hands under his tee shirt and jersey, helping him wriggle out of both. Justin's breath picked up.

She stretched back on the bed and he followed, laying on his side facing her. He stroked his fingers gently up and down the side of her breast. Gradually, his hand wandered lower, inching slowly towards her belly.

Courtney unbuttoned his jeans.

He sighed, and relented, scooting on top of her and kissing her.

JUSTIN HAD no idea what to make of the conversation he'd had with Courtney earlier. He'd tried to make it clear that he wanted kids. Not just someday, but that he'd be happy with it now. He had expected Courtney to find that reassuring, or maybe even romantic. He'd hoped she would then tell him the news she'd been withholding. Instead, she seemed determined to talk him out of ever having kids. He couldn't figure out why.

Courtney was exhausted by that evening, but Justin convinced her to head to another restaurant with him and Keith. They managed to sneak out of the hotel and hit the streets without being noticed or stalked, but a few minutes later, Justin apparently was recognized.

"Justin!!!!!!!!!!!!!!" They heard the desperate squeal from a block away.

"Should we run?" Keith joked.

Justin turned warily. Two twenty-somethings were chasing after them. "They seem harmless."

Keith rolled his eyes. "Once you stop, you're going to get swarmed, especially now that she yelled."

But Justin didn't care. He turned and waved, letting the girls catch up.

"Oh boy," Courtney mumbled to Keith. "It might be a while. We should've gone sightseeing without him."

Justin turned. "Hey, I heard that! You better not ditch me. I got the tickets for the game."

"He's right," Keith said.

"Omigod omigod omigod," the shorter girl said. "Can I get your picture?"

Justin nodded. "Don't you want to be in it?"

The girls glanced at each other and Keith stepped up to take their phones. He snapped one quick photo with each and returned them.

"Are you in town for long?" the taller girl asked.

"Just through Monday morning, then I'm back to New York for a film."

"Omigod," the shorter girl said.

Justin was trying not to laugh. The girls were both attractive enough, but they seemed to be a tad too obsessive.

"I can't believe you're actually this hot in real life," the taller girl said.

Courtney and Keith both giggled, making it even harder for Justin not to laugh.

"Are your eyes naturally blue?"

Justin nodded and gazed at Courtney. She'd asked him that when she first met him too. It was an obvious question, really. He had the kind of eyes that look mysterious and beautiful on TV, ads, or movies, where you could assume it was a trompe de l'oeil. In person, though, his eyes were still very bold, which led everyone to believe it was contacts.

"Can I give you a hug?"

Justin nodded and hugged each girl. The second one held tight a little too long. "I better let go now, or my fiancée might get jealous," he said.

The girl released him. "She wouldn't have to know."

He laughed loudly. Courtney was giggling so hard that she buried her face into the shoulder of Keith's coat.

"She's right over there," Justin said, pointing. Then he added, "Although she might be moving in on my friend anyway." He approached them. "Hey there, enough of that," he joked to Keith.

They all laughed and waved to the girls. Justin interlaced his fingers with Courtney's, tucked her hair behind her ear, and kissed her on the cheek. He wondered if she'd ever get used to the insanity.

Later, when Courtney and Andi were off chatting about something, Justin approached Keith.

"I talked to Courtney earlier today. I told her I thought she'd look hot pregnant and that we should have a baby."

"And?"

Justin shook his head. "She seemed disgusted. I just don't get it."

Keith shrugged.

"Listen, so when I go back to New York, will you keep an eye on Courtney?"

His friend made a face.

"I mean, just, look out for her. Call me if something seems off."

"Off?"

"Yeah."

"I don't know what is normal for pregnant chicks. How will I know if something is off?"

Justin considered that. "I don't know. I'd just feel better if I knew that someone who's aware of her...condition...was keeping an eye on her and making sure she seems okay."

"Yeah, I guess I can do that," Keith finally agreed.

～

THE NEXT MORNING, Courtney and Justin both slept in, although with the time change, it still felt to Courtney like the seven-thirty wake up that it was in California. Justin pulled on her hand, clearly hoping she'd stay in bed with him a little longer, but she stepped into the bathroom. She brushed her teeth while the shower heated up.

"Can I at least join you?" Justin asked.

She smiled, perfectly happy to share some quality time with Justin in the shower.

They were just drying off when there was a knock at the door, followed by a "knock knock."

Courtney grabbed a robe and peeked out at Andi. She was wearing a robe as well, but her long hair lay straight over her shoulders.

"Oh good, perfect!" Andi exclaimed, tugging Courtney by the hand. There were two women in the common area of the suite watching expectantly. Andi pointed to the lady standing by a makeshift salon chair. "This is Kirstin, and she does hair and makeup, and that's Mia, and she's going to do our massages."

Courtney was bewildered.

"Don't worry, my treat. Now sit down. You can do hair first, and then we can trade. Since yours is already wet, you could get it cut. Maybe add some layers?"

Courtney gazed around the room, as if searching for help. She spotted Keith in the corner, fully dressed and reading the paper. Their eyes met, and he shrugged. Then they both turned to the massage table, where Andi stretched out on her stomach and then tossed the robe to the ground, flashing a brief view of her breasts before the masseuse pulled the thin sheet over her. Keith's eyes widened, and he exhaled hard.

Courtney sighed and plopped into the chair by Kirstin. "I don't spend a ton of time on my hair," she said. "I'm not sure layers are the way to go."

"Long layers, Kirstin," Andi said, popping her head up. "Trust me, Court, it'll be gorgeous. Want some highlights too?"

"No!"

Kirstin finished the cut and was drying Courtney's hair when Justin emerged from the bedroom. Courtney didn't see him at first, but realized something had happened when Andi exclaimed "ouch" at the exact time Kirstin dropped the hairdryer. Courtney turned and saw both Mia and Kirstin staring wide eyed at the corner of the room.

Justin froze in the doorway, apparently oblivious to the commotion in the common area. His short hair had dried, but he was still wearing the thick white towel wrapped around his waist, and nothing else. "Sorry," he mumbled. "I just wanted to see about breakfast."

"I had coffee and a grapefruit at eight," Andi said, relaxing back onto the table.

"I ate too," Keith said, returning to his paper.

Justin glanced at Courtney. "Oatmeal, fruit," she said.

"Coffee?"

Courtney nodded, and Justin ordered the food from the phone in the common area. Kirstin retrieved the hairdryer, but Courtney could tell she was still ogling Justin from the way that only one section of her hair was getting dried.

Justin hung up and approached Courtney. "Okay, what's the deal here?"

"We're getting pampered," Andi said, her voice muffled. "Or at least trying to. Could you go put clothes on? You're distracting everyone."

He fake pouted and kissed Courtney on his way back to the bedroom. Kirstin switched off the hairdryer and fanned herself.

Courtney turned to see her, raising an eyebrow expectantly.

"Sorry," Kirstin mumbled. "I didn't know... I mean that was...

Oh my God. He is so hot. And he kissed you. How did you not just pass out?"

Andi started giggling. "Yeah, we get it. It's Justin Erikson. He's hot. And for some reason he's parading around naked."

Courtney turned to face her.

"Why don't I get that kind of reaction from men? Like ever?"

Courtney smiled.

"He's engaged, you know," Andi continued, addressing Kirstin. "I'm pretty sure he's done more than just kiss her. Although come to think of it, we haven't gotten a lot of details."

"I've gotten more than enough details," Keith chimed in. "And I'm going for a walk now. It smells like a spa in here."

"That's the point," Andi retorted, but Keith was gone.

Kirstin straightened and styled Courtney's hair in five minutes flat, and then Courtney traded places with Andi. She remembered reading something about massage during pregnancy, but was pretty sure it didn't apply till later on.

"Are you really engaged to him?" Mia asked her a few minutes into the massage.

Courtney held up her ring finger in response. Thankfully, Mia was quiet and let her relax until her breakfast arrived. It still made her uncomfortable to witness the effect Justin had on other women. It wasn't just that he had fans—it was that women literally drooled in his presence and fanned themselves as he walked through a room.

When there was a knock at the door, Justin magically reappeared, as though he hadn't eaten in weeks. He was wearing jeans, but still no shirt, as he answered the door. Mia stopped rubbing Courtney, so Courtney sat up and pulled the robe around her. She was hungry anyway.

"You are going to get dressed today, right?" Andi asked him.

He turned to Courtney sheepishly. "I can't decide what to wear to lunch. I wanted your input."

Courtney laughed. "You want my input on your outfit? That's a first."

"Ooh, where are we doing lunch?" Andi asked.

Justin shook his head. "You and Keith are on your own. Courtney and I are going to Harry and Izzy's."

"I hear it's good. Why can't we come? Is this like a date?"

"Yes," Justin said, plopping onto the couch with a plate of eggs.

Courtney sat beside him with her oatmeal, chugging the coffee. "His mom is coming and my parents are coming," she explained to Andi. "They haven't met before." She turned to Justin. "Can't you just wear whatever you're wearing to the game?"

A horrified expression crossed Justin's face. "Nevermind. I'll dress myself."

Courtney laughed. She realized she should be nervous about the lunch, but oddly enough, she wasn't. Having met Justin's mother, she knew her parents would like her and that they'd all get along.

As it turned out, she was right. Their parents all got along so well that they might need to worry about the parents ganging up on them. For now, though, it was a relief to Courtney. She didn't want to risk ruining her last twenty-four hours with Justin by accidentally blabbing about the pregnancy. She just wanted to enjoy her first—and possibly last—Super Bowl experience with him, and then have a relaxing stress-free night.

After all the weird comments he'd made over the weekend, two things were very clear to Courtney. Justin's life would be ruined if they had a baby now, and Justin would never forgive himself if he knew she got an abortion.

16

After the big game, Justin got back into the grind quickly. He enjoyed the project he was working on, and it was nice having an apartment in New York while he filmed. It just sucked being away from Courtney. She was going to spend the following weekend with him, but sharing a phone call with his fiancée on Valentine's Day wasn't ideal. Especially since she used the call as an opportunity to cancel their weekend together.

"You promised you'd come see me," he reminded her. "It was a condition of me repaying your loans." He was teasing, of course. But it was killing him being away from her, and he'd convinced himself that she had planned to tell him about the baby when she visited. The timing made perfect sense. He'd even taken the liberty of making celebratory reservations at a few different restaurants in the city.

"Seriously, Justin?" she snapped. "That's hardly an enforceable legal agreement and I never would've agreed to let you do it if I'd known you'd hold it over my head."

"I was joking. I miss you. Don't you miss me?"

There was a lengthy silence, but when she spoke again, her

tone was sincere. "Of course I do, babe. I just can't travel this Friday. I have...a really big appointment at work in the morning."

"You could come later," he suggested.

"I'll come a different weekend, when I can spend more time with you. Okay?"

He reluctantly agreed. "Will you do me a favor in the meantime, though?"

"That depends on what it is."

"Will you stay at my house until I'm back?"

She paused again. "Is Keith not there?"

"No, he is."

"Okaaaaaay, so why..."

"I feel like you're pulling away lately, Court. And you're moving in soon anyway, right?"

"Yes."

"Well, it would make me feel a lot better about everything if I knew you were at the house now. You can call me crazy, but..."

She interrupted with a soft laugh. "Yes, Justin. I will shack up with your roommate until you're home. Does that make you happy?"

"It actually does," he replied with a laugh of his own.

WHEN SHE'D RETURNED to L.A., Courtney could no longer put off the appointment. If she was calculating the timing correctly, she was running out of time to get the abortion. She'd made the appointment for Friday morning. It worked out, since she had already planned to take the day off work to fly to New York for the weekend. Then, she'd have the whole weekend free to recover. But she hated lying to Justin. Hearing his disappointment on the phone when she told him they needed to postpone a couple weeks was heartbreaking.

She felt so bad about the lying that when he asked her to stay at his house until he came back, she agreed. She'd been working so much the first two days back that she was barely there, though. But on Wednesday, she left work early. She'd been having insane stomach cramps off and on since the night before, but it had gotten worse at work. She hoped it wasn't the onset of some horrific stomach bug. Probably, it was karma punishing her for what she was about to do Friday.

Keith was stretched across the larger sofa in the living room when she got home. Courtney felt so awful that she really just wanted to curl up in a ball on the bed, but she reasoned he might distract her.

"Hey, you're home early," he said as she walked in. "Slow day at the shelter?"

She considered lying, but a stabbing pain low and to the side knocked her breath out. She focused on her breathing and lowered herself to the couch. "No, really busy actually, but I'm not feeling great."

Keith's eyes widened. "Are you okay? Do you need to go to a doctor? I can take you to a doctor."

His extreme concern was more than a bit off putting. "I'll be fine," she insisted. "So what are you up to?"

He gazed at her for a long moment as if trying to decide if she was telling the truth before answering. "Writing. Trying to work on this screenplay, but not sure how realistic this one character is."

"What's the screenplay about?" Courtney asked. She had known Keith was working on one, but she had never asked him about it. She hated how self-absorbed she could be. He knew what she did and she never really even tried to learn more about him.

Keith started talking about the movie, just as another sharp pain hit. The sensation passed as quickly as it hit, but Courtney knew she needed to lie down.

"I'm sorry," she said, slowly rising to her feet. "I think I'm going to take a nap. I just don't feel right today." She sighed, wishing Justin was there to rub her back soothingly while she rested. He'd have made her feel better instantly.

The stabbing pain returned, this time quickly intensifying to the point that she heard herself cry out. Keith shot to his feet.

"Courtney! Are you okay?"

She felt his hand on her back, but she couldn't even answer with the pain so intense. Courtney felt overwhelmingly warm, like she was burning alive, and the room got darker and darker until she just gave up trying to see and closed her eyes.

When she opened her eyes again, Courtney was in bed. She glanced around the room, quickly ascertaining it was a hospital. She was alone in the room and fully clothed, a scratchy white sheet thrown over her lap. She remembered talking to Keith, remembered standing up, and then nothing. She was so tired and her stomach hurt.

Suddenly, she remembered the pregnancy. *Oh God.* She really should have told someone she was pregnant. Before she could figure out how to call a nurse to the room though, the door clicked and in walked a doctor she didn't recognize, followed by Keith. The doctor smiled professionally, his mustache momentarily distracting Courtney from the pain in her abdomen.

"Oh good, you're awake," he said.

"How did I get here?"

"I drove you," Keith answered.

Courtney turned to him. He looked really stressed out. She'd seen him tense before, it was practically his M.O., but she'd never seen him this tense. That couldn't be a good thing.

"You fainted," the doctor explained, stepping closer and lifting Courtney's left wrist off the bed, checking her pulse.

Courtney opened her mouth to tell the doctor about the pregnancy, then realized she couldn't say anything in front of Keith.

The doctor's hand brushed against her engagement ring as he set her hand back on the bed. "Your fiancé here mentioned that you are pregnant ..."

"He's not my fiancé," Courtney said, at the same time as Keith said it.

The doctor cleared his throat uncomfortably. "Oh, right. Well, I was telling the father..."

"He's not the father either. My fiancé is the father," Courtney shrieked. Then she turned to Keith, realizing the implication of the doctor's words. "Wait, how do you know I'm..." she couldn't even bring herself to say the word 'pregnant' out loud.

The doctor frowned, too confused to speak now.

"I, um, work for her fiancé," Keith finally explained. "He's out of town. He asked me to keep an eye on her."

"Did you talk to him?" Courtney asked. "Does he know?"

Keith nodded, the pained expression on his face tensing more.

"Well, I'm afraid if you're not family, you need to step out," the doctor said to Keith.

Courtney shrugged. "It's fine. I don't mind if he stays," she said. "Unless you don't want to," she said to Keith.

"Justin asked me to stick around," he said, then he glanced at the doctor. "I'll go get a soda and come back. You need anything Courtney?"

She shook her head and turned back to the doctor.

"How are you feeling?"

"I'm really tired and I've had a stomachache all day and lots of cramping."

"How far along are you?"

Courtney hesitated, then gave her best guess. "I haven't had an ultrasound or anything yet. I was supposed to a couple weeks ago, but the office was running behind, and then it was rescheduled for later this week."

He nodded, solemnly, and a nurse came in to help her up. "I'll give you a minute to change into the gown, and then I'd like to do an exam to see if we can pinpoint the problem. We'll get an ultrasound in here too."

Courtney nodded and quickly changed into the gown, shoving her clothes into a bag the nurse brought.

The doctor returned and performed his exam, silently except for the occasional request of the nurse. When he was finished, he threw his rubber gloves in the trash.

"So am I going to live?" she asked awkwardly, desperate to dispel the tension in the room. Courtney still didn't feel quite like herself, was still tired, and ached to just see Justin again. Luckily though, the stabbing pains had subsided. She actually didn't feel much cramping at all now.

"Do you know if your fiancé will be arriving soon?" the doctor asked. "It might be better if I wait and talk to both of you at once."

"He's in New York, working. He's not supposed to return for a few more weeks."

The doctor swallowed audibly, something that even Courtney knew was never a good sign. "Courtney, it's possible you're in the early stages of a miscarriage. We won't know for sure until we get the ultrasound, but it's definitely something we should rule out. At this point, there is nothing we can do to prevent it, but I'd like to keep you here overnight for observation and rest. I don't want you to get your hopes up, but resting won't hurt. I'd also like to rule out an ectopic pregnancy."

Courtney turned to the ceiling, unable to tolerate the tense expression on the doctor's face for another moment. She wondered how she was going to explain this to work. Or to Justin, for that matter.

"Courtney, did you hear what I said?"

"I'm tired," she replied, lifting her eyes even higher to dodge the doctor's stare. "Is it really necessary to keep me overnight? The pain is gone now."

"The nurse will be back to draw some blood and we'll know more after we have those results and the ultrasound. But regardless of what caused the pain, the fact that it was intense enough to cause you to faint is concerning to me. I'd like you to stay the night."

She sighed and nodded, then let her eyes shut again. It was just too much to think about.

Courtney jumped as she heard a man clear his throat. She looked up expectantly, hoping against the odds it would be Justin, but it was just Keith.

"Sorry," he mumbled, "but they wanted me to come back in here and talk to you. You okay?"

She snickered. "I said I was tired, so they sent you in for a chat? Figures."

He sighed. "Yeah, they uh, well, they had some concerns that you weren't yourself, but they don't really know you, so they asked me to see if you seemed all right."

"I'm fine," she retorted, pulling the crappy white blanket up to fully cover the hideous green hospital gown.

Keith sat on the chair beside her. "Do you want to talk to Justin?"

Courtney didn't answer. What would she say to him? She didn't want to talk with him, she wanted to see him. She wanted him to hug her, to completely envelop her in his strong arms, and to take her out of this place.

"Courtney, if you don't want to call him now, I think I should. He's waiting on an update."

"So call him. Or don't. I think I might take a nap. I'll just talk with him later."

Keith stood, then leaned over the bed. She turned to him briefly, but his short curly black hair covered his eyes and she couldn't decipher his expression. "Courtney, are you sure you understand what the doctor said?"

Courtney heard herself laugh, wondering if it was too late for her to take back what she said about not minding Keith sticking around.

Keith sat on the bed beside her. "Courtney, the doctor thinks you're losing the baby. Are you sure you don't want to talk to Justin now?"

She closed her eyes tightly, felt him rub her back gently for a moment, and then he left. She had less than a minute alone before the nurse returned with a wheelchair. Courtney moved from the bed to the chair, careful to be sure the gown fully covered her. She clutched the bag of clothes and her purse on her lap as the nurse steered her through a series of winding halls and onto an elevator, before finally arriving at a small, yet blissfully private, room.

After some paperwork, the nurse set up an IV in her hand. She drew a blood sample and then gave Courtney some medicine to help her relax. Courtney found it ironic that they thought she needed help relaxing when, in reality, this was probably the most relaxed she'd ever been, with her entire body and mind numb.

17

Courtney was abruptly jolted from her relaxation by the screech of tiny wheels against the linoleum. An alarmingly perky redhead dragged a large piece of equipment into the room, with the nurse Courtney recognized trailing behind.

"Hi there, I'm Alex, and I'll be doing your ultrasound," she said, way too peppy. "We are going to start with an internal ultrasound then we'll do an external one to get some additional photos." She explained how it would work then proceeded to slide a condom over a large plastic wand.

Courtney cringed and looked away, not daring to glance at the machine or the tech while the cold probe was violating her. Several minutes passed without the tech saying anything, but just as Courtney started to worry, she withdrew the offending device and set it aside.

"You're doing great," she said as the nurse lowered the head of the bed until Courtney was lying flat. "This will feel cold," she warned.

A plop of cool gel squirted onto Courtney's lower abdomen. And then another probe pressed against her skin. Alex used it to smear the gel around, then pressed a bit harder and moved slowly around the lower right corner of her abdomen, pausing to type something on the computer.

Courtney dared to gaze at the computer screen once, but didn't see anything recognizable. She wasn't sure what she was supposed to see anyway.

"Is everything okay?" she asked, realizing how dumb she sounded.

"You're doing great," Alex repeated, not answering the question in the slightest. "The doctor will come in and talk with you after I'm done."

Alex kept moving the probe around against Courtney's abdomen for a while longer, then finally wiped the gel off.

"I'm going to get the doctor," the nurse said, sighing. "Can I get you anything to drink or eat?"

Courtney shook her head. The nurse's expression was easy to read. Nothing they'd seen was good news, or at least that was their interpretation. Maybe Courtney should be relieved. If she were being honest with herself, she thought she was. She'd basically decided on the abortion anyway. Now she didn't have to decide. And she didn't have to deal with the guilt over having done something so drastic.

She decided food poisoning was the best excuse for her boss and texted April, letting her know the name of the hospital where she'd been admitted just in case. Less than a half hour passed before April replied, blissfully sympathetic. After that, Courtney barely had time to check her email before the doctor came in. The look on the doctor's face removed any doubt in Courtney's mind about whether the pregnancy was viable. She stared straight at him, ready to hear the words aloud.

The doctor slowly lowered himself to the backless stool near the foot of the bed then rolled a few inches closer. "I've reviewed your scans and the results of your bloodwork. I am so sorry to tell you that you are not pregnant."

She averted her gaze. The sorrow in the doctor's face compounded the guilt she felt over the relief flooding her system.

"False positives on a pregnancy test are extremely rare, but a corpus luteum cyst can cause a positive reading on a test. They're a normal part of the menstrual cycle but occasionally grow excessively large and can even cause abdominal pain, pelvic pain, or bleeding. We see an increased frequency of them in women who are taking progesterone-only birth control pills."

Courtney repeated his words in her head then turned back to face him. "Wait, false positive? What does that... You're telling me I had a miscarriage, right?"

He shook his head. "No. It appears you were never pregnant."

Courtney wanted to laugh out loud at the ridiculousness of it all. She'd been so stressed, so miserable, and all over nothing. Except, it still didn't make sense.

"I used a test at home and it was positive. Then my doctor told me I was pregnant. They did the test in their office."

He nodded. "Yes, and that is considered an accurate way to determine pregnancy, but honestly without bloodwork or an ultrasound, there's no way to be certain."

"But I didn't get my period."

"That could be from the cyst as well. Or from your birth control pills or stress, really. A number of factors can cause that."

Courtney wished he'd stop saying the word "cyst." It had to be up there as one of the most annoying words in the English language, right along with 'moist' and 'hubby.' Although, what if he was using it instead of an even worse word? Something scarier. "You don't mean I have a tumor, right?"

He shook his head. "No, it's called a corpus luteum cyst.

Generally harmless and we often do see them along with an early pregnancy. In your case, it seems to have grown larger than we'd like. From your scans and the pain you felt, my suspicion is that the cyst grew to the point that it caused your ovary to twist and could have cut off blood flow to the ovary. It then ruptured."

Courtney waited for him to say more, but it was clear he thought his job was done. "So...what does that mean? How do you fix it? Am I going to live?"

"You're fine. It seems to have resolved itself. We will do another scan in the morning to check on your ovary, and I'm sure your regular gynecologist will want to see you in the office soon for a follow-up appointment and ultrasound."

Courtney had no idea what to say to any of this. Five minutes ago she'd thought she was pregnant and now she was...just fine? It was all so unexpected.

"Most likely you should be fine to get pregnant right away if that's what you want," he continued.

"I don't," she said quickly, before even registering the words leaving her mouth.

If this surprised him, he hid it well. "I'm going to prescribe a traditional combination birth control pill with estrogen then. You can discuss alternatives with your doctor when you go for your follow-up appointment, but in the meantime, that should prevent any future cysts from growing."

Courtney suspected she should have dozens more questions, but the doctor clearly was ready to leave. And, in his defense, it was well past normal business hours. She supposed that was par for the course in that line of work. He probably had to be at the hospital to deliver babies anyway.

She thanked him and he left. She closed her eyes, relishing the peacefulness she felt from whatever drugs they'd given her. She must have fallen asleep at one point, only to be awakened by a nurse checking on her. It was dark outside, and quiet in the halls. Courtney realized Keith was seated in a chair across the room, seeming like he'd probably been awakened at the same moment she had.

"You can go home, Keith," she said. "It's late."

But he shook his head, and Courtney fell back asleep.

JUSTIN TOOK a cab from the airport straight to the hospital, shaking his hand dismissively at the two girls that stopped him and requested autographs just outside the airport. He hated doing that, but it was already after four o'clock in the morning. He couldn't stand the thought of Courtney waking up and still being all alone. It was bad enough that she'd had to go through it all alone thus far. Keith had given him the room number, so he was able to go straight there room. He shuddered as he walked down the cold, sterile halls, remembering the visits to his dad all those years ago. Clenching his fists nervously, Justin realized that nothing good ever happened in a hospital. The guilt hit him. Why had he left Courtney all alone? She needed him more now than ever, and he was thousands of miles away. She was all alone.

And not just physically, either. Courtney was completely alone emotionally, too. She didn't even know he knew about the baby. God, he was an idiot. Why hadn't he just been honest with her from the start? She wouldn't have been upset at him for ruining her surprise. It would have been fine.

When he reached the room, he relaxed. Courtney was asleep, looking calm and peaceful. Keith, who had been sleeping in a chair, popped up when Justin arrived. The two stepped into the hall.

"How's she doing?" Justin asked.

Keith rubbed his eyes. "She's been sleeping a lot." He

paused. "And when she's awake, she's not, well, I don't know man. She doesn't seem right. I don't think she gets any of it. And then they gave her some medicine to relax her, so she stopped making any sense at all." He looked tired, and pitiful.

"Get some sleep, dude," Justin said, patting him on the back and then pulling him in for the briefest of hugs. "Thank you so much for bringing her in and staying with her. I don't know what I'd do without you. Seriously, you're awesome."

Keith nodded again, gazing to his shoes. "I'm really sorry, man."

Justin forced a smile, then tiptoed back into the room. He stood beside the bed, uncertain of how to proceed. He didn't want to wake her, but he also didn't want to sit way across the room from her. He just wanted to hold her. She looked so fragile and so alone, curled up in that stupid hospital bed.

He slowly pulled off his jacket and shoes and then quietly lowered himself onto the bed behind her praying she didn't wake. He awkwardly rested his head beside her, delicately brushing her dark hair out of the way, and wrapped his arm around her. She sighed and relaxed into him but didn't wake. Justin was exhausted. Counting his workout and time in the makeup chair, he'd had an eighteen hour work day the previous day, and he had been too worried on the plane to sleep any. Courtney seemed so peaceful that he wished he could sleep now, but instead he found himself anxiously awaiting the sound of her every breath.

It couldn't have been more than an hour when she sighed again, then shifted, slowly at first, but then flipping her head to the side when she realized she wasn't alone.

"You're here!" she squealed.

He sat up quickly, wincing from the numbness in his arm. Courtney began to sit too, but seemed thrown by the needle taped into her hand and draped up the other side of the bed.

Justin helped her onto her back, then scooted closer and leaned over her.

"I'm so glad you're here. I missed you so much."

She seemed so genuinely content at that moment, Justin realized that either Keith was right—Courtney really didn't understand what had happened—or she'd momentarily forgotten. He wasn't sure which was worse. He leaned in and kissed her on the forehead.

"Why aren't you in New York? Don't you have to be shooting now?"

"Don't worry about it."

She frowned, then glanced around the room. "Keith was here."

Justin nodded. "He left when I got here."

"He was really nice," she said, and then she wrinkled her brow.

Justin was thankful he'd asked Keith to look out for her. Although, then again, Keith would've taken Courtney to the hospital and stayed with her until he arrived anyway. He was just that nice of a guy.

"He mentioned that you thought I was..." she began. Then she stopped. "There's no baby," she said softly, her voice like a child's. "I'm not pregnant. I'm sorry I..."

Justin held his breath now, uncertain of how to respond. He leaned forward and kissed her again, and smoothed her hair back off her forehead. "I know," he finally said. He felt like he should say more, like reassure her somehow. But he knew better than to say it was okay, since it really wasn't. She'd just been through a traumatic experience, and all alone. And it wasn't okay. She'd been happily anticipating this new life, and now...

He had so many questions for the doctor, like how it happened or what caused it. Would they be able to have children down the road or would this happen again? He wondered if the doctor had already told Courtney all of these things, but he didn't want to make her relive the trauma by catching him fully up to speed.

She didn't speak again, and it wasn't too long until a nurse came in.

The nurse started into the room quickly, then stopped abruptly, clearly not having expected to see someone else next to the patient. Justin hopped up quickly, unsure of hospital rules about him sitting on the bed.

"I'm her fiancé," he explained. "Justin."

The nurse glanced him up and down and then froze, mouth open. Justin knew she must recognize him and prayed she took that whole confidentiality thing seriously. Course, who knew how many people had seen him arriving the night before, but he wasn't even going to think about that now.

The nurse blushed. Finally, she spoke. "I'm so sorry, I just assumed that the, well, there was, um…"

"The guy here last night was my manager. I asked him to stay with Courtney until I could get here. I've been in New York filming." Normally, Justin wouldn't have offered such a lengthy explanation, but given the circumstances, it seemed like confirming her suspicions about his identity might get them to more important questions faster.

The nurse nodded. "I'm so sorry." She turned to Courtney. "I just need to take your vitals. The doctor should be by in a few minutes."

"Dr. Patel?" Courtney asked.

Justin assumed that was her regular doctor's name. He recalled seeing it on some of the papers he'd found in her purse that day.

She shook her head. "No, she's not on call today. It's Dr. Lammers."

Justin waited patiently until the nurse started out of the

room. Then he followed her out, telling Courtney he'd be right back.

"Do you have a moment?" he asked the nurse, pulling the door shut.

She turned and nodded, blushing.

"Look, I don't know if you recognize me or anything..." he began.

"I do," she said. "I've seen all the *Days End* movies."

He smiled. "Well, so you understand my concern about confidentiality. It's really important that as few people as possible know I'm here, and, if possible, could we keep everyone out of the room except maybe you and this Dr. Lammers?"

The nurse nodded. "That should be okay. We usually have a whole team of nurses, but I can put a note on the file."

"That would be great. And if there's any way you can keep my name off of everything, you know, just keep it all under my fiancée's name, that would help too." He paused, hoping that didn't sound like he was embarrassed to be associated with Courtney. "I just, well, given the nature of the situation, I'd really like to keep this out of the tabloids." He sighed, rubbing his forehead.

Her lips parted and she frowned, but just as it appeared she was going to say something, she simply nodded again. Justin ducked back into the room, eager to get out of the hallway before someone spotted him. Courtney seemed more alert now, but he didn't want to press her for details. She, however, seemed perfectly content to interrogate him.

"Why did Keith think I was pregnant?" she asked.

"I told him," Justin said, trying to keep his tone as apologetic as possible. "I was worried about you when I was so far away. I wanted to make sure he'd look out for you."

Justin figured that was close enough to the truth. He could've told her how he needed someone to talk about it with since she, for some reason, hadn't said anything to him yet. But he didn't want her to feel like he was blaming her for anything, certainly not now. It's not like it mattered anyway at this point. Him having known sooner wouldn't have changed anything.

"Yeah, but why would you tell him that? What made you think I was?" she asked.

Justin couldn't think of any way to tell her without coming off as an asshole, so he just went with the truth. "I spilled something on your purse, and when I was making sure everything dried, I found some papers about pregnancy. You've been acting different, so..."

She cringed and he stopped talking, instead reaching over to touch her hair again. But she shrugged away from his hand.

"Why didn't you tell me?" she asked. "If you thought I was... you should've said something."

Justin chewed his lip to hide the frown. Sure, he should have. But she should've told him first. He shouldn't have had to find out that way.

Except, he couldn't exactly say that while she was lying in a hospital bed sad and in pain. "I'm sorry," he said instead. "I thought maybe you wanted to surprise me, and I didn't want to ruin it."

Any explanation he gave sounded weak now. Looking back, he had no idea why he'd acted the way he had. "Are you feeling okay now? Do you need anything?"

She shook her head. "I'm fine. I...the pain was really intense yesterday, but it's gone now. The doctor said it all resolved itself."

He suppressed a grimace at the callous way she referred to it all. "I'm glad you're feeling better. I'm so sorry I wasn't here. I never should have traveled across the country when you were..."

Courtney turned to him again, her bright eyes filled with thought. "Justin, I'm not pregnant. You understand that, right?"

He nodded. "Yeah, it's okay. I get it. This happens, and it's not your fault." He didn't know much about any of it, but he was sure that was true.

"No, Justin, I was never pregnant," she said.

He felt his jaw drop, but there was no time for follow up questions before the door swung open. An older, blonde doctor walked in. She introduced herself and greeted them both, then turned to Courtney and said she wanted to do a follow-up exam.

"This is my fiancé," Courtney said.

Justin realized the polite thing to do would be to introduce himself, but he was too dazed still by what Courtney had just said. He was tempted to ask the doctor if they could have a minute alone before she did her exam, but he figured that wasn't appropriate. Still, he had so many questions for Courtney.

The doctor asked how she was feeling, and then an ultrasound tech came in. Justin left as they began the exam. He promised Courtney he'd be right outside.

Justin needed to contact Keith and figure out something with work, but talking with Keith would depress him, so he texted instead.

"Courtney's ok. We'll be home later. Can u call Marty and tell him I need to be here the rest of the week?" He hit send, and the reply from Keith was almost instantaneous.

"Yes. On it."

They discharged Courtney later that morning, with instructions to take it easy and then follow up with Dr. Patel in two days.

18

Courtney seemed fine the first day they were home, but Justin struggled to mask his disappointment. He'd always been that way, even as a kid. Once he got excited about something, well, it just took him a while to get over the letdown. He assumed that however bummed he was, though, that Courtney felt infinitely worse. So he tried to act chipper around her, but she wasn't having any of it. As soon as Courtney picked up on his true feelings, she started acting sad.

Justin hated knowing his inability to move on so quickly was making the whole ordeal even harder for her.

"I'm so sorry, babe. I don't want you worrying about me. I'm supposed to be taking care of you this week. I will be just fine."

Courtney wrinkled her face.

Justin tried to pull her close to comfort her, but she shook free.

"Justin, stop. I...this is all my fault."

He cringed. "Courtney, you know that isn't true. You didn't even tell me, so you certainly can't blame yourself if I'm disappointed now."

She made a sour face, and he realized how bad his words

had come out. That hadn't exactly been what he'd meant, only that it wasn't like she'd tried to get his hopes up. But before he could explain, she spoke again.

"I should've gotten an ultrasound sooner, so I knew for sure."

"That wouldn't have changed the end result," he reminded her, although the doctor had mentioned they could have put her on medicine to treat the cyst before it became so painful. She still looked guilty, but he had to know the truth about some things. It just didn't make sense.

"Why didn't you, though?" he asked.

"Why didn't I get the ultrasound sooner?"

Or at all, he wanted to say. Instead, he nodded.

She flung up her hands then made her way to the couch, sitting on the end with her leg curled under her. "I don't know. I had planned to, but then they were running behind, and I was so nervous about missing work. I'd just joined the executive team and then I was taking time off and if I had a baby, I'd be missing a bunch more work..."

"If," he repeated. "So you weren't even sure you were pregnant? That's why you didn't tell me?" Suddenly, it all made sense.

Courtney crossed her arms over her chest before shifting so one hand supported her chin. She sighed, her lips pursed. "No. I thought I was pregnant. From the moment I saw the first positive test..."

"And that was when?" he asked, lowering himself to the couch beside her.

"What does it matter, Justin? I'm not pregnant. Never was. Can we just forget all of this and move on?"

That seemed like a mature thing to do, but he couldn't. He needed it to make sense in his mind. "I want to know. It's like...it feels like this big thing. And you and I have always talked about everything but then there was this huge thing and you never even told me."

"Which is it, big or huge?"

"Court, come on." He reached out and rubbed her leg. He couldn't remember her ever being this defensive about anything.

She weaved her fingers through her dark hair, leaving them clasped around the tips. "I took the test on the day you were flying with Ryan. When I'd gone to take my pill earlier, I'd realized I missed a couple when I was sick, so I figured it was smart to check. But I honestly didn't expect it to be positive... until it was."

"So why didn't you tell me?"

"I don't know. You were thousands of miles away, not to mention really busy." She paused, shaking her head. "And I was freaked out. It was unexpected. I was terrified. You know?"

"Not really. Because you never told me," he said. He instantly regretted his tone.

He apologized immediately, as did she. Then, neither of them spoke for a minute. Courtney gradually relaxed back against Justin and he shifted to rope his arm around her. He knew he should just let it drop, but he couldn't. It still didn't make sense.

"When were you going to tell me?"

She took her time answering. "I don't know. I didn't want to tell you over the phone."

"But you found out before I left for New York," he reminded her. "And we were together in Indiana."

"Well, I said I was sorry. I should've told you right away, should've gotten the ultrasound, and then we wouldn't be here right now. Like I said, it's all my fault."

Courtney pushed off the couch and started up the stairs. He waited a couple minutes, then followed her. She was seated on the corner of the bed, gazing at the door as if she'd known he'd come for her.

"It just seems like the sort of thing you'd tell your fiancé," he said, leaning against the wall facing her.

She nodded. "You're right. And I planned to tell you at first."

"At first?"

"Justin, I was terrified. Everything in our lives was so perfect. We were happy, your career was going so well. My career was going so well. We had this perfect rhythm. A baby would've ruined everything."

He didn't know how to respond to that. Those same thoughts had gone through his mind when he'd found out, too.

"I wanted to make sure it was for real before I told you, so I went to the first doctor's appointment. And then, I didn't want to tell you until I figured out what to do."

"Like, how to tell me?"

She shook her head again. "I never wanted to have a baby, Justin. Not now, anyway. In five or ten years, sure."

He pushed off the wall, walking closer to her. "I would've understood that. It's not like I would've thought you did it on purpose. You know that, right? And it's not like I'm ready for kids either. The timing sucked. I agree."

Courtney tilted her head to the side. "You started going on about how wonderful babies were or how great it would be when we had kids."

"Only because I thought you were pregnant and scared to tell me!"

"Okay, well, after hearing how much you wanted a baby, how was I supposed to look you in the eyes and tell you I didn't want a baby?"

He didn't have an answer for that.

"When I found out I was pregnant, I wanted to get an abortion. I planned to get it done before you were even back in town. I'd already scheduled it. It was supposed to be yesterday."

Justin's breath caught in his throat. "You weren't even going to tell me?"

She shook her head. "I thought you'd talk me out of it. Or that you'd let me go through with it and be all supportive and wonderful and then spend the rest of our lives resenting me or feeling guilty for doing it, even though it was the only solution that made sense."

"You were going to abort our baby without ever even telling me?" Justin's stomach tightened as he heard the words aloud.

Courtney was crying now, but Justin didn't feel even a hint of the sympathy he usually felt when she cried. Instead he felt sick, betrayed. Justin felt his entire body tense as his heart pounded furiously.

"No. I had already decided to cancel the appointment. I couldn't have gone through with it, without you. You were just so confident whenever you talked about us as parents. I figured you wanted that baby so badly and I just thought I could be happy about it too for your sake."

Justin took a moment to ponder the full ramifications of what she was saying. She reached for his arm, but he backed away from her.

"Jesus, Courtney, you don't have a baby for someone else. What was your fucking plan, were you just going to go along with it the whole time, have a baby you didn't want, and then what, resent me the rest of your life?"

"No! I wouldn't have resented you. I would've done it for you but would have been happy when we actually had the baby. I didn't even realize I still felt that way until I saw how disappointed and sad you were and all I felt was relief."

He shook his head, speechless. The past two days he'd been through hell. Yeah, he'd been sad about the baby, but mostly it was killing him to worry about Courtney. Was none of that real? Justin was overcome with the urge to throw something, to punch his fist through the wall, something, anything.

Courtney's tears were pouring down her face, smearing her eye makeup across her cheekbones. "And now you hate me because this is all my fault and I'm so sorry. I really wished I could feel the way you did, that I could want that baby like you did, and I can't stand having you mad at me. I wouldn't have gone through with the abortion."

"I'm not mad that you didn't want the baby, Courtney. I'm mad that you didn't tell me how you felt. I'm not some one-night stand. I'm going to be your husband. You should have told me you were pregnant. You should have told me you wanted an abortion."

"I'm sorry," she repeated.

There was a sick silence between them. Courtney's eyes pleaded with him and Justin knew she was waiting for forgiveness, that she really expected him to just pat her on the back and say it was all okay.

"I have to go," he said instead. He grabbed his gym bag and left. He wanted to be alone and he wanted to hit something, hard. Might as well go do some boxing.

Justin stayed at the gym for two hours. When he was too exhausted for anything else, he showered, then climbed into his car, unsure of what to do next. It was eight o'clock, too early to go home. Justin knew he couldn't face Courtney again today. She'd lied to him. She'd betrayed him on the single most important thing in their lives.

He'd been ready to marry her, and he'd gone above and beyond trying to show her he was happy about the pregnancy. Justin had meant every word he'd said to her, but all Courtney had done was lie. She said she wanted to have a baby with him, but now he knew she didn't. She said she wanted to marry him, but now he didn't know. Had she only accepted his proposal out of pity for him?

Justin needed a drink. He tried to think of someplace—other than his house, where Courtney was—that he could drink alone. Someplace where no one would recognize him or harass him. He couldn't come up with anything, so he drove to his friend David's. David, a successful fashion designer who'd created many of Justin's favorite shirts, lived alone in a modern-style house about twenty minutes from Justin's, practically next door by L.A. traffic standards.

David answered the door on the second knock, wearing fitted jeans with designer-cut rips in the knee and a patch on the thigh, but no shirt.

"You alone?" Justin asked.

David nodded.

"I need a drink," Justin said.

David motioned for him to come inside. David grabbed a shirt and handed Justin a cold beer. They sat on barstools in the massive kitchen.

"Huge fight with Courtney. Don't want to talk about it. Don't want to go home until she's asleep," Justin said. David nodded, and that was the last they discussed it.

EACH TIME COURTNEY awoke that night, she was acutely aware of Justin's absence in the bed. It was his bed, and while she'd slept in it alone plenty while he was out of town, that was different. Now, he was avoiding her. Twelve hours earlier, he'd felt the same way she did. They both shared the familiar urge to touch each other. Even in sleep, their bodies would find one another. They'd always awaken pressed up against each other, or with Justin's arm around Courtney, or with Courtney curled against Justin's chest, or even simply with their fingers entwined.

Now, Courtney was alone. She'd only told him the truth because he looked so hurt. She knew he was suffering mostly because he thought she was upset, and she'd wanted to relieve his pain by letting him know the whole story. But instead, she'd just made it worse. Now he'd not only lost his baby, but his trust in her.

Courtney wasn't sure if he'd stayed away all night to punish her or because he really couldn't stand to be around her. She hoped it was the former.

She climbed in the shower before the water warmed up, needing the cool blast of water to calm her puffy, tear-soaked eyes. She twisted her hair into a bun instead of drying it, dabbed on the most cursory level of makeup, and then dressed for work. She tried not to think about where Justin went the night before. He knew lots of people in town, but he didn't have lots of close male friends, at least not the kind that he'd barge in on last minute. Probably he'd just stayed in a hotel.

Courtney tiptoed out of Justin's room, hoping not to wake Keith. She made it to the front door and then glanced out the window as she slipped into her coat. The silver Audi was there, in the driveway. She turned to look at the long narrow table along the side wall of the foyer and realized Justin's shoes, coat, and car keys were there too. So he had come home last night. She started towards the guest room, just beyond the kitchen, and then stopped. If he'd slept in the guest room in his own house, Justin obviously didn't want to see her.

"David dropped him off around two and then took a cab home," Keith said, walking down the stairs in long pajama pants and a tee shirt.

Courtney nodded. "I'm going to work," she said, her voice cracking.

Keith rubbed his eyes sleepily. "Any reason he didn't sleep in his room?"

"He's mad at me," Courtney answered, leaving for work before she started crying again.

Justin wasn't flying back to New York until Monday, so Courtney convinced herself she'd have time to make things right. He'd have the whole day away from her, and he could sleep off the hangover. That night, he could yell at her, and get it out of his system.

Tomorrow, they'd make up, and everything would be back to normal by Sunday night.

Courtney had figured she'd be safe at work on a Saturday. Normally no one else was working in the business office part of the shelter, so she could give Justin plenty of space. But then April showed up, apparently with the same idea of catching up on work. Courtney didn't feel like chatting or explaining her absence the prior day, so she packed up and went back to Justin's.

19

———

When she drove up to Justin's, there was loud music coming from the patio and several other cars in the driveway. Courtney opened the front door tentatively, unsure of what she'd find, but the house seemed empty. She started towards the kitchen and nearly ran into Cathy, who was on her way out.

"Oh, hi," she said. "Is Justin out back?"

Cathy nodded, a clear look of disapproval in her eyes. "I'll see you Monday," she said, grabbing her purse and heading for the door.

Courtney winced and blew out a sigh. That didn't seem like a good sign. She left her soft, black leather Coach briefcase—a gift from Justin—on the front table by her keys and went to the back patio. She immediately spotted Keith, dancing on the opposite side of the pool with two girls in bikinis. She peered out the window longer, seeing one other guy and two other girls, these two both dressed, albeit in super tight-fitting clothes. She still didn't see Justin, and, as much as Courtney would love to believe it was Keith's gathering, it seemed a lot more Justin's style.

She took a deep breath and headed outside. Everyone

turned to stare at her as though she was an alien. It took Courtney a moment to remember that she was wearing pinstripe pants and a fitted blouse, which probably made her look like a tax auditor to the drunk girls by the pool.

Keith waved enthusiastically, sloshing his beer all over the place. It was barely three o'clock, and Keith was drunker than she'd ever seen him. Courtney sniffed a few times and hesitated. Maybe Keith wasn't just drunk. The patio area was smoky, and not in a cigarettes-only way.

She swiveled around and saw Justin off to the side, straddling a patio chair. He wore a grey knit cap on his head, faded blue jeans, and a white sleeveless ribbed undershirt. His necklace lay right in the center of his chest, drawing the eye to his massive pecs, and the shirt did nothing to hide his shoulders or biceps either. Courtney couldn't deny that he looked incredibly sexy, except for one small detail. He held a joint in one hand, a Corona in the other.

Justin saw her approach and passed the joint to the guy seated beside him. The guy turned, grinned dopily, and walked away. The blonde on Justin's other side was slower to move, first giving Courtney an unimpressed once over, and then slowly sauntering past.

"Hi," she said, sitting awkwardly on the chair beside him. He made no move to kiss her or touch her. Instead, he finished the rest of his beer and dropped the bottle to the ground. It hit the pavement with a loud clank but didn't shatter.

"I passed Cathy on her way out."

"I should've had her go buy more Corona first," Justin said.

"I'm sure you have plenty of other beers inside."

He shrugged, avoiding eye contact. "Mexican weed warrants Mexican beer."

"Maybe I should go pick up some tacos for dinner," she said icily.

Justin laughed so hard he nearly fell out of the chair. "That'd be awesome, babe. Thanks." He glanced over at Keith. "Yo Keith, toss me the tequila!"

Keith threw a bottle in their direction, missing by about fifteen feet, so it flew into the pool. "Sorry!" he shouted.

Justin rose to his feet. "It's cool. I'll just swim to it," he said, starting to unzip his pants.

Courtney heard the girls whistle. She glanced down and realized with how low his jeans were, she should be able to see the top band of his boxers. "Justin, the pool is freezing and you're not wearing anything under your jeans."

He frowned, stuck a hand down his pants, and snickered. "Oh shit, you're right." He kept laughing but backed away from the pool.

"Justin, you're wasted. You're drunk and stoned. It's the middle of the day."

"So? It's Saturday. Lighten up. I need more tequila," he said. He snatched the joint back from the other guy and wandered into the house. He took a long drag and then retrieved an unopened bottle of Cuervo Gold from the pantry.

Courtney followed, shutting the patio door behind them. The afternoon was not going according to plan at all. They were supposed to talk, or at least to fight, to get it all out there. Justin was not supposed to be high. At the rate he was drinking, he wouldn't even know her name in another hour.

"You shouldn't smoke that in your house," she said. "And you should probably stop altogether. It can make you really sick if you're not used to it." Courtney knew that from watching friends of hers, not from personal experience. She'd never even tried weed at any point in her life.

"How do you know I'm not used to it?" He leaned in closer then slapped his hand onto the counter. "Oh, right, because *I* tell *you* everything."

Justin took a step forward, causing Courtney to responsively inch backwards. She stopped when her back was flush against the kitchen wall. He leaned forward and placed one hand on each side of her head, trapping her. A week ago, he could've done that precise move and caused her knees to wobble with excitement, overwhelming her with desire. Then, she'd have known exactly what he would do next. Now, Courtney had no idea what he was thinking, let alone what his next move would be.

"You know this shouldn't surprise you," he said in a deep voice, his rancid breath hitting her nose. "The girls, the booze, the weed...I thought you read up on me in the tabloids? This is all old news. I might've changed, been on my best behavior for you for a little while, but now I'm not so sure it's worth my effort to give all this up. Especially when you just want to mess with my head, apparently."

Courtney bit her lip. Maybe he wasn't as trashed as she thought. Or maybe his bitterness was just that resilient. "Who are all these people?"

He shrugged and pulled back, releasing her. "Friends." Justin held out his hand. "You want some?"

"No," Courtney replied.

"Come on, no reason not to. It's not like you're pregnant or anything. And even if you were, a little weed doesn't matter if you're not going to have the baby anyway, right?" The cavalier tone in Justin's voice made Courtney's stomach lurch.

She waited, certain he'd apologize, but he raised the joint to his lips again instead. She exhaled hard. The smell was starting to nauseate her, and she knew she'd cry if he said another awful thing to her.

"Justin, I said I'm sorry. I understand that you're still hurt and angry, but I don't see how this is helping. We need to talk."

"I don't have anything else to say to you," he said, his blue eyes piercing into hers. "I don't even fucking know you."

Courtney swallowed hard, but the lump in her throat kept rising back up. "Yeah, I'm beginning to think the same thing about you."

He stared back at her without saying anything, a glossiness coating his eyes. Courtney couldn't tell if it was tears or just the weed. Probably the weed, she decided.

"I'm going to go shower and change, since I now smell like pot, and then I'm going to pack up my stuff. If we can't even talk about what happened, then I guess we need a break. I don't think I should stay here while you're back in New York."

He shrugged.

"If you want to talk, call me later tonight. Or tomorrow. Otherwise I'll just see you when you're back in town."

She waited for him to answer, but he simply stared back, his face devoid of all emotion. After a minute, he blinked, then grabbed the tequila and went outside.

Courtney did exactly as she said, going upstairs and showering, then packing up all her stuff. Some of it she could leave, since she had extra makeup and stuff at home, but she'd need her clothes while Justin was out of town.

Courtney considered that she might never be back, but she didn't let herself dwell on it. She knew she'd hurt him, and yeah, Justin was being a jerk now, but it was because he was high. He wasn't himself. He'd come to his senses and figure that out soon enough.

She carried the last load of her stuff to the car, passing Keith as she paused by the front door to leave her key. Courtney made her way to the patio, ready to say goodbye to Justin, but stopped. He was on the patio still, a non-Mexican beer in his hand, dancing, or more precisely, grinding, in between two of the girls.

Courtney watched for a moment and then turned, knowing nothing good could possibly come out of her interrupting that.

"Are you leaving?" Keith asked, frowning.

As he stood closer, Courtney could tell he was high too, not a good sign since he was the rational one of the pair. "Yeah. And I'm moving out, at least while Justin's gone."

"His flight's not till Sunday evening."

Courtney gazed over to the patio. "It doesn't look like he needs me around right now."

Keith seemed panicked. "Does he know you're going now?"

Courtney shrugged. It was hard to tell what Justin knew.

"Hang on, don't go yet," Keith said, scurrying outside. Courtney watched him pull Justin away from the girls and whisper something. Justin said something back, Keith replied, and then Justin returned to the girls. Keith paused for a moment, glanced over at Courtney, then came back inside, looking dejected.

Courtney nodded, knowing exactly what Keith didn't want to tell her. "It's okay," she said, even though nothing was further from the truth. "Take care of him tonight, will you?"

"Yeah."

And then, as Keith pulled Courtney in for a goodbye hug, Courtney realized the situation was even worse than she'd thought. She hurried to her car and drove as far away as she could before she was crying too hard to see the road. She pulled into a parking lot about a mile from Justin's house and cried until there was nothing left.

THE NEXT MORNING, Justin awoke to a pounding headache. He was still wearing the clothes from the night before—jeans and a sleeveless undershirt, and they reeked. He had been sprawled out on top of his covers and, as best as he could tell, he'd slept alone. That was a relief, at least.

He stripped off his clothes and lingered in a steamy shower before the growling of his stomach finally prompted him to shut off the water. He dressed for the gym, although he couldn't imagine a successful workout with the way he was feeling so far, and opened his door. Keith's bedroom door was still closed, but the single red leather pump outside his room suggested he might have enjoyed some overnight company.

Downstairs, Justin started the coffee, poured himself a bowl of Raisin Bran and then glanced into the guest room while he ate. The door was open, revealing two guests—Sarah and Evelyn. Both were fashion models he vaguely knew from various work events. Both were also single and straight as far as Justin knew, but based on the way their bodies were positioned in the bed, Justin couldn't help but wonder if there was something else going on. Sarah was on her stomach, the sheet pulled up to her waist, but Evelyn was sprawled out on her side, her perky bare breasts completely visible from the hall.

A few years ago, if faced with this opportunity, Justin would've gone into the room and joined the two of them in bed, no matter how hungover he felt. But now, he simply watched them sleep for a minute and then closed the guest room door as he returned to the kitchen. It was Courtney's fault, he knew. Even now that he was pissed at her, he couldn't bring himself to enjoy a couple of girls more than willing to enjoy some fun with him in his house.

Justin finished his cereal, poured a cup of coffee, and grabbed two hardboiled eggs from the fridge. He couldn't remember exactly how he'd left things with Courtney. He knew he'd been a dick, but she deserved it. Course, she probably didn't even know how mad he was, likely thinking it was just the beer and pot making him treat her that way. Courtney probably expected him to sober up and then apologize, just like he always did whenever they fought.

Well, this time, he wasn't apologizing. Not yet anyway.

He needed to be back in New York soon, and Justin knew that leaving town without calling her was by far the best way to let Courtney know exactly how pissed he was. If they were going to get married, he needed to know she'd never again lie to him over something so important. And if they weren't, well, it'd be just as easy to start their time apart while he was mad.

After a few days, they could talk and maybe he wouldn't be so angry anymore. He'd be busy enough in New York to keep his mind off Courtney, and maybe the break would even convince her she needed to pick a date for the wedding.

He walked to the foyer and fingered the key she'd left on the table, hoping he was right as he wedged it into his pocket.

THE APARTMENT HAD BEEN empty when Courtney returned. She carried her bag up to her room, relieved to find it just as she'd left it, but left her purse by the front door so Erica would know she was there as soon as she came home. She changed into pajamas and took one of the pain pills they'd given her at the hospital, even though it probably wasn't appropriate for the type of pain she currently felt. Then she curled up in bed.

When she awoke, it was light outside. Based on the wafting aroma of coffee and bacon, Courtney knew Erica was home. She crept downstairs, still in her pajamas, uncertain of what to expect. Erica was at the kitchen table alone, eating bacon and an orange and drinking coffee. She glanced up from the newspaper she was reading when Courtney appeared.

"Hi," Courtney said tentatively.

Erica proffered a timid smile, the kind you give someone who's clearly fragile, and although Courtney knew it was supposed to be comforting, it made her feel infinitely worse. She looked around and didn't see Erica's girlfriend, who'd been staying at the apartment more nights than not the past few weeks. "Where's Kaylee?"

"She's at her place. I know you had a rough couple of days and that you don't like her, so..."

"I don't dislike Kaylee," Courtney said.

Erica appeared skeptical.

"Oh God, I'm sorry. Is that what you guys thought?" Courtney shook her head and shuffled over to the coffee pot, helping herself to a large mug. "She's welcome to come back. I can talk to her if you want. That's not why I was staying at Justin's."

Erica snapped her bacon strip in half. "You were really out when we came home last night."

Courtney sighed. She wasn't sure how to respond.

"I'm really sorry about what happened. I felt like I should've done something else after Justin told me you were in the hospital, but I didn't know what would help."

Courtney nodded. "No, it's fine. It's not like you could've done anything to change what happened."

"Are you doing okay? Can I do anything now?"

"No," Courtney said, answering both questions at once.

Erica swallowed audibly. "Is Justin..."

"He's headed back to New York to finish filming. I thought I'd stay here for a while."

"Of course," Erica said, nodding. "So...um...how did he take the news?"

Courtney wasn't even sure which news Erica was referring to. "He had been thinking I was pregnant for weeks, apparently since he found some pamphlet in my purse. So he was pretty bummed to learn that I wasn't. And even less thrilled that I never told him."

"I'm sorry."

Courtney could tell Erica was thinking by the way she chewed her lip. She didn't have the energy for any other opinions on her life. "I'm going to shower," she said, shuffling back upstairs.

Courtney stood under the spray of water until the temperature changed from scalding, to comfortably warm, to tepid, not shutting off the faucet until the cold water was stinging her skin. When she got out of the shower, she checked her phone, futilely, and then dressed, styled her hair, and applied makeup, just in case Justin came by on his way to the airport.

Once she was dressed, she returned to her room, closed the door, and sat on the edge of her bed, trying to decide what to do next. Nearly an hour passed without her moving, and then her phone buzzed. It was a text from Justin. It read: "Landed in NY safely."

Courtney sighed and set her phone down. It buzzed several more times, again notifying her of the same message, and she knew it wouldn't shut up until she clicked on it. She opened the message, wincing as she glanced at the prior texts he'd sent her, back when he didn't hate her.

"Okay," she finally typed back, quickly adding, "I really am sorry."

Nearly a minute passed without a response from Justin, but then finally his answer popped up. "Me too," it said.

Courtney wasn't sure what to make of that, but since he was already on the other side of the country, there was no point in her being dressed. She stripped down to her underwear and crawled under the covers, staring at the ceiling until she finally fell back asleep.

Over the next several days, Courtney spent as much time as

possible at work. When she came home, she'd microwave a frozen Lean Cuisine while changing into her pajamas. Then she'd watch TV while eating and go straight to bed. Justin didn't call or text her anymore, and Courtney wasn't sure what that meant. She still followed him on Twitter, and he'd post the occasional update there, tweeting, "started filming at 5a.m. today. That's like 2 for us Cali guys," or, "NY traffic is insane." Nothing too personal, but then again, the messages were intended for his 950,000 followers, not just her.

20

Justin kept busy with work since returning to New York. The directors and the rest of the cast and crew had done some serious reworking of the schedule to accommodate his sudden extended disappearance, and he felt obligated to repay them by working his ass off for the rest of the project. Aside from the lead director and the producer, no one knew why he'd disappeared.

He was relieved to have the apartment in New York, since a hotel room was always lonely. But now, even the apartment felt empty. Andi wasn't in town, and he didn't have any close friends on the cast. So when he wasn't filming, rehearsing, or working out, Justin was alone with nothing to do but think.

He was trying to avoid thinking at all costs, because it wasn't presently productive. Wherever his thoughts began, he always ended up with the same feelings—guilt for how he treated Courtney, and anger at how she'd lied to him. The confusion was there, too, and not just about how things currently stood with him and Courtney, since Justin had no idea. She'd left her house key but kept the ring. What did that mean? Justin wanted to believe she kept the ring because they were still engaged, even though they weren't currently speaking. But Justin couldn't be certain about that, because he was still confused about how Courtney felt about him before the fight, how she'd felt months ago when she first started keeping secrets from him.

Justin had nearly another month in New York. He knew it was pointless to worry now. He just needed to keep busy. So the following Thursday night, he was ready to hit up a runway presentation for a designer's spring line. Justin had been invited to countless shows during New York's fashion week, but since he was actually in New York filming and not just hanging out and watching the runway, he'd picked the five that interested him most and ignored the rest.

Thursday's show featured the spring lines, both men's and women's, for an upcoming designer. Justin sat in the front, left after the first half, and caught up on sleep before shooting Friday. He only had one scene to film Friday, so he got up at five and hit the gym before arriving on set. He chugged his coffee and ate a protein bar from the makeup chair, then miraculously finished with his scene by two. That night's show was much more interesting, and he'd toyed with the idea of participating in a print ad for the designer, so he wanted to get a good feel for the line.

He stayed for the full show, swinging by the backstage area beforehand to chat with the designer. After the show, he found the designer again and dropped some hints about his interest. Then he texted Marty to give him a heads up and headed out to a party. For a lot of the shows, the after party was more interesting than the main event. And in a way, it was a different type of fashion show.

Saturday evening was the Victoria's Secret show, featuring their new spring line. Not surprisingly, backstage at that show had tighter security, so Justin waited just outside the dressing room with the other schmucks hoping to run into someone familiar. After a minute, he spotted her.

"Is that Justin Erikson?" she shrieked, rushing forward to hug him.

"Jasmine," he said with a smile, the familiar greeting feeling awkward based on her attire. He stepped back and gave her a once-over. He couldn't help but grin. "You look good," he said. She was all ready for her first pass down the runway, he assumed, in a beige lacy bikini and matching bra, paired with spiky high heels. Her body was lean, tanned, and shimmering. She had the long legs and perky breasts of, well, a twenty-three-year-old lingerie model.

"You think? They've got me looking so conservative tonight," she said with a pout.

Justin shook his head. Jasmine was a knockout in any outfit. She had long, platinum blonde hair and dark, sultry eyes. A guy would have to be dead not to notice her. They'd hooked up once, years ago, before becoming strictly friends, but the flirty banter had continued.

"I don't know. It's still pretty hot. You got a second outfit?"

She nodded. "Hot pink and black next, and then I'm actually wearing a bathing suit in the last one."

He frowned. "I thought you'd do a separate swimwear show."

"Yeah, we will. This is just a preview, I guess." She glanced behind her. "Why don't you come on back? I know some of the other girls would love to say hi. Anne still wants to talk to you about getting involved with your friend's line."

"Hey, how come you won't ever do any modeling for David?

Jasmine laughed. "He can't afford me. And besides, I don't like wearing clothes." She winked mischievously and pulled him by the hand.

Justin stood his ground, certain nothing good could come from joining her in a room of half-naked (or worse) models for a casual chat before the show. His whole look-don't-touch policy was easier to abide by when he stayed in the audience for the show. "Nah, I want to be surprised during the show. I'll catch up with you ladies after, when you're dressed."

She rolled her eyes and angled her head so her eyes were pointing downward as she glanced up at him. "Is this about that girlfriend of yours?"

Justin laughed. "Fiancée."

"I'd love to meet her. Is she here?"

Jasmine actually had met Courtney, or at least seen her, back when he and Courtney first started dating, but he didn't want to bring that up. He started to say that she was back in L.A., but before the words left his mouth, Justin realized that he didn't know exactly where Courtney was. Presumably she'd gone back to her apartment when she moved out of his place, but he couldn't be certain. Aside from a few short texts, they hadn't spoken.

Justin realized he hadn't answered. "Sorry, Jas, no, Courtney isn't here tonight."

She smiled. "I better get back there. Stick around after the show, right?"

He nodded and took his seat.

The show was awesome, of course, but the more scantily clad women he saw in their bras and panties, the more he kept thinking about Courtney. This was the first fight they'd had for a while, and the first official "break" they'd ever taken.

During the two years that Justin had been with his ex, Kinzie, they'd fought all the time and were on breaks about as much as not. They'd argue, not speak for days or weeks, then make up and have sex. That, plus a few publicity-stunt dates was about the extent of their relationship.

With Courtney, it had always been different. Early in their relationship, they were apart frequently because of his work, but they still talked. And Justin knew a break was different when you were engaged. Part of him was still pissed off at her, and the other part figured she was just as mad at him. It seemed best to give it another week or so before they tried to work things out, but Justin wasn't sure how many more lacy bras he could see without going crazy.

As soon as the show was over, Justin climbed into a limo with Jasmine and a few other friends to head to an after party. He downed some champagne in the limo, followed by two quick shots at the party. He knew a few guys at the party, some other actors, and a couple of musicians, so he was at the bar chatting with them when Jasmine came up and tapped on his shoulder.

"Dance with me," she begged, playfully swatting him on the butt.

Justin raised his eyebrows. "Not if you can't keep your hands to yourself," he teased.

"Damn, dude, I'll dance with her," one of the other guys mumbled.

Jasmine smiled and shook her head at the guys. "He's just being silly because he has a fiancée. But she isn't here, and I happen to know you are a good dancer." She pulled him to the dance floor.

Justin knew he was drunk as soon as he started to dance. Jasmine probably knew it too, but didn't seem to care, as she twirled around the floor in her super-short super-low-cut white denim skirt and off-the shoulder tee shirt. After the first song, he started to wonder if she was drunk too since she was even flirtier than usual. Since she rarely ate, it probably wouldn't take much to get her sloshed.

A slow song came on and Jasmine slung her arms around his neck, pulling him uncomfortably close. She smelled like cigarettes, the perfect reminder of why he'd never sought a repeat of their night together. He felt her sigh against his chest.

"Come on, Jus, work with me here," she said.

"What?"

"You don't have to grab my ass, but could you at least get your hands a little closer? I feel like we're in Junior High."

"Jas," he started to lecture her, but then figured it out. Jasmine didn't really want to sleep with him, and if she was throwing herself at him this obviously it had to be for someone else's benefit. "Are we trying to get someone's attention here?"

She giggled and pulled away from him long enough to nod yes. "Do you feel used?"

He considered this, but immediately remembered how hard it was, trying to meet the right person, or really just anyone decent at that age, when you had any degree of fame. He inched his hands down and cupped her butt cheeks. "No, but if Courtney finds out about this, you're dead," he whispered, kissing her on top of the head.

By the time the song ended, Justin needed another drink, and Jasmine seemed to think she'd succeeded at making whomever she was after jealous. He ambled back to the bar and ordered a Jack and Coke.

While he waited for his drink, he turned and noticed a redhead standing next to him. She was staring straight ahead, a mostly empty clear drink in her hand. He recognized her but couldn't decide for sure who she was. He nearly laughed with the realization that her name probably wouldn't come to him unless he saw her in her bra and panties again.

"You were in the show tonight," he said, accepting his drink from the bartender.

She nodded. She had thick, shoulder length red hair and bright green eyes. She was nearly Justin's height, but a quick glance to her feet confirmed that was only due to high heels. "Are you dating Jasmine?"

Justin coughed. "No, definitely not." He paused, knowing he

should say that he was engaged to someone else, but the words didn't come out the way he planned. Instead, he said, "We're just friends."

"Us too," she said with a coy smile. "I'm Isabela."

"I have a dog named Bella," Justin said, wondering how he was already drunk enough to blurt that out. He swallowed nervously. "Your accent is beautiful."

"Brazilian," she said. "I just moved here."

Justin had never been with a Brazilian woman, but he'd heard great things. Of course, he realized it wasn't likely that an entire nation's women were super talented in the sack, but he also figured a stereotype had to be based on something. He stuck out his hand. "Justin Erikson."

She nodded. "You're an actor, right?"

He nodded.

"Will Jasmine mind if you dance with me?" she asked.

He glanced over at Jasmine, now happily giggling and flirting with a tall guy across the room.

Justin chugged his drink and followed Isabela to the dance floor. They danced and drank together over the next hour. By the time he climbed out of the limo at the end of the night, Justin realized he wasn't at his own apartment.

"You guys are roommates?" he asked Isabela, pointing to her and Jasmine. They both nodded, and the next thing he knew, he was alone with Isabela in her bedroom.

Her shirt was on the ground, but he wasn't sure which of them had taken it off. He stared at her perfect breasts and smiled. "You've still got glitter on," he said, tracing his finger across her cleavage. She laughed and kissed him hungrily. Justin felt her hands slip under his shirt and he stepped back, pulling it off for her. She smiled and slowly unzipped her skirt.

"You were not wearing those earlier," Justin said, pointing at her ultra-skimpy thong underpants.

"I don't think I'll be wearing them later either," she said, unfastening her bra and raising his hand to her breast.

They kissed for a minute longer before Justin moved his lips to her neck, then slowly tracing his tongue along her collar bone and working his way lower.

And then he stopped, panicked. Nothing about her was familiar. She didn't smell like Courtney. She didn't taste like Courtney. And she definitely didn't feel like Courtney.

Justin stared up at Isabela, who was still gazing back seductively. He instantly felt sick. "Shit," he said, scooting back. "I've gotta go."

He glanced around the room, quickly locating his shirt and jacket and then noticed the confused look on Isabela's face. "I'm sorry. I have a girlfriend. I'm fucking engaged. I've got to go." He scrambled out of the room, out of the apartment, and started walking down the street at a brisk pace while he pulled out his phone to call a cab.

The next morning, Justin awoke to his phone ringing. He groaned, rubbed his eyes, and answered after checking the caller ID.

"Dude, you sound terrible," Keith said.

Justin cleared his throat. "You woke me up. I had a late night."

"Sorry. Want me to call back later?"

"No, I'm up now." He sat up in bed and glanced at the time. It was eleven a.m. Shit! How had he slept that late? He dragged himself out of bed and went to the bathroom to piss while Keith was talking.

Keith went over some business stuff he'd gotten from Justin's accountant and the newest stack of papers from the publicist and agent. Justin tried to listen, but none of it seemed too important, and he couldn't keep his mind from drifting to thoughts of what he'd almost done the night before.

"Have you talked to Andi?" Keith asked suddenly.

"Andi Taylor? No, why?"

"She's coming to New York for a couple days. She wanted to see if it was okay for her to stay at the apartment."

"Yeah, of course it is." Justin was relieved at this news. Andi would definitely cheer him up. And maybe she could help him figure out what he was doing with Courtney too. "Wait, why did she call you to tell you that? She could've just called my cell."

There was a long pause. "We've been talking some lately," Keith finally said.

Justin recognized that uneasy tone in Keith's voice. "Talking? You've been *talking* with Andi?" He laughed out loud, knowing exactly what Keith meant by 'talking.'

"Dude, don't fucking tell her I said anything. I mean it."

Justin laughed again. How had he not seen this coming? They were perfect for each other. "You didn't tell me anything." He paused. "But you're going to tell me everything, right?"

"Maybe after she leaves New York," he finally said. "She gets in Wednesday and leaves Friday night. Her guy is coming with her."

"Her guy?"

"Oh, you know, Jeff. Her bodyguard-slash-driver."

"Oh. Right."

"So, Justin, about your late night," Keith said.

"I can't get into it. I haven't eaten anything yet."

"That bad?"

Justin sighed. If he couldn't tell Keith, there was no one to hear his confession. He shuffled into the kitchen and started to make scrambled eggs. He was too tired to separate out the yolk, so he just dumped three whole eggs into a bowl, stirred, then plopped it into a still-cool skillet. "I drank too much and almost hooked up with a model after the fashion show."

"Jasmine?"

"No!" Justin was insulted that Keith would even think that, but then again, it was her roommate.

"What do you mean by almost?"

He scraped at the eggs in the skillet. "I went back to her place. We made out. Clothes came off. And then I left."

Keith was quiet.

Justin suddenly felt defensive. "She was one of the models in the show, so I'd already seen her in her bra and panties. It wasn't like I saw much more." Since attending the show was a legitimate activity, surely nothing that failed to surpass the limits of the show could be considered cheating.

"So her bra and panties stayed on at her place?"

Justin closed his eyes, distinctly remembering the shape of her nipple as it brushed against his bare chest. "Fuck, dude. I don't even," he sighed. "I wasn't thinking. As soon as I realized what I was doing, I left. I didn't even get my shirt back on before I left."

Keith didn't answer. Justin dumped the cooked eggs onto a plate, grabbed a fork, and began eating standing up.

"Say something, Keith."

"Like what?"

"I don't know. What are you thinking?"

"I guess I'm just surprised. I wasn't real sure how you left things with Courtney, but even if you broke up it seems soon for this, after everything you guys went through."

"Who said we broke up?"

"You're still with Courtney?"

Justin sighed. He needed coffee. "I don't know. I don't think we broke up. We're not exactly speaking now."

"What?"

"It's a mess, okay? We'll figure it out when I'm back in town." Justin glanced at the clock. He was supposed to go to another fashion event this afternoon. He still needed to shower and get dressed.

"Well, maybe don't fuck any models until you figure it out. That probably won't help your position with Courtney."

Justin had already felt pretty shitty for what he'd done, but hearing the judgment in Keith's tone was a slap on the face. Keith was his friend. He was supposed to be on Justin's side, no matter what.

"I gotta go," Justin mumbled.

WITH HER STRICT schedule of work, cry by the TV, then sleep, Courtney managed to avoid all social interaction most of the week. She wasn't necessarily trying to avoid Erica and Kaylee, but she felt better being alone. By Thursday, though, she felt ready to talk, at least if only to assure Kaylee that she didn't hate her.

Courtney came home from work at a reasonable hour and slipped into jeans. She hung her suit pants in the closet just as she heard the door open, and she knew Kaylee had returned home. She bit her lip nervously, eager to get the apology out of the way. She stood to find Kaylee in the living room, but Kaylee was already heading into the kitchen.

"Courtney," Kaylee exclaimed. "You're back."

Courtney nodded. "Justin's in New York. I'm going to be staying here for a while."

Kaylee nodded, expressionlessly, and retrieved a SoBe Tea from the fridge. "Erica told me about, you know, and I just wanted to say I'm sorry."

"Thanks." Courtney swallowed. "Do you have a minute? I wanted to talk to you." She followed Kaylee into the living room and sat beside her on the couch. Erica was curled up in the armchair across the room, pretending to read, but Courtney assumed she was listening, too.

"I actually wanted to apologize. I wasn't staying at Justin's because I don't like you. I didn't mean to give you that impression. I actually do like you, or at least what I know about you. I guess I don't know you very well, but you seem really good for Erica." Courtney sighed, desperate to stop her rambling.

"I had been planning on moving in with Justin anyway, so..." she trailed off as she realized she didn't even know if that was still going to happen. As much as she loved her independence, the thought of never living with Justin physically pained her.

Erica sat across from them on the floor. "Are you sure you're okay? You seem a lot more, I don't know, off, than I would've expected. I thought you'd be relieved to learn you weren't pregnant."

Courtney caught the glance that Kaylee shot Erica, a clear stop-being-insensitive-glare. After witnessing Erica remain single throughout law school, it was sweet, actually, to see Erica in that sort of mind-reading relationship with someone.

"Well, yeah. I was."

"You're not now?"

That hadn't been what Courtney meant, but now that she thought about it, maybe that was the truth. If she were pregnant now, she and Justin would still be together. Sure, she'd be in the same quagmire of having no time for her career, but now it seemed that she had all the time in the world for work and she was miserable. What she wanted was Justin.

Erica cleared her throat. "You seem really depressed, Courtney. Maybe if you told him you were having a hard time, he'd take a little longer off work. You don't seem like you should be alone now."

"Justin isn't speaking to me," Courtney said, her voice dry.

Erica's eyes widened, but she didn't speak.

"I finally told Justin that I hadn't wanted to keep the baby at first," Courtney admitted. "I just thought he'd feel better about the whole situation if he knew I wasn't as crushed as he thought, but instead he felt betrayed and said he can't trust me."

She wiped away a tear. "He said the whole last two months of our relationship have been a big lie and he couldn't believe I was going to have a baby just to avoid telling him the truth and then I'd resent him the rest of our lives."

"But you wouldn't have," Erica said, her eyes sad now too.

Courtney nodded. "I know. But he was mad and he said he needed some time, so I left and now he's in New York for a few more weeks."

"Wait, you didn't break up, did you?"

Courtney gazed down at her ring. "I think maybe we're taking a break. I don't know. I tried to talk to him that Saturday before he left, but he had friends over and he was drinking and smoking pot and being a total dick. So I just left my key on the table and took off. I thought maybe he'd call before he left town, but he didn't."

Erica squeezed Courtney's hand, and then they went back over each of the precise details of that day, up through the exchange of texts the Sunday he left.

Kaylee and Erica exchanged glances again. Courtney immediately regretted ratting Justin out. It had taken her a while to convince Erica that Justin wasn't the womanizing party-guy the tabloids portrayed him as, and now she'd just undone all that work.

"He's not like that normally. He really is a sweet guy," Courtney sighed. "He was a little wild before we got involved, but he's changed a lot in the past two years."

"So have you," Erica said.

Courtney didn't agree. "How so?"

Erica laughed. "When I met you, you were wearing Old Navy

sweatpants, a tee shirt from your high school, a ponytail and flip flops."

Courtney shrugged. "So?"

Kaylee started laughing. "Wait, really?"

Courtney glanced down at her outfit sheepishly. She had changed after work, but still looked decent. She'd straightened her hair, applied makeup, and was wearing designer jeans that cost close to two hundred dollars, a Banana Republic sweater and Coach ballet flats. "Okay, so I dress better now."

"And your nails," Erica said. "You used to bite them, and now you have manicures and pedicures year-round."

It wasn't a battle Courtney could win, and she didn't want Erica to notice the layers in her hair. Thank God she hadn't let Andi talk her into highlights. "Okay, you're right. I don't like looking shloompy when I'm with Justin. People photograph him all the time."

"And who pays for this new look?"

Courtney rolled her eyes. Erica knew she worked at a women's shelter—not exactly high-paying lawyer work. "You know Justin does, Erica. He also bought my car, more shoes and purses than I'd ever know what to do with, and he paid my rent. He gave me a credit card with my name on it that goes to some account where he doesn't even see the bills; his accountant just pays it."

Erica smiled smugly.

"I'm not saying you're right, though. We're not law students anymore. I didn't have money before and now I'm engaged to a guy who has loads of it. So yes, I have a higher caliber of stuff now. But that doesn't mean I'm any different."

Erica shrugged. "The old Courtney wouldn't just let a guy treat her like crap."

Courtney felt her face burning. Kaylee popped up from the

couch and mumbled something about needing to make a call as she scurried up the stairs.

"He doesn't treat me like crap," Courtney said. "And besides, you just finished implying he buys me too much stuff. Which is it, he spoils me or treats me badly?"

"I think you let him act like a jerk because of his money."

Courtney had no response to that. It was ridiculous. Justin's money had never been a part of the equation for her.

Erica's expression softened. "I'm not saying you're only with him for the money, just that you don't hold him to the same standards you might otherwise."

Courtney shrugged. "I guess I don't get what you're trying to say."

"Okay, so pretend your fiancé is just some regular guy, living in a crappy apartment in a bad neighborhood with a couple of roommates. You come home from a hard day at work just days after suffering an emotional trauma and he's grinding up against some other girls, wasted beyond recognition, smoking dope, and cursing at you. You're telling me you'd just let it go?"

Courtney nodded. "He said he was sorry."

Erica rolled her eyes. "He texted 'me too.' That's hardly a heartfelt apology."

"He's not that guy, Erica. I really hurt him, and he just, he reacted badly. Very badly. But I still love him."

"I think you could do better."

"Better than Justin Erikson?" Courtney scoffed.

"See? Listen to yourself. How can you be so sure you're not just with him because you think he's supposed to be the best? Since when does fame even matter you to?"

"It doesn't. Erica, you don't know how much easier everything would be for me if Justin were just a regular guy. I would give up the fancy car and clothes in a heartbeat if he could just blend in like anyone else."

"Then tell him that. If he really loves you, he'd give it up for you, right?"

Courtney frowned, shaking her head. "Yeah, he probably would. But then he'd be miserable. Justin loves acting. He loves being recognized. I've never met anyone else so happy with a job. I could never ask him to give up his dream just so I don't have to deal with tabloids."

Erica shrugged. "Fine, I give up. I guess I just don't get it." She moved to the couch beside Courtney.

"You do too, Erica. I've seen you with Kaylee. She makes you happy. It's the same for me with Justin." She paused. "I know it's hard for you to see because you're the one I vent to about all the crap he's done, but," she sighed. "Every time Justin looks at me, I feel like the most important person in the world. He would jump in front of a train for me. I can come home after the worst day ever and just one simple kiss from him, and none of it matters."

Courtney was crying again, but she didn't care. "I know he's not perfect, but he tries so hard. He never had money growing up, and he's just not comfortable with it. He donates a ton and then he tries to stay uninvolved with the rest, letting Keith or his accountant deal with it. But he still has it and he really doesn't know what to do with it."

"I guess that would explain the gambling," Erica said. "But what about the drinking? The weed?"

Courtney shrugged. "He normally doesn't do drugs, really. I don't know what all he might have tried in the past, but the pot last weekend was definitely an aberration. And it's not like he's an alcoholic. He'll go weeks without drinking when he's working, and then he drinks too much when he's stressed out or angry."

Erica didn't answer.

Courtney curled her knees to her chest and slumped her

head down. "I want to be mad at him still, but I just miss him so much. I hate knowing he's mad at me. I can't stand not talking to him. Why couldn't he have come by on his way to the airport and just given me a hug? He could still be angry, but at least tell me that it's going to be okay so I could stop stressing about it." She groaned and closed her eyes.

After a minute, she felt Erica gently rubbing her back. "Because he's a man, Courtney. And men don't think that way," she finally said, eliciting a small chuckle from Courtney in between tears.

After several minutes, Courtney lifted her head up. "So what do you think? I should just dump him? Break off the engagement because he has one bad day when he's pissed off about something I did?"

Erica blinked calmly several times before responding. "Maybe, maybe not. But the old Courtney would have at least talked to him. Now it's like you're just waiting around for him to forgive you or apologize."

"What if this isn't a break? What if he thinks we've broken up?"

"Do you think that's what he wants?"

"I don't know," Courtney said. "He was really upset that I hadn't told him how I felt about the baby, but I can't imagine that would be the end for him. I don't think he'd give up everything we have over one stupid lie."

"So why don't you talk to him?"

Courtney sighed. She'd thought about calling him a million times since he'd left town, and yet, so far, she hadn't. Part of her was scared to call when she didn't know what he was thinking, and part of her was worried that she did know what he was thinking, and that she just didn't want to hear it out loud.

"I can't read him over the phone. I need to see his eyes to know what he's really thinking." Courtney finally said. "He doesn't always say what he means and he can conceal whatever he's feeling with his voice."

"He is an actor," Erica said, the corners of her lips turned up in a small smile.

Courtney tried to smile back, but then another nagging thought popped into her head. "What if I'm not good for him? What if he's better off without me?" She paused. "I mean, all this stuff lately, the drinking and the partying, that's a reaction to things I did and said. If I'm not in his life, maybe it would be simpler."

Erica shook her head. "Courtney, if you're not good for him, who is?"

Courtney knew it was a rhetorical question, but an answer came to her immediately. "Andi."

"The actress you thought he was cheating with?"

She nodded. "He wasn't, for the record. They're just friends. But she's perfect for him." She sighed. "Andi's beautiful and smart and nice and funny. Dating her would do wonders for his career, and I don't think he'd have half the drama I cause since they're both on the same page with the whole publicity thing."

"But he doesn't love Andi. He loves you."

Courtney wasn't certain either of those statements were true. She knew that at least until a week ago, Justin had loved her, but she wasn't positive how he felt now. And while she believed he'd never been romantically involved with Andi, she suspected he would have at least considered a relationship with Andi if she had been open to it. Courtney still remembered, nearly two years earlier, when Andi told her Justin wasn't her type.

"Courtney?"

Courtney turned to Erica, aware that she'd spaced out for a minute.

"Why don't you fly to New York to talk to him?"

21

The first two days Andi was in New York, Justin was so busy with filming that he didn't even see her. He noticed signs of her around the apartment, like a half empty mug of tea on the coffee table, luggage in the closet of the second bedroom, and small grey slippers beside the couch. But it wasn't until the third day that they were both awake in the apartment at the same time.

So naturally, they ordered takeout.

They busied themselves sharing details of work and other small talk until the food arrived and was divvied up, but then Andi went in for the kill.

"How's Courtney doing?" Andi's tone was nonchalant, but Justin knew Keith had probably told her some details already.

He shrugged. He honestly didn't know how she was doing.

She plopped two plates down on the table. They began to eat quietly.

"You're not going to tell me what's going on with you and Courtney?" she finally asked.

Justin glanced at her. "Depends. Are you going to tell me what's going on with you and Keith?"

Andi smiled. "Touché." She chewed a bite of fish. "And no, I wasn't going to, because I'm sure Keith already told you."

Justin shook his head. "He didn't tell me anything."

"He obviously told you enough to make you ask."

He sighed. "I haven't spoken to Courtney since I got here. We had a fight before I left. She moved out."

Andi's expression didn't alter. "Keith told me all that. What was the fight over?"

Justin hadn't told anyone this yet. "I found out she had thought about getting an abortion but never told me. She was just going to have a baby she didn't want, just because she thought I wanted her to."

Andi sipped her water daintily. "I wouldn't want a baby if I got pregnant now. It's not that unreasonable of a position. Besides, none of that matters. She wasn't actually pregnant, right?"

"She should've told me. She can't seriously be planning on marrying me if she can't even be straight with me."

Andi chuckled.

"What?"

She hesitated. "You have that adorable little doe-eyed expression, and I saw the way you looked at her when you thought she was pregnant. Telling you she didn't want your baby probably would be a lot like shooting Bambi's mom."

Justin exhaled an exaggerated sigh.

"Fine. I'm just saying," Andi said.

They continued to eat in silence for a minute.

"Wait, so are you still getting married?"

Justin shrugged.

This clearly surprised Andi. "Wow, really?"

"I haven't talked to her. I don't know." He paused. "She still has the ring. That seems like a good sign, right?"

Andi frowned. "So you still want to marry her, but you don't know if she wants to?"

"I'm still mad, or, I don't know, hurt? She's always been honest with me, and this time, when it mattered more than ever, she wasn't. But I tried to move on and it didn't feel right. I don't want to be single and I don't want to date anyone else. I just want things with Courtney the way they were before...everything."

"Why do you like her so much?"

He rolled his eyes. "You like her too."

"I'm trying to be helpful Justin, but I can't give you the woman's perspective on this if you won't talk to me. Tell me what you like about her."

"She's nice. Not just in that generic way, but really nice, to everyone. She's really aware of how things impact other people." He paused before continuing.

"She's funny, honest, and she likes sports. She's not judgmental or preachy. She's beautiful, obviously. And it doesn't hurt that she'll have sex with me whenever I want."

"Justin, nearly any woman would have sex with you whenever you want," Andi interrupted.

He rested his fork on the plate. "You wouldn't."

Her jaw dropped. "I never said that. And besides, it was years ago. I hardly knew you, and you were with Kinzie then."

"You said I wasn't your type and you didn't trust me."

"Both true statements," she said with a smile.

"Keith is your type, though."

"I like Keith. He's a sweetheart." She paused and raised her eyebrows. "But, of course, you already know that."

Justin laughed. Keith and Andi made perfect sense as a couple, and he wondered why he'd never seen it before. He didn't even want to think about what would happen when they broke up, though. They were two of Justin's closest friends, and he wasn't good at awkward situations.

"Don't worry, Justin. Keith's a big boy. He can take care of himself. And I promise I'll be nice."

He smiled and took both of their plates to the kitchen, rinsing them and dumping them into the dishwasher. When he turned around, Andi was gone. He poured himself a drink, took a shower, and then collapsed into bed in his sweatpants and a tee shirt. He figured he should go over his lines for the next day, but he was exhausted. He closed his eyes for a moment, and apparently he fell asleep.

Justin awoke suddenly and turned to see Andi stretched out beside him. She had snatched the script out of his hands and was shooting him a condescending stare. She had changed into her pajamas as well, and had placed a tall glass of water on the nightstand beside the bed.

"I'm betting you're supposed to be reading this, not snoozing," she said.

He smiled, guilty as charged.

Andi sighed. "Come on, sit up. I'll practice with you."

He sat up and rubbed his eyes. He'd been so messed up about the whole Courtney thing that he just hadn't been sleeping well lately. But Andi was right, he did need to learn his lines.

Andi went over the first page with him, then paused.

"What?" he asked. It was clear she was thinking something.

She rested her hand atop his. "I think you should marry Courtney."

"Do you think I should call her?"

Andi considered this, then shook her head. "Keith said you were a total jerk before she moved out. Actually, he didn't call you a jerk. He said something much worse, but I'm a lady and I can't repeat that."

Justin winced, praying Keith hadn't told Andi everything.

"I think you should give her a little more time, and then tell her how you feel. I've seen how she looks at you, so I'm sure she'll forgive you." She paused. "But you need to make sure you forgive her by then, too."

He kissed her on the cheek. "You're a good friend," he said. "But if you fuck over Keith, I'll slip Nair in your shampoo."

She smiled and returned to the script.

FOR A SMALL FEE, Courtney was able to change the ticket she originally had to visit Justin so she could depart immediately. As soon as Courtney's flight landed, she caught a cab to Justin's apartment. She rehearsed her apology during the entire cab ride, taking a deep breath and excitedly climbing out when they pulled up to the curb. She climbed up the large stone steps to the main door of the building and smiled at the doorman, then froze. She didn't even know what floor Justin's apartment was on.

"Can I help you, Miss?" the man at the counter asked.

She nodded and stepped closer. The man's name tag read "Jerry." Not exactly the stereotypical doorman name. "Yeah, I just flew in to surprise my fiancé and I know his apartment number, but I'm not sure which floor it's on."

Jerry nodded. "What's his name?"

Courtney froze. Obviously she knew his name, but what she didn't know was what name he'd used for the apartment. Surely it was in his real name, right? But if it wasn't and she blew his cover, well, then she'd feel horrible. "It's number 1805," she finally said instead, resting her hand on the counter.

"That's the fifth floor," Jerry said, his eyes darting down to her massive ring.

"Great, thanks," she said, picking up her bag.

"He's not in now, though. Do you have a key?"

"Oh. No." She had known there was a good chance he wouldn't be there, and that was the main reason she'd been tempted to call first.

"I can let you in if he authorizes it."

Courtney shook her head. "I really wanted to surprise him."

Jerry shrugged.

"You don't happen to know where he went or how long he'll be, do you?"

He shook his head. "He was with Ms. Taylor, though."

Courtney frowned, not having realized Andi was in town, too. She remembered seeing a coffee shop up the block and decided to head there. Hopefully she could watch for their car from there.

Courtney ordered a decaf white chocolate latte and plopped down at a table by the window. Glancing around the place, Courtney felt out of place. There were three couples, clearly on dates, and two guys seated separately, both wearing headphones and engrossed in work. She rummaged in her bag and pulled out her book. She tried to read but quickly grew restless and instead decided she should keep an eye out for Justin.

By the time she finished her coffee, Courtney was exhausted. She left the shop, hoping the fresh air would invigorate her by the time she returned to the apartment building to check if Justin had returned without her noticing.

Luckily, right then, a black town car pulled up to the curb in front of the building and a man stepped out of the driver's seat. It was dark, but the car was only about twenty yards away, and Courtney had a strong hunch that the man was Andi's driver. She watched eagerly, and sure enough, a small-framed brunette stepped out of the car. Seconds later, a man climbed out, too. Courtney was certain that it was Justin. She nearly shouted out to him, but before could say anything, he had wrapped his arm tightly around Andi's shoulder.

Courtney froze, watching with a perverse intrigue as Andi and Justin both laughed, glanced up at the sky, and laughed again. And then Justin kissed Andi on the cheek, swept her up into his arms, and dashed into the building carrying her. Courtney swallowed the lump rising in her throat and realized she'd been clenching her hands together, causing her diamond to press into her middle finger and pinky, leaving a jagged outline of its shape on both fingers.

Why was the image so unsettling? She knew they were friends. Close friends. And Justin was a physical guy. Him kissing Andi on the cheek probably meant nothing. That was just how he greeted female friends. She just needed to go in and say what she'd planned to say. So why weren't her feet moving?

Courtney reached her hand to wipe a tear off her cheek and realized the dampness on her face wasn't just tears—it was raining. Andi's driver climbed back into the car, but he didn't drive away. That must've meant Andi wasn't staying the night. Of course, even if Andi didn't come back out, that didn't mean anything. It was her apartment too.

She had no proof that Justin had done anything wrong, yet an icky feeling flooded her body. Courtney scurried towards the car and tapped on the driver's window. He rolled it down slowly.

"Hi, I don't know if you remember me, but I'm Courtney. I'm a friend of Andi's."

His face remained expressionless. "She's inside."

Courtney nodded. "I'm sorry, I don't remember your name."

"Jeff."

"Right, thanks. Do you remember me?"

Jeff stared at her for a long moment. "You're Justin's girlfriend?"

"Fiancée," she corrected.

"He's inside too." He began to roll up the window.

"Wait!" Courtney stuck her hand in the window. Jeff's eyes

widened with irritation. She backed her hand away. "Sorry. I actually had a question for you, though."

He waited expectantly.

"Justin and I sort of had this big fight before he went to New York, and we haven't been talking, and so I just flew out here today to apologize and, you know, reconcile. And I was waiting in a coffee shop over there so I saw when you pulled up and I saw him and Andi get out."

"So you already know they are inside?" The tone of his voice displayed confused irritation that she was talking to him despite that knowledge.

Courtney frowned. "Do you know what they're up to? I mean, were they acting normal? Did they seem like friends to you?"

"Why don't I call Miss Taylor and tell her you're here?" He started to push a button on his phone.

"No, don't!" she shrieked, startling him into dropping the phone. "Sorry," she mumbled. "I really wanted to surprise Justin."

His eyes narrowed. "If you're going to her apartment, I'm going to call her and let her know."

"Is that because you're afraid I'd be interrupting something?"

"It's because that's my job," he said.

"Right, I know you're like her bodyguard or whatever, but it's not like she needs protection when she's inside her own apartment, right?"

"I work for her. I think she'd like to know if you're on your way up, so I am going to call her."

Courtney considered this. "Okay, if I go up, you can call. But can I ask you a question first?"

"The car interior is getting wet," he said.

"Do you want me to get in?"

"No!"

"Okay. I just want to know if there's something going on with Andi and Justin."

His face was blank.

"I promise I'll go away if you just tell me."

"I don't follow Miss Andrea's personal life."

Courtney rolled her eyes. The man was with her constantly. Obviously, he knew every detail of her personal life.

"Please. I flew here all the way from L.A. I saw him carry Andi inside and they looked, well, they looked like Justin wasn't exactly waiting around for me. I just wanted to surprise him. I don't want to go up there and, um, interrupt him, though."

He sighed. "I'm taking Miss Taylor to the airport late tonight. You can surprise whomever you want after we leave."

Courtney turned, leaning against the wet car. She heard Jeff clear his throat loudly. "I know, I know. I'm going," she mumbled. "I just have to figure out where I'm going. I don't know my way around New York, and I don't have money for a hotel." She still had Justin's credit card, but no way was she going to rely on him financially if he had moved on.

"I can call you a cab," Jeff said, his tone hopeful.

She nodded and searched for her brother's contact info in her phone. She called him, but he didn't answer. Hopefully, he was just asleep and not out of town. The cab arrived before she had time to worry, so she gave the driver the address, thanked Jeff and left.

By the time the cab pulled up to Jack's building, Courtney was a mess. She couldn't stop crying and she hated the feeling that she had no one to blame but herself for her current situation.

She glanced up and noticed the cab driver eying her warily. She wiped her nose on her jacket sleeve, lacking a tissue, and sniffled loudly.

The driver told her the fare and her eyes widened. If she

gave him that, she'd have virtually no cash left, which didn't seem like a good thing since she was alone in New York City at night. "Hang on," she mumbled, dialing her brother again. Thankfully, this time, he answered.

"Courtney, do you have any idea what time it is here?" he said when he answered. "It's nearly eleven o'clock."

"Sorry. I called earlier, but..."

"Can I call you back tomorrow morning?" he interrupted.

"Um, well, actually, I'm here, and I..."

"You're where?"

"Here. In New York. Outside your apartment."

"What? You're outside my building?"

She glanced up and saw a half-dressed man pull the curtain back and stare out the window. She waved tentatively. "Can I, um, borrow some money for the cab?"

There was a long silence. "Yeah, I'll be down in a minute. Let me grab a shirt."

He hung up and she climbed out of the cab. It had stopped raining, at least. A moment later, Jack appeared. Although she hadn't seen her brother for nearly six months, he looked about the same—tall, clean shaven, with short brown hair. He was wearing suit pants and a tee shirt and looked tired. He leaned in the cab window, paid the driver, then turned to her.

"They take credit cards, you know."

Courtney winced. She hadn't known that, actually. In L.A., she either drove her own car or used the drivers Justin kept on retainer. "I'm sorry it's so late. Were you asleep?"

He shook his head, and she sensed some hesitation. Instead of explaining, though, he grabbed her bag and started back inside.

"You look terrible," he said. "What happened?"

Courtney sighed. She didn't know how to answer that. Honestly, she didn't know exactly what happened, or where to even begin thinking about it, but also, she wasn't sure she could even tell him. Jack was four years older than her, and they didn't have the sort of relationship where they'd share dating failures with each other. Of course, until about a minute ago, they also didn't have the type of relationship where they'd just show up at each other's house unannounced in the middle of the night.

He showed her into his apartment. "Do you want a drink?"

"You mean like coffee or booze?"

Jack laughed. "Either."

"Alcohol would be good."

He showed her to the cabinet, and she selected a bottle of vodka. He mixed it with some OJ and was just handing her the glass when Courtney sensed someone behind her. She jumped and turned abruptly, coming face to face with a cute blonde.

"Kelly, this is my baby sister Courtney. Courtney, this is Kelly."

Courtney stood, flustered. "Oh, I'm sorry. I didn't realize you had company. I can go."

"Where? You obviously have no place to go, or you wouldn't have come here," Jack said. "Anyway, it's fine. Now you get to meet Kelly."

The woman smiled. She looked a couple years older than Courtney with a medium build, a pleasant smile, and her blonde hair pulled back into a tight ponytail. She was wearing boxer shorts and a tee shirt, both of which appeared to belong to Courtney's brother. Clearly, she'd interrupted something much more interesting than sleep.

"Nice to meet you," Kelly said.

"You too. I'm really sorry to barge in here." Courtney said.

"I didn't even know you were coming to New York," Jack said.

Courtney snorted. "Me neither, until earlier today. I decided I wanted to surprise Justin, so I bought a ticket and flew out here on a whim."

"Did you change your mind about surprising him?"

Courtney took a generous sip from her drink. "Yeah, you could say that." She noticed Jack and Kelly exchange a familiar stare and felt even more uncomfortable. How long had her brother been seeing this woman, and why didn't she even know about it? Had she really been that caught up in her own life?

"Give me just a minute, Courtney. Make yourself comfortable." Jack stepped into the bedroom with Kelly, closing the door behind him.

Courtney poured herself a second drink and then, finding a box of herbal tea in the cabinet, microwaved a mug of water so she could have some tea to relax as soon as she was comfortably buzzed.

Jack returned alone to find Courtney on the couch, clutching the tea in her hands.

"There's a guest room, you know," he said. "You can stay here as long as you want."

"Thanks. I'll probably fly out tomorrow, though."

He nodded and sat down on the chair across from her.

And then, without warning, Courtney burst into tears again. Jack scooted over to the couch, uncomfortably slinging his arm around her. "I think Justin's sleeping with Andrea Taylor," she finally blurted out.

"Andrea Taylor the actress?" Kelly asked, apparently having emerged from the bedroom for a glass of water without Courtney noticing.

Courtney nodded, ignoring the look of amazement on Kate's face.

Jack cleared his throat. "Kelly, um, Courtney's engaged to Justin Erikson, the actor." He turned to Courtney. "You are still engaged, right?"

Courtney shrugged, waving her ring finger in the air.

"I'll give you guys some privacy," Kelly said, backing into the bedroom.

Within minutes, Courtney had blabbed the whole crazy story to Jack. He was quiet the entire time, and he didn't speak for a minute or two after she paused.

"Courtney, I'm sorry. I didn't even know you thought you were pregnant."

"I didn't really tell anyone."

"Did Mom and Dad know?"

"No. I didn't even tell Justin, so of course I didn't tell them."

He grimaced. "So you came out here to apologize to him and found him and Andrea..."

"I didn't catch them in the act, or anything. They just seemed a little too cozy."

"And you're sure he was bringing her up to his apartment?"

"It's technically her apartment too."

He choked on his drink. "Wait, he lives with her?"

"It's a nice apartment. They're just roommates." She paused. "Or at least they were."

"But you didn't confront him, so does he even know you're in town?"

She shook her head. "I don't know what to do."

"What do you want to do?"

"I want to fly home and pretend this never happened. Maybe I'll call him tomorrow and apologize over the phone."

"Wait, so you still want to marry him?" Jack's tone did little to hide his opinion.

"If he fooled around with Andi, it's my fault. I mean, I was a total basket case, and then we had a big fight and I forced him away. We're technically on a break or something." She cringed. "I don't even know if he'd want to marry me anymore. Maybe he'd be better off with Andi. They do make a cute couple. And I think it would be easier for them, since they have so much in common."

Jack's judgmental expression didn't alter.

She rolled her eyes. "Oh, come on Jack. I'm just being honest. What do you want me to say?"

He sighed. "Look, Courtney, honestly I see what you're saying. I mean, I know tons of people that have either cheated or been cheated on and they stay married, but that's different. They're already married. And if you're saying you were on a break, then I guess there's the argument that he wasn't even cheating."

He paused. "But this is you, Courtney. I know we don't talk that often, but you've never struck me as the type to just look the other way. And it only complicates things that he's so famous and always traveling. How are you going to feel if you do marry the guy and then in five years read in a tabloid all about some other affair he's had?"

She nodded solemnly, not actually needing his input. She already realized she was a fool for thinking things could ever work out between her and Justin. They were two worlds apart to start with, and now that she'd hurt him, he'd never forgive her.

"You should get some sleep. Thanks for letting me crash here."

JUSTIN WENT to bed as soon as Andi left, but he couldn't fall asleep. It wasn't the time change; he'd already been in New York for nearly two weeks, giving him more than enough time to adjust. He just had a lot on his mind. It didn't help that the entire weekend loomed in front of him, completely empty, the first opportunity he'd had since leaving L.A. to even think about the shambles of his personal life.

He wished Andi could've stayed longer. When he was with Andi, Justin didn't feel so lonely. Somehow, Andi managed to make him laugh again, something that had been so absent from his life the past few weeks that he'd nearly forgotten the sound of his own laughter.

Justin kept replaying part of his conversation with her in his head. Instead of comforting him when he detailed Courtney's plan to simply have a baby she didn't want without ever telling him the truth, Andi had simply shrugged, saying she would've just had an abortion without telling the guy if it'd been her.

He had shuddered at the thought. Justin could never imagine Courtney doing something like that without talking to him first.

Justin sighed and flipped onto his left side, squishing the pillow before plopping his head back onto it. He still couldn't believe Courtney hadn't told him her worries about a baby. She told him everything. That was their thing—communication. Even when they were apart, they always told each other anything and everything. Except lately.

Andi said he should give Courtney time. His instincts told him to call her, but Andi was insistent. "She's been through a lot," she'd said. "And you're a lot to handle. Give the poor girl some time."

Justin never pegged himself as a handful, but his mom would probably agree with Andi. Still, it didn't seem right that he wasn't even talking with his fiancée. And he hated not knowing if she even felt the same way. Justin reached for his phone and tweeted "can't sleep," desperately hoping Courtney would happen to see it and call him. Instead, some random girl with a photo of her dog as her profile picture replied to let him know he was "super hawt." Great.

22

———

A week later, Justin was back home. After weeks away, he had plenty to catch up on around the house, so he was able to keep his mind off Courtney for the first day. He posted on social media often upon his return, though, making it abundantly clear that he was back in hopes that she'd take the first step.

On his second day back, he was scheduled to do a public appearance and interview at a nearby mall. He used to love that sort of publicity stunt, where he could really interact with the fans, but lately, it just seemed like a hassle.

"You got a package," Keith said as he walked in from the gym.

"Leave it on the counter there," Justin replied, heading upstairs to shower. His interview wasn't until four that afternoon, but he planned on doing some shopping before and then getting there early to do autographs.

"It's from Courtney," Keith said, his voice strange.

Justin stopped short of the top step. He paused, then retreated down the stairs. Keith handed it to him, along with

249

scissors. He turned the box over in his hand. His address was there, but not his name, and there was no postage.

"Did she drop it off herself?"

Keith shook his head. "A courier. I had to sign for it."

He sliced the box open and glanced inside. There was no note, just another small box, which Justin didn't need to open to know was her engagement ring. He threw the box onto the counter.

"Damn it!" He jogged back upstairs and stepped into the shower without waiting for the water to heat up.

An hour later, he was dressed and ready to go. He hurried down the stairs and into the kitchen, made a sandwich, and scarfed it down in record speed. No way was he going to dawdle long enough to change his mind.

"Am I okay to wear this to the interview?" he asked Keith.

Keith nodded and shrugged. "Yeah, you look good. I thought you were coming back here first, though, so I could drive."

Justin shook his head. "I'll meet you there," he said, snatching the ring box out of the package and wedging it into his pocket.

"Are you sure this is a good idea?" Keith asked, popping out of his chair and following Justin to the door.

Justin snorted. "No." He opened the front door.

"You already told people you'd be there early to sign autographs," Keith reminded him. "Don't be late."

He drove straight to the shelter, speeding more than he should have and running a fair share of orange lights. He parked the Audi and scurried into the building, knowing his hat and sunglasses weren't a foolproof disguise. He started back to Courtney's office when he realized there was a new receptionist.

"Can I help you?" she asked, her voice trailing off to a mere whisper by the end of the question, her cheeks turning a crimson shade nearly matching her shirt.

Justin was in no mood to be charming. "I need to see Courtney. Is she in?"

"Courtney..." The receptionist paused for him to supply the full name.

He was fairly certain there was only one Courtney at the shelter's business office, especially since they had less than ten employees there anyway. "Courtney Robbins."

The receptionist nodded, fumbling with the phone. "Um, who should I say is here?"

Now he openly rolled his eyes. This was getting ridiculous. He tugged off his sunglasses. "Charlie Brown," he replied dryly.

The girl cleared her throat and spoke into the intercom. "Um, Courtney, you have someone here to see you," she said timidly.

Justin couldn't hear Courtney's response, but he was growing irritated. "Can I just go back there?"

"She'll be out in a minute," the girl replied, shaking her head nervously.

He tapped his foot impatiently, then checked his phone. Aside from a text from Keith reading "Dude..." there was nothing of interest. Justin wondered if Keith knew what he was really about to do, or if he just assumed based on his familiarity with Justin that it had to be something he'd regret.

He turned right as Courtney appeared. She had a mug of coffee in her hand, and looked very lawyerly, with a black suit skirt and pale pink blouse. Her hair was pinned up.

"Justin," she said quietly and without emotion, as though answering a question.

"Hey," he replied.

They stared awkwardly at each other, Justin acutely aware that the receptionist was still gawking at them.

He finally realized she was waiting for him to talk. "I got your package," he said.

She glanced down. "Oh, right. Sorry it took me so long to get it back to you."

"I don't want it."

She faced him again, confused.

"I gave it to you. It's yours," he said, walking closer and holding the small box out for her to take.

Courtney didn't move. "Technically speaking, since we didn't get married, I'm supposed to give it back."

Justin wasn't sure what to make of that. It was very Courtney-esque to know the proper legal procedure for dumping someone, but her response also seemed to suggest she didn't really want to give it back.

"Well, I'm telling you to keep it, so..." he picked up her hand and placed the box there, folding her fingers up over it.

"Justin, I'm just not sure I should..." Her voice crackled and her bright eyes were starting to tear up.

"Look, Courtney, I gave it to you, and there's no one else I want to have it. If you don't want to keep it, sell it." He'd intended to storm off after this line, but instead he found himself frozen, staring back at her sad, blue eyes.

He willed her to speak, to move, to do anything at all, but she just stood there, too.

Finally, he ran his thumb gently under her eye, wiping a tear off, and took a deep breath. And then he turned and left, wondering if that was the last time he'd ever see her.

If he hadn't had a full schedule that day, his next step would have been to drink. Justin was definitely in no mood to shop before his publicity appearance, so that left him with more than an hour to kill before he needed to head over to the plaza.

His phone buzzed. It was another text from Keith, different from the first only in punctuation, reading "Dude?"

He started the car and called Keith to meet him for a drink

before the appearance. At least if Keith was with him, Justin wouldn't be allowed to go overboard.

Two drinks, three breath mints and ninety minutes later, Justin was in the courtyard of an outdoor shopping mall. They hadn't finished roping off a clear line for fans waiting for photos and autographs when he first arrived, so Keith stood beside him along with the two security guards there for crowd control. Justin smiled till his cheeks hurt, wondering if his grin looked as unnatural as it felt today. He posed for countless photographs, wrapping his arm around the girl requesting each photo, and signed photos of himself until his hand cramped up.

Normally, Justin liked this sort of appearance. It was exactly the kind of attention he craved, combined with an abundance of cute ladies he could harmlessly flirt with. Today though, he wasn't feeling it. He wasn't in the mood to be cheery, and he'd never been great at faking that.

"Can I get a picture of you with my daughter?" A woman asked, catching his attention. She didn't look much older than him, but she was holding a young toddler. The little girl had a head full of curly brown hair and bright blue eyes.

Justin glanced up, catching the panicked look in Keith's eyes. Yeah, like he was going to lose it over a stupid baby that happened to have blue eyes. He nodded at the woman and accepted the toddler. He tried, unsuccessfully, to get her to smile at her mother, or even to look in the direction of the camera, but instead the kid just gazed right at him. The mom snapped a photo anyway, and he started to hand back the child, but she held tight to his necklace, nearly ripping it off. The mom looked mortified, but Justin just laughed. It was nice to have a distraction.

He crouched down to sign two more autographs before standing and stretching his neck side to side. Then, out of the corner of his eye, he caught a glimpse of dark brown hair in the back of the crowd. The girl had her back turned to him and was saying something to the security guard, clearly hoping to bypass the line. He rose to his toes and as soon as he saw a corner of the girl's pale pink blouse, he knew it was Courtney.

He turned and tried to get Keith's attention, but Keith was engaged in some in-depth discussion with Jamie and didn't see him. Frustrated, he tried Keith's cell, but he didn't even answer. Keith was less than fifteen feet away, but about a hundred women stood between them, making it virtually impossible for Justin to reach him on foot. He didn't want to risk Courtney leaving before he even found out why she was here.

He turned to the fans standing closest to him. "Hey, guys, I'm trying to get my friend's attention, the guy with the dark, curly hair over there," he gestured. A few of them turned to see him, but the rest just stared at Justin, seemingly excited that he was saying something real. "On the count of three, can you help me out and yell 'yo Keith'?" Several nodded, so he counted, and they all yelled together.

It worked.

Keith laughed, then came over to Justin. "What's up?"

Justin nodded his head in Courtney's direction. Keith turned and immediately saw her.

"Did you know she was coming?"

"No, but I don't want her to leave. Can you get her closer?"

Keith nodded, then started off through the crowd. Justin signed a few more autographs, and then Courtney was there.

"Hey guys, I need a quick break, and then I will be ready to sign some more autographs here right after the interview, so stick around," he said to his fans.

He grabbed Courtney by the hand and pulled her off to the corner where Keith had pointed, a security guard planted nearby to keep people from following. He dropped her hand as soon as they were out of earshot of the crowd.

"I didn't expect to see you here," he said. He noticed she had unclipped her hair, letting it hang in loose waves over her shoulders.

"Maybe I wanted an autograph," she teased.

He wasn't sure what to say. She nervously glanced down, then back up at him. She reached into the purse and pulled something out. Justin felt a knot in his stomach. If she'd driven all the way over here just to give him that fucking ring again, he'd probably toss it into the damn crowd.

But she didn't show him what was in her hand. Instead, she spoke. "Justin, I just wanted to tell you I'm sorry. I really screwed things up this time and I know you're mad at me, and I hate knowing it's probably too late to fix it."

"I'm not mad at you," he heard himself say, surprised at how much he meant it.

"All I ever wanted was to make you happy, and that's the only reason I didn't tell you how I felt about the baby from the start. You were so sweet whenever you talked about us having kids that it just made me fall more in love with you, and then once I saw how excited you were, I didn't want to ruin it. If I'd actually been pregnant..." she paused, "I mean, if it had turned out differently, I wouldn't have resented you. I know that. I would've been happy."

Her voice wavered and he saw that she was crying. Again.

She sniffled, then continued. "I pictured her just how you did, and I still sometimes have these dreams where we're together and we have the baby and we're just so happy. I still want that someday. I want children. With you. I know you'd be the best dad, and..."

Courtney stopped abruptly right before a tap on the shoulder caused Justin to jump in the air. It was Jamie.

"You're on in less than five minutes, Justin. They need you now."

He turned to Jamie. "Two minutes." He must have looked serious, because for the first time ever, his publicist listened to him without a fight.

"I shouldn't have come here," Courtney mumbled apologetically.

"It's fine," he said, his tone impossible to read.

She took a deep breath, knowing she had to hurry up. "I just wanted you to know that I'm sorry, and that I still want that with you. I came to New York last week to tell you that, but when I was waiting outside your apartment I saw you and Andi..." her voice trailed off. "Look, I don't even care about whatever happened with Andi. I still love you, and none of that matters."

Jamie reappeared just then. "Let's go, you're on," she said to Justin, tugging at his arm.

Justin turned back to her, his expression a combination of confusion and panic. He shook Jamie's hand off him. "You were in New York? Why didn't you come see me?"

She hesitated. "I went by the apartment to talk to you, to apologize, but Andi was there. I ran into her driver outside."

"Justin," Jamie repeated, now bordering on irate.

"Hang on," he snapped at Jamie. "Courtney, nothing happened with Andi. She was only in town a couple nights. She took me out to dinner one night to cheer me up. She told me I was being a jerk and should give you some time and then beg you to take me back."

Courtney knew she was blushing now, wondering how she could have ever thought anything else had happened.

"I thought we were on a break, not broken up." He sounded flustered. "Wait, so what you saw with Andi, is that why you gave me the ring back?"

She nodded, and dropped the ring into his hand. "Justin, I only want to keep it if I'm wearing it. I can't bear to have it if we're not getting married, if you're not even speaking to me. It hurts too much to have that reminder of everything I messed up."

Before he could answer, Jamie dragged him away.

"We'll discuss that later," Jamie snarled at Justin before escorting him in front of the cameras where a chipper, thirty-something blonde was waiting with a microphone.

Courtney watched nervously, her hand feeling numb from squeezing tightly around the ring as she held it. She startled as someone patted her shoulder. It was Keith. He smiled knowingly, handed her a tissue, then nodded for her to follow him closer to the stage. They stood off to the side of the makeshift stage, about ten feet from where the informal interview was being conducted. Courtney noticed that, in addition to the TV program's cameras, there were dozens of fans filming on their phones.

If Justin was distracted by their conversation, he didn't show it. He was upbeat and charming with the interviewer, the answers rolling off his tongue like he'd rehearsed it. Courtney tried to listen to the interview, rather than focusing on the fact that she'd just made it through most of what she'd planned to say and that he'd said nothing in return.

Justin started pacing with the mic while telling a story about his childhood. It was one she'd heard before, about a fight he and his brothers had over turkey drumsticks. When he finished the story, and the audience laughed, Justin jogged off to the side quickly. He spun Courtney so they were facing away from the cameras, and leaned in so close that she could feel his lips on her ear as he whispered.

"Then I think you should be wearing it," was all he said.

Then he pinched her hand and scampered back on stage, apologizing briefly.

Courtney was confused, and as soon as she glanced up and saw the look Jamie was shooting at Justin, she was a little scared too. Then she glanced down and realized he hadn't been pinching her—he was putting her ring back on her finger.

She felt instantly lighter, and a little dizzy too. She caught Justin's eye and saw his dimples flashing as he aimed that perfect grin right at her. Courtney covered the ring with her hand, as though she feared it would fall off, and then scraped her thumb along the stone, the pale red scratch along her skin the validating proof that her diamond was really back where it belonged, and that he'd put it there.

She felt a hand on her back and nearly laughed to see it was Keith nervously steadying her. Courtney wondered if she really looked that dazed, that close to fainting, or if it had just been so long since anyone had seen her truly happy that they weren't sure what the expression looked like.

Courtney tuned back in as the interviewer thanked Justin for his time, and he flashed one more grin at the audience before jogging back to her.

"It looks good there," he said, clasping her hands in his. "I'll let you keep it if you promise never ever to take it off again." He paused and leaned forward. "No matter what."

Courtney smiled haplessly, wishing so desperately that she could kiss him without causing even more of a nightmare for his publicist. "What if it needs a cleaning?" she asked.

His eyes narrowed. "Fine, but I don't ever want to open my mail and find that sucker in it. Deal?"

She nodded. "So you still want to marry me?"

"Of course. I'll marry you right now if you want. I bet there's an ordained minister somewhere in this crowd," he teased, glancing around.

Courtney smiled and bit her lip, too elated to speak.

He laughed, shaking his head. "I can't believe you thought I moved on to Andi. Courtney, I haven't stopped thinking about you. I mean, I was pissed, but mostly I just felt bad that you didn't think you could talk to me about something." He kissed her forehead. "I missed you so much."

She smiled. "I missed you too. I just, well, I thought you didn't love me anymore. I wanted to make things easier on you."

"Courtney, I think I've always loved you, and I know I always will love you."

"Oh, Justin, I love you too. So much." Courtney realized people were starting to stare at them. She hoped they couldn't hear, but she wasn't sure. "I want to marry you more than anything. I want to raise children with you."

"Six?" he asked, a sly grin on his face.

She winced. "Two. Okay, maybe three if you promise they'll never fight over turkey legs."

But Justin didn't answer. He wrapped his arms around her back and kissed her hard and long, squeezing her so tightly that she could barely catch her breath, then lifting her toes off the ground. Courtney heard wild shrieking, clapping and whistling, but she didn't even care. When he finally set her back down, Courtney couldn't stop smiling. Justin delicately kissed her left hand, winked, then made his way back over to where he was signing autographs. The crazed squeals from the audience increased.

Justin glanced at Courtney again, and she realized proudly that he was blushing. "Sorry guys, I just had to finish up a little chat with my number one fan over there."

23

s soon as Justin finished signing a respectable number of autographs, he grabbed Courtney by the hand.

"Let's get out of here," he whispered.

She hesitated, just long enough for him to pray she wasn't going to insist on returning to work for the day. That just wouldn't fit with what Justin had planned.

He waved to Keith, but intentionally dodged Jamie's glares. He was already on her shit list, so what difference would it make if he skipped out without chatting with her? He pulled Courtney closer as they stepped outside. Keith caught up to them just in time to point in the direction of the SUV waiting to drive them.

"Where are you going?" Keith asked, holding the door open and using his body as a barricade between the fans who'd followed them out. "When will you be back?"

"Don't know, Mom," Justin replied, pulling the door shut. He whispered directions to the driver, switched his phone to vibrate, and snuggled closer to Courtney.

"I'm not dreaming, am I?"

She smiled. "Keith and your publicist didn't look very happy to see you sneak off."

"Do I look like I care?" Justin knew he was still grinning. He was smiling so hard his cheeks hurt.

Courtney shook her head. "So do I get to know where we're going?"

Just then the vehicle slowed.

"We're here. Aren't I romantic?" Justin joked as she saw that he'd taken her to a hotel, of all places. Then he realized he probably couldn't walk in and get a room without someone recognizing him.

"Crap," Justin mumbled out loud.

Courtney leaned in and kissed him, soft and slow. "I'll check in, and I'll text you the room number."

"I don't want you to have to pay," he began, reaching for his wallet.

She flashed her sparkling blue eyes at him. "Seriously, Justin?"

He fidgeted in the backseat for about five minutes, waiting for her text. Justin received—and ignored—two calls and three other texts before Courtney finally wrote. Jamie had clearly figured out Justin was going off the grid for a few hours and she wasn't happy. The second Courtney's number popped up, Justin flew out of the car and zipped through the lobby so fast he didn't notice if anyone was staring.

She opened the hotel room door right as Justin reached it, and within seconds his mouth was on hers and their bodies were pressed against the closed door. "God, I missed you," he said, sliding his hands up the back of her blouse, feeling the smooth skin on the small of her back.

Courtney followed suit, leading her hands up his shirt, then eagerly tugging it off. Justin picked her up and carried her to the bed, careful not to crush her as they collapsed onto it together.

Justin missed kissing her more than anything, but he had a more pressing need that was distracting him from fully focusing on her luscious lips and soft tongue. He rose to his knees, unfastening his pants before working on undressing Courtney. She happily complied, and within moments his mouth was back on hers. He worked his way down to her chin then lower and lower.

Suddenly, she pushed him back. "Wait."

"What?" Justin panted.

"We need a, um, condom," she said nervously.

"What? Why? You're on the pill."

She shook her head. "Not since, well, you know…I stopped taking it when we found out about… The doctor switched me to a new kind, but I haven't been on it long enough for it to be effective."

He slumped back on the bed. Of course. She wasn't on birth control because she'd thought she was pregnant. Justin knew without looking that he wouldn't find any condoms in his wallet.

"Well, shit," he said.

"Justin you have to have one."

"I don't. Why would I? You haven't been talking to me, let alone sleeping with me."

She frowned. "You mean you weren't, I mean, there wasn't anybody else?"

"Of course not."

Justin knew he should've been offended at how surprised she looked, but he was still too damn happy to have her back by his side.

"So you haven't had sex at all with anybody since…"

"I didn't want anybody else, Courtney. I wanted you. And now that I have you, we're sitting here talking instead of…" He paused. "Wait, were you with someone else?"

She stood and started to dress.

"Wait, Courtney, I didn't mean…"

She brushed his hand off. "I know Justin, and no, I wasn't with someone else."

"Where are you going?"

"To the lobby. To buy condoms."

He rose to his knees and pulled her close again. "Hurry back?"

She grinned.

He scrolled through eight angry messages from people expecting him to be various places before switching his phone off. After what felt like an eternity, Courtney returned.

She locked the door behind her and tossed a bag onto the bed. Justin reached into the bag and pulled out two boxes with 12 condoms each.

"Was there a buy one get one free sale or something?" he asked, laughing.

"I didn't want to run out," she replied, climbing on top of him, her long dark hair tickling his face.

"I just fell in love with you all over again," Justin said, flipping her onto her back and kissing her.

THEY SPENT the night at the hotel, but sadly didn't make a dent in the second box. Justin ordered room service in the morning, then climbed back into bed, just as the room phone rang.

Courtney glanced at Justin, uncertain whether he'd want her to answer or not, but he simply shrugged. He hadn't discussed it much, but it was clear that he had skipped out on something and that his people were trying to find him.

Courtney answered the phone.

"Courtney? Thank God. It's Keith. Can you put Justin on?"

"It's Keith," she mouthed to Justin. He grimaced.

"Is everything okay?" she asked Keith.

He sighed loudly into the phone. "I know he's with you, Courtney. Come on, I had to call ten hotels before I tracked you down. You know he skipped a gala last night? Jamie had to tell them he had food poisoning. He's got something else tonight, and an interview tomorrow. How long are you planning on hibernating?"

Justin snatched the phone away before she could answer. Courtney retreated into the bathroom, trying to give him privacy, but she still overheard some of the discussion.

After a bit, Justin tapped on the bathroom door. "Will you come with me tonight? It's a movie preview and charity thing. There will be photos, drinks, dancing, more photos..."

"I have nothing to wear."

"Courtney doesn't want to go, so I'm not going," he said into the phone.

"Justin," she scolded. "Ask if Jamie can find me a dress. Then we will go."

THAT EVENING, with Courtney by his side, Justin posed for photos on the red carpet, waved to fans, and happily sat through the entire film. Normally at movie previews, his eyes were glued to the screen, since nothing was more thrilling than watching what might become a new favorite for the first time. Nothing except Courtney, apparently, since that night, Justin couldn't keep his eyes—or hands—off her.

She looked like a princess, in a casual, flowing pale pink gown. Jamie had gotten her a last minute appointment to have her hair and makeup done, but Justin was happy to see that Courtney had insisted it all still look natural. She was gorgeous, and smiling, and all his. Somehow, they'd both managed to forgive each other, and just being with Courtney tonight, well, Justin had a feeling that whatever came their way, they could handle it as a team.

Justin was expected to stick around and socialize for a bit after the preview, maybe even offer some positive feedback on the production, but he was counting down the minutes till he'd be alone with Courtney again. Although, he had to admit he was enjoying himself even more with Courtney by his side. She seemed more comfortable than she used to at this sort of event, and he found himself laughing and smiling often.

Courtney tugged his elbow, pulling him towards one of the empty cocktail tables.

"What's up?" he asked, concerned something was wrong. He knew tonight had been too good to be true.

"In case I forget to tell you later, I had a really good time tonight," she began, rising to her toes to kiss him softly on the cheek. "And also, I had an idea. For the wedding."

Justin felt his jaw drop. "Our wedding?"

She nodded eagerly. "I don't want to get into it here, but I was thinking about it during the movie, and I really think my plan will work."

He was still stunned. For a bride who hadn't seemed even remotely interested in choosing a date, let alone making other key decisions, developing a full plan seemed pretty surreal. "I'm gonna need more information," he said.

"Not here. Later, I promise. But how would you feel about giving me a wedding for my birthday?"

24

———

Twelve days and seven months later, it was beginning to look like they had pulled off the surprise of the century. Okay, maybe not of the century, but it sure felt like it with all the work they'd put into it. They'd decided to let no one except Keith in on the secret, and that was only because they both knew Justin stank at surprises.

Obviously, it would've been easier for them to just plan a small, dignified destination wedding, bringing only their closest family and friends along. But Justin's family was so big that it seemed impossible to keep the guest list small enough to be practical, and besides, he and Courtney had both always wanted a big, traditional wedding. The guest list settled in around 250, which, by Hollywood standards, really was miniscule. They'd sent out invitations for a surprise birthday party for Courtney. That seemed plausible to everyone who knew them, since Justin, apparently, had earned himself a reputation for his big romantic gestures.

Oddly enough, people generally didn't question why the surprise birthday party was more than a month away from Courtney's real birthday, and those who did question it quickly accepted the explanation that it was just to ensure she really wouldn't be expecting it. And, whenever anyone asked about the wedding, they said they were planning a long engagement, with a small, private ceremony in the fall.

The way Justin saw it, the only drawback of this plan was that he had to be the public face of any final details. Courtney was responsible for the majority of the plans, selecting the location, caterer, florist, baker, and so forth, all under the guise of making plans for the "real" wedding in the fall. But when it came to actually calling the caterer, decorator, or florist to arrange specific details for the surprise "party," Justin or Keith had to do it, since the surprise was supposedly for Courtney.

The hardest decision had been to keep the secret even from their families and the bridal party. But Courtney had been sneaky about the attire, having her bridesmaids get fitted for their dresses early, claiming the dresses would take forever to be hemmed. David even hooked them up with a designer who did women's formal wear so everything looked perfect.

In the end, they told Jamie the truth six weeks before the big day. Justin had been all in favor of keeping her in the dark, actually a little amused at the thought of seeing her face when she realized he'd handled his own publicity for once, but Courtney was frankly just too scared of Jamie to keep up the ruse. As predicted, Jamie had been pissed that she wasn't in on the secret to start with, but as they filled her in on the details, she and Courtney started to bond. Justin realized he was probably going to have them teaming up against him in the very near future.

The morning of the big day, he and Courtney had awakened early in bed together at his house, which, for the past four months, had technically been their house, although Keith had only moved out the month before. He'd expected her to be frazzled, to immediately shift into high gear, flitting about the house frantically, but instead, Courtney had simply turned to him calmly and smiled.

"Today's the day, huh?" she said, kissing him softly.

He frowned and glanced at the calendar on his phone before shaking his head. "Nope, I don't see anything scheduled for today. Maybe I'll get some guys together for a poker game."

"You're bad," she teased, staring back up at the ceiling. "But you know, this might be your last chance to have sex with a single woman."

He was tempted to spit out a sarcastic retort to that too, but figured, based on past experience, that the joke might hit too close to home. So instead, he seized the opportunity, slipping Courtney's tank top up over her head before she could protest.

Twenty minutes later, they both tromped downstairs to find a tasty feast prepared by Cathy, who was eying both of them suspiciously. They'd invited her to the party, of course, but she of all people seemed a bit more wary of the surprise element than anyone else.

COURTNEY KNEW if even their own family and closest friends hadn't figured out the surprise, the rest of the guests were in for a shock. Still, Courtney found herself shaking with nervousness. She didn't think it was pre-wedding jitters since she had zero doubts in her mind about what she was about to do, but she just still wasn't accustomed to all the attention.

Generally, whenever she was with Justin, the majority of people were focused on him. Today, she figured some of the attention might go to the bride. Besides, it was going to be pretty hard to ignore her in the dazzling, strapless gown with a twelve-foot train.

Courtney glanced at her father, who was clearly more

panicked than she. Her mother, along with all the groomsmen and the minister, was already in the ballroom where the ceremony would be held. Just then, Keith poked his head in the door. "He's about to make the announcement. You ready?"

She nodded, sucked in one last, deep breath of air, and exhaled slowly. A minute later, she heard Justin tapping on the microphone in the room next door, where they would return for a cocktail hour after the ceremony before moving into a third room for the dinner.

"If I could have everyone's attention," he began, eliciting a few claps and whistles before he'd even finished. "I have a little announcement to make. It's more of a confession, really." He paused, and Courtney wished she could see his face right now.

"You see, there was a typo on the invitations tonight," he continued. "Not so much a mistake as an outright lie, I guess." She heard Justin pause longer this time, taking in the audience's initial responses, although she could only hear muffled voices.

"There is a surprise tonight, but the surprise isn't for Courtney, and she's been in on it from the start. The surprise is actually for all of you." He finished his spiel, and Courtney knew he had to be looking proud now. "So if you'll all follow me into this room, we'll go ahead and get started with the real reason you're all here tonight."

And then, as the footsteps and rustling of people moving into the next room, ushered along by Justin's loyal brothers, grew louder, Courtney heard excited voices and shrieks as people figured it out. The harpist began playing, but it took another ten minutes before everyone was seated. Finally, the processional began, and the doors to the room where she'd been hiding opened, allowing her bridesmaids to slowly make their way down the aisle, one by one.

"If I forget to tell you later, congratulations!" Erica whispered before starting the slow walk.

Courtney's dad squeezed her hand and, right as the Bridal March began, they walked down the aisle. She realized later from watching the video that all of the guests stood and turned as she passed them, gasping and cooing over the dress, but in the moment, Courtney was oblivious to it all. The only thing she focused on was Justin, and his adorable dimples, warm blue eyes and perfectly contented grin watching her as she approached.

The closer she got to him, the more it all came flooding back to her, from the moment she'd first spotted him at a dance club, hoping to get his autograph, to that first of many jogs on the beach with him, to the interview where he'd first confessed he loved her. She remembered his excitement each time she'd dropped by his house unannounced and that comforting way he could hug her where she felt completely protected by his arms.

By the time Courtney reached Justin, her eyes were tearing up. Her father kissed her cheek and sat beside her mother. Justin quickly wiped the tear from beneath her eye and kissed her softly on the forehead as he took both her hands in his.

"You look beautiful," he whispered.

"You too," she gushed. "Handsome, I mean."

Justin smiled and gently pressed his lips into her forehead again.

"The kissing is supposed to happen last," the minister joked, eliciting chuckles from the audience.

Courtney tuned out during the ceremony, knowing none of it really mattered until the end. And when she finally, finally heard those words, "I now pronounce you husband and wife," she realized that what she'd been waiting for all these years had finally happened.

Justin kissed her instantly, lifting her off her feet and spinning around until her shoe fell off and they were both tangled in the long train. Erica and Andi straightened the train and stuck her shoe back on for her right before she and Justin sauntered back down the aisle together.

The rest of the night was similarly perfect. It was a typical reception, with drinks, dinner, cake, and dancing, except that several of the people giving toasts had been nominated for an Emmy, Oscar, or People's Choice Award. Well, and there were two performances that Justin had saved as a true surprise for Courtney. One of his friends performed a rap from his second album and another serenaded the couple with a love song from his first album. And there was a bit more security than perhaps the average wedding. But other than that, it was all pretty normal.

If anyone had asked Courtney five years prior if she'd ever envisioned having a popular hip hop artist rap at her wedding, she would've laughed hysterically. She similarly would have never predicted more than ten of their guests bringing along a bodyguard.

But Justin, well, he was exactly the type of man she always knew she'd end up with.

EPILOGUE

Seven years after the wedding, Courtney and Justin were back at St. Thomas for the second time since his proposal, the first return trip having been the honeymoon, of course. Despite the hurricane a few years before, the resort hadn't changed much. They planned to spend their days the same as the last two trips—evenly divided between having sex, lounging at the beach, and eating, with the distinction, of course, that Courtney wouldn't be drinking this time given that she was almost four months pregnant.

This baby wasn't their first. After the wedding, they'd waited a few years before diving into parenthood. Then, when they'd decided it was time to go for it, Courtney had gotten pregnant immediately, thrilling both of them. The pregnancy had been blissfully easy.

They'd agreed to wait another three years before trying for a second, but were both happy when they found out Courtney was pregnant with Savannah about a year ahead of plan. Savannah seemed to like surprising them from the start, arriving three weeks early and about seven hours after the premiere of the first action film where Justin was the lead. He'd told people his acting was just so amazing that it shocked Courtney into early labor, but she always knew Savannah was just too eager to meet them. They didn't know the gender of the third baby yet, but they were in agreement that it should probably be their last.

They'd left Aiden, now four, and Savannah, almost two, at home with their full-time nanny. Courtney had dropped down to a flexible part-time schedule at the shelter, but she was still practicing law and attempting to right the world's social injustices whenever she could. She was a frequent guest lecturer at various continuing education seminars and now had aspirations to teach at a law school once the kids were a bit older. Justin's career had skyrocketed since the final *Days End* film hit theaters, so he was now able to be pickier with his films, selecting a couple of bigger projects each year.

About two years after the wedding, they'd moved into a new house in the same neighborhood as Ryan and Audrey, and Justin had finally sucked it up and hired one full-time security guard. Mostly, the bodyguard stuck with Courtney and the kids, since Justin was still ripped like the twenty-six-year-old hunk she'd fallen in love with.

Keith was still Justin's manager but had taken on one additional client too: Andi Taylor. Courtney was pretty sure he'd broken some manager-client rules at some point, though, since he and Andi had quickly become the cutest couple she knew.

Life was good. As she lounged on the beach, virgin mojito in hand, handsome movie star husband at her side, Courtney smiled at the realization that somehow, amidst the chaos, they had accomplished a real life Hollywood love story

The End

ACKNOWLEDGMENTS

Phew...this part gets harder with every book. I am blessed with an amazing editor, Kimberly, and a truly patient cover artist, JD Designs. I also truly appreciate my parents, who've babysat their grandkids many, many times during this crazy virtual school year, therein allowing me time to actually work on this book. I'm grateful for all the friends who indulged my celebrity-stalking habits back in the day and for all the gossip sites that help lighten our "news" feed these days. Finally, I owe a huge shout-out to all the readers and bloggers who help promote my books and spread the word about my stories.

ALSO BY LIZA MALLOY

Sixty Days for Love

For Love and Italian

Forbidden Ink

The Brothers' Band

The Brothers' Band: The Next Track

Hollywood Endings

Legacy: The Awakening

Legacy: The Revelation

Coming Soon... Supporting Roles (*Hollywood Romance Book 3*)

Movie star Andrea Taylor is a magnet for the wrong type of guy. After being hurt too many times, Andi's accepted that she isn't the relationship type. Men are handy when she needs a fun night, but other than that, her focus is on her career as one of Hollywood's most successful actresses.

As the manager for one of Andi's co-stars, Keith has known Andi for years. He'd even go so far as to describe them as friends. But the last thing he expected was to end up in bed with *the* Andrea Taylor.

Fresh out of a relationship, Keith isn't looking for anything serious, and Andi assumes Keith has his own agenda just like every other man in her life. But as the chemistry between them builds, Keith sets out to prove to Andi that good guys do exist.

Can Andi let down her guard or has she been burned one too many times?

ABOUT THE AUTHOR

Liza Malloy writes contemporary romance and women's fiction. She's a sucker for alpha males, bad boys, dimples, and muscles, and she can't resist a man in uniform. Liza loves creating worlds where her heroine discovers her own strength and finds her Happily Ever After. When Liza isn't reading or writing torrid love stories, she's a practicing attorney. Her other passions include gummy bears, jelly beans, and the occasional marathon. She lives in the Midwest with her four daughters and her own Prince Charming. *Hollywood Beginnings* is her ninth novel.

Visit her website at www.LizaMalloy.com

Join her email list at http://eepurl.com/gnuROD